A Lady Never Surrenders

REGENCY BEST FRIEND'S BROTHER ROMANCE

SISTERHOOD OF SCANDAL
BOOK ONE

BRONWEN EVANS

Bronwen
Evans

Copyright

A Lady Never Surrenders
Book #1
Sisterhood Of Scandal Series

This book contains an excerpt from the prequel *A Lady Never Concedes* by Bronwen Evans. Copyright © 2022 by
Bronwen Evans

Copy Editor: Angela Bissell
Cover: Forever After Romance Design

❀ Created with Vellum

C ornwall, England, 1802

The carriage slowly rolled to a stop in front of an imposing country house. No, her mind was in a muddle; she remembered it was actually a castle—Marlowe Castle. Tiffany Deveraux's eyes felt so heavy they refused to obey her command to stay open. She wanted to see her new home, but after the twelve days it had taken to travel from Yorkshire to Cornwall, she was exhausted. Besides, she'd seen it once before, be it a long time ago.

"Wake up, Tiffany," Susan, her late mother's lady's maid, said. "We are finally here and your cousins have gathered to welcome you."

Tiffany did her best to obey, but her tiredness sucked her under and fighting it was like trying to swim in a sodden cloak. She'd had little sleep since her parents murder, trying to comprehend the horror. Her days passed completely numb with grief and disbelief, while her nights were spent sobbing at the loss.

The carriage door opened, letting in mild midnight air. How odd, she drowsily thought. In Yorkshire the air would have had a bite to it, even though it was spring.

1

There were voices, and she felt rather than saw Susan exit the carriage.

A man's voice carried over the others. Her uncle's?

Two weeks ago, a highwayman had killed her parents and her life would never be the same. Gone was the mother and father she loved with all her heart. Gone was the happy family filled with devotion and now... now she didn't know how to get over her loss.

Her uncle, the Earl of Marlowe, was now her guardian. As from today she was to live with him and his family. She had not seen her cousins since her tenth birthday, seven years ago now. She had no idea why the visits between their families had suddenly ceased. She missed seeing Claire, even though they still wrote regularly. As an only child, she'd had her precious books but little else for company over the past few years.

"She's exhausted, poor dear." This voice was lovely. Warm and feminine. "Fane, you'll have to carry her."

"I would love to, Mother. But I wrenched my shoulder on the hunt this morning when Hero threw me."

A deep masculine laugh skittered over her skin like a pleasant caress. "I never thought I'd see the day, Fane. A horse threw you."

"And what man comes to the country to paint?" Fane mocked.

The older male voice she thought was her uncle's interjected. "That's enough you two. Wolf, I know you are our guest, but you'll have to do the honors. Dayton is still away at school, and my knees won't make it up the stairs."

"Yes, sir."

The carriage tilted under someone's weight—the man with the smooth voice and goosebump-inducing laugh, presumably. Tiffany wanted to open her eyes, but they wouldn't cooperate.

"Come now, my belle au bois dormant."

Why was a Frenchman calling her his sleeping beauty?

Strong arms gently lifted her, one under her knees, the other around her back. She wasn't exactly tiny, but he carried her as if she were no heavier than a feather filled pillow.

Tiffany snuggled closer to his warm hard chest and clutched the lapels of his jacket.

"Can you reach her pocket? Something's digging into my ribs."

She felt a hand rifle in her pocket.

"Her glasses."

The man's steady gait lulled her deeper toward sleep, and the sounds of excited voices faded away as he carried her up the stone steps of her new home.

She let her head rest against his shoulder, her thoughts drifting in and out. Odd that she should feel comforted, protected, in a stranger's arms. The sensations were so delicious that when he laid her down on a soft mattress, she only reluctantly released her grip on his jacket lapels. Soon the heavenly feel of a soft mattress and warmed sheets seeped into her bones. But she felt the absence of his arms. She wanted to see him. This man who'd carried her as if she were the most precious cargo in the world.

She fought the fatigue and finally her eyelids lifted, and all her breath left her body in one long sigh as she took in the beauty of the masculine face staring back at her with an amused expression.

Handsome. Oh, he was so handsome it hurt to look at him.

She reached out her hand and stroked his chiseled cheek. "Are you my prince?" she whispered.

That throaty laugh again. "No, my sleeping beauty. I'm the big bad wolf. Sleep now."

And, as if swallowed by a swirling mist, he faded away and she could no longer see him.

She drew the scent of him into her lungs and fell asleep, dreaming of the handsome prince who would rescue her from... from the one thing she'd endured all her life. Loneliness.

3

Chapter One

L ondon, 1808, six years later

Miss Tiffany Deveraux stood between two of the most sought after bachelors in all of England. Her guardian and cousin, Fane Deveraux, the Earl of Marlowe, flanked her left side, while Marlowe's rakish best friend, Slade Ware, Marquess of Wolfarth, stood at her right elbow.

Every woman in Lady Rutherford's ballroom envied her. The armor piercing stares were wholly undeserved and Tiffany took no joy in the attention.

What the envious debutantes did not understand was that she was all but invisible to both men. Marlowe's mother had always insisted on Fane escorting Tiffany and his sister, Lady Claire Deveraux, to every ball, and where Fane went, Wolf followed.

Since Lady Marlowe was no longer living, the thought of her gone cut deep. Tiffany still felt the loss. It had been like losing a second mother. The absence of Lady Marlowe also meant the men would soon deposit Claire and Tiffany with Lady Vale, a society matriarch, before heading to the sanctuary of the card room. Tiffany could almost smell the men's fear. Mothers with marriageable daughters were closing in. Like a well-planned military advance, every mother present was maneuvering to introduce their daughters to the men.

Tiffany pushed her glasses back up her nose, feeling more and more invisible as the two men talked over her head, while Claire, who stood behind them, was busy filling her dance card. Her cousin was popular with men looking for a wealthy and pretty young lady of quality to marry, and also with the young ladies, who were eager to befriend her in order to meet her brother.

Tiffany was not bitter or jealous of her cousin. She herself was neither wealthy nor pretty: a fact that could not be disputed. What she had, thank the lord, was intelligence. She did not need to marry, or marry well. Her gift with numbers saw to that. Soon she would not even *need* Fane's charity. She hugged her smug secret to herself, armor against those who looked down their noses at the penniless orphan.

"I suggest we see the girls safely to Lady Vale's side before Lady Rutherford has us roped in as dance partners." Wolf's words flew over her head since she stood no taller than his shoulder. "Are you listening, Fane?" he persisted in that husky, innately sensual voice that always shook her feminine sensibilities.

"You go along. I think I see Lady Saline Porter," her cousin replied.

She turned in the direction the men were now staring and noted the beautiful young widow with a flock of gentlemen surrounding her. *She* was certainly not invisible.

"I thought your actress was enough woman for you," Wolf said, then glanced sharply at Tiffany as if he'd only just realized that she was in earshot.

Fane cleared his throat and smiled down at her. "Isn't that Miss Valora standing with her mother? Look, she's waving at you."

Yes, Valora was standing next to her mother, Lady Vale. "I'm waiting for Claire," she replied. Just then, Claire swung toward her.

"Tiffany, Lord Donahue was just saying that he'd love to beg a dance from you if you have any free?"

She inwardly sighed. Lord Donahue was a nice but dim and pimply young man who had taken a shine to her. Most likely because she'd been kind to him one night at the beginning of the season, and he'd sought her company ever since.

He stammered over her hand, his face turning a mottled red. "Miss Deveraux, ma-may I have the pleasure of the f-f-first waltz of the evening?"

She could feel Wolf and Fane's amusement without needing to look at them. "That would be lovely, thank you, my lord," and she held out her card for him to complete.

Once Lord Donahue had taken his leave, Fane shook his head. "Why do you encourage the man, Tif? You can do so much better than him."

Claire slipped her arm through Tiffany's and squeezed her hand.

Anger made her bite when really she should have ignored him, but it didn't help that Wolf was there as well. "Not all of us are blessed with looks or money, Fane. You do not know what it is like to go unnoticed. Most of us mere mortals make the most of what God has given us. Lord Donahue is a delightful man." She looked away from the two men beside her. They had never, ever had a moment's doubt about how the world perceived them. Handsome and desirable were their middle names.

She shifted her weight, intending to set out across the room to greet her friend Valora, but before she'd taken a step, Wolf bent to whisper in her ear, "I think when God made you he knew exactly what he was doing."

She stiffened. What was that supposed to mean? Was it a compliment? Her heart hiccupped and she looked at Wolf and found herself pinned by his crystal blue eyes. They weren't, as she'd expected, mocking her. Instead, they were filled with something much worse: pity. She wished the floor would crack open and swallow her whole. Lowering her gaze, she tugged on Claire's arm and escaped around the edge of the ballroom before tears welled.

She knew Wolf was only trying to be kind, but she'd been infatuated with him since that day six years ago when he'd carried her into her new home. But Wolf was not for the likes of her. Love did not easily find women of her ilk. She didn't inspire poets to write sonnets or artists to paint her portrait. Her heart clenched tight in her chest. Love—oh, how she wished for a man to find her worthy of love.

Yet that was only partly true.

She wanted one man to love her—Wolf. But she was far too intelligent; she realized that was but a dream. Wolf could have any woman he wanted. Why would he want *her*?

"I could thump my brother. In fact, I should do so every morning until he learns to think before he speaks."

She gave Claire a weak smile. "It's not his fault. The world has always been easy for him. He does not understand what it is like for those not so blessed."

Claire shook her head as she waved out to Valora. "No. That's not it. He is shallow. He does not look deep enough. He is distracted by the beauty of a woman rather than what is in her heart, or in her soul. I'm hoping he grows out of it before he finds himself shackled to a woman who, when her beauty fades as we know it will, is empty and boring. Married for the rest of your life is a long time."

Tiffany thought of the way the two men had drunk in Lady Saline. "We are shallow too," she said. "You're assuming a beauty like Lady Saline does not have a heart, yet I know she does."

When Tiffany was a child, books were her best friends, as they were now. Tiffany read widely and because of that was worldlier than many of her age, and because she was one of those people who observed rather than partook in life, she had seen the way Lady Saline and her companion, Miss Murphy, interacted. The lingering of fingers as their hands brushed, the little smiles that only lovers understood, and the fact not one of the handsome gentlemen surrounding her, not even Tiffany's cousin Fane, drew her complete attention away from Miss Murphy.

She snorted at the absurdity of life. "They think because we are younger, and female, that we don't think at all. When in reality we see far more than they do."

"What do we see?" Valora asked as they arrived at her side.

Tiffany pressed kisses to her cheeks. Valora would not understand, as she was beautiful beyond words. "Oh, nothing. It's just that Fane annoyed me."

Valora peered around her to stare at the men before they disappeared into the card room for the rest of the evening. "Well, something has upset them. Wolf is remonstrating with Fane rather vigorously."

Tiffany glanced over her shoulder. The two men did appear to be arguing.

Valora soon lost interest and sighed. "I find most men are fairly annoying, especially those who insist on proposing when they are well aware I shall not accept."

"You are getting quite the reputation for saying no," Claire stated. "If you're not careful you'll wake up one day and find that every man is too scared to ask."

Valora sniffed. "Then he is not the right man for me. Anyway, you can talk."

Tiffany privately thought that perhaps there was not a man alive who would ever be right for Valora. She'd turned down handsome rogues, attractive dukes, and wealthy lords. She glanced at Lady Saline and wondered if her good friend Valora was that way inclined. She hoped not, as Valora's brother Lord Vale was hell-bent on seeing her wed this year.

"Oh, I say," Valora exclaimed, tapping Claire's gloved arm with her fan. "Your brother and Wolf are dicing with danger. They're coming this way and Fane looks most put out."

The soft hum of female mutterings and twitching fans rose until the sound was like a swarm of bees in a hive. The men were not seeking the safety of the card room this evening. What were they about? Women were jumping to conclusions—dangerous conclusions. Tiffany hoped they were mistaken conclusions. Wolf could not possibly be announcing to the *ton* that he was looking for a wife. She knew Fane wasn't.

Lady Rutherford, seeing her chance, gathered her two daughters and shooed them in the men's direction.

Wolf continued on with purposeful strides, while Fane looked as if he'd like to shove a dagger in his friend's back.

"The Wolf looks as if he's hunting," Claire said.

Tiffany thought the description very apt. Wolf's lips were curved in a sly smile. She could imagine a snarl taking its place at any moment. His black hair, cut short to frame his face, gleamed blue-black in the candlelight, and his broad shoulders cast black shadows on the walls as he strode the length of the room. As he drew nearer, the sharp contours of his face, the aquiline nose and the chiseled cheeks added to his predatory appearance. People around them took a step back. Wolf *did* look like he was hunting. His gaze was hard and focused and—her heart began to pound in her chest—fixed exclusively on her.

Her legs were suddenly made of jelly.

He stopped directly in front of her, took her gloved hand and, bending low over it, brushed his lips across the material.

Tiffany's knees knocked.

"Miss Deveraux, I would be honored if you would allow me the next dance."

Her eyes narrowed. What was he about? She couldn't begin to imagine, but with everyone watching she had no choice but to curtsy and find a reply. "How lovely to see you wish to dance this evening, my lord."

His smile widened and she almost forgot to breathe.

Loud enough for all to hear, he said, "Only with you, Miss Deveraux. Only with you."

Shock struck her dumb, and when the music started for the quadrille, the only thing that stopped her panicking was Fane escorting a scowling Valora onto the floor so as to form a foursome. She pinned her gaze on Valora. Her friend merely shrugged and soon Valora and Fane were gliding across the floor, all the while snapping at each other, which was nothing unusual.

When Wolf's arm came round her back to glide her over the floor, her stomach clenched. When he twirled her she could smell his sharp woody scent, and it made her more lightheaded. When he drew her close she could see the perfect cleft in his chin, and his eyes, the palest of blue set off by long, black lashes, were mesmerizing. He was so beautiful.

She tried to think of something to say but he had her senses in a whirl. By the time the dance ended she could not think. She could only feel, and when she stepped away from him, she noticed the loss of his warmth as if she'd stepped naked into the snow. Yet she knew her face was flushed, because heat radiated from her cheeks. She pushed her glasses up her nose and tried to get her brain to focus.

Before she could say a word, Wolf brought her gloved hand to his lips and whispered, "Thank you for the dance, Miss Deveraux. You'll never go unnoticed again."

With that he turned and made his way with Fane to the card room, guests parting before them like the sea parting before Moses.

～

"What on earth was that about?" Fane asked Wolf as they made the safety of the card room.

Wolf wished he knew. He had no idea what had prompted him to make such a public spectacle, least of all on Tiffany's behalf. But there was something about the hurt he'd seen in her eyes.

"Your asinine comment about Lord Donahue," he replied.

"What comment?"

Wolf turned on his friend. "Sometimes you can be such an arse. Tiffany was right. Some of us have been blessed more than others in this life and we should not look down on anyone else because of it."

"I don't look down on anyone." At Wolf's raised eyebrow: "Well, perhaps I do." Fane paused before adding, "Tiffany could be a pretty girl if she didn't dress her hair so severely and didn't wear those glasses so often. I did wonder for a moment if you had decided to accept my offer."

Wolf almost laughed. He and Fane had got drunk at a family gathering last year, and Dayton, Fane's younger brother who was now in India, had casually suggested they marry each other's sisters.

"Tiffany is not your sister."

"No, she is my cousin and we discussed this. My poor cousin, and I am worried about her chances of making a match. She's already three and twenty."

"Hardly on the shelf."

Fane sighed. "I cannot understand why she refuses to let me offer a larger dowry."

Likely because she didn't wish to be sold off like livestock. Wolf's mind flashed to his two sisters. He wanted them to find a good match but he also wanted them to be happy. Ashleigh had already suffered heartache, and while Fane was his best friend, Wolf wasn't blind to his faults. Ladies were toys to Fane, and he'd left many with a broken heart. So had he, if truth be told, but he hoped he was more of a gentleman than his friend.

"Let's play cards and hope the ladies do not wish to stay too late tonight."

"I don't know what's put you in such a mood."

Wolf grimaced. "I apologize. I'm sure you have Tiffany's best interests at heart."

Fane broke into a grin. "I do. I like the girl. A tad too percep-tive, but at least she does not prattle on at the dinner table. I just hope she doesn't think she has to settle for the likes of Lord Donahue."

Tiffany did deserve a man better than Lord Donahue.

He motioned for a servant to bring him a drink. A dead weight settled in his gut. He had never felt this disconcerted. He took a seat at the faro table but could not concentrate on the cards. He knew he should not have come out tonight. He'd rather be home painting. He only had three months to get a piece ready for the Royal Academy exhibition. He'd promised a painting that could be auctioned off to raise money to set up a Royal Academy scholarship.

He wanted to ensure the British Royal Academy of Art was the best in the world. Better than the French, in particular, for they had just employed a new director who had laid down a challenge. Another challenge, like the ongoing hostility with France, which surely was heading toward another war.

He was thankful Rockwell, his younger brother, had made it through the Irish Rebellion unscathed, or as unscathed as any man could be. He often heard the screams at night from his brother's nightmares. The British had lost good men fighting in Ireland. Men like Viscount Furoe. He hoped there was not another war, especially with France. He would do everything in his power to ensure the French did not better them in the arts—or in anything.

As he lost yet another game, he admitted the truth. It was the news Rockwell had delivered this afternoon that saw him unsettled. Another creditor had come calling regarding their uncle, Lord Melville, and his latest debt. Wolf knew he'd have to do something to curb his uncle's spending, but why did this have to occur when he had a painting to deliver?

He would have to cut Melville off and also advise his mother not to give her brother more money. Handling his mother would be the difficult part. She loved her brother, faults and all. Wolf hated to upset her, but it wasn't just his life Melville's spending affected. If he didn't rein in his uncle the family would eventually be put in financial peril.

While his skills lay in the arts, he was thankful that Rockwell had a head for numbers. He also owed Fane's father a great debt.

The late Lord Marlowe had been his guardian after his father's death. Wolf was only eleven when his father broke his neck falling from a horse in the hunt. Lord Marlowe had honorably held his estates together until Wolf had been old enough to learn the skills to manage them.

His thoughts veered back to Fane's offer. Marry Fane's sister, Claire, or his cousin Tiffany. Why did Tiffany's face, and not Claire's, flash in his head? He did owe the Marlowes a lot, and whomever he chose it would repay his debt to them. And he was reaching that age where a wife would be a wise move. Plus, if Ashleigh's scandal could not be forgotten, then he could call on Fane as a last resort to marry his sister—if Ashleigh agreed.

Claire or Tiffany? Claire was the prettier of the two but her tongue was sharp. Besides, it would help Fane more if he offered for Tiffany.

A wave of heat washed over him as he thought about dancing with Tiffany earlier. He could not get the images of those enticing emerald eyes, full of spark and intelligence, and her soft lips, slightly open in invitation, from his mind.

He shook his head. Perhaps a match could be arranged. At least Tiffany, as a poor cousin, would not be expecting a love match. She would be sensible and calculated in her approach to marriage. As for him, after the tragedy of losing Margo, love was an emotion he would never indulge again. He had only one true love in his life now—his art—and it took all his focus.

Margo's death had almost destroyed him. It had warped him, and the idea of sleeping with his future wife filled him with dread.

This time, when he married, it would be a marriage of convenience, and sleeping with his wife would be for the purpose of a child only.

One all-destroying love in a lifetime was more than enough.

Chapter Two

Although tired from the late end to the ball, Tiffany went ahead with her planned visit early the next morning. As she traveled across London, she relived the memory of Wolf singling her out for a dance. Rumors had circulated all night, making her the center of attention for once, and she'd hated it. Staying unnoticed was a skill, and one she needed—especially today.

She alighted from the hackney, pulling her widow's veil down over her face. She furtively glanced up and down the crowded street, praying her widow's weeds disguise would work. If she was recognized... Well, to be seen without an escort would ruin her. She'd become a social outcast. At that thought, she had to stop herself from laughing out loud. Society's likely reaction to hearing that a Miss Tiffany Deveraux was seen unescorted at the London Stock Exchange would be—*who*? A scandal was surely the only way she'd be noticed at all. She'd often wondered if that alone was reason enough to throw caution to the wind and let her secret out.

Blow Wolf's attentions last night. Hard to stay unnoticed when one of London's most eligible bachelors dances a waltz with you.

Normally she never visited Mr. Sprat, her stockjobber, in person. Women were not encouraged to invest. It was currently scandalous to do so, and had been ever since the South Sea debacle. Few stockjobbers would take a woman as a client. Her age was also against her. At three and twenty, no stockjobber took her seriously. Sprat had been her father's stockjobber and hence had agreed to help her.

Usually they communicated by missives, or she would arrange to meet Mr. Sprat in the park with her lady's maid in tow. All very respectable. There was less chance of scandal, or of her cousin finding out about her investments. Fane would be hurt to think his orphaned cousin, whom he so generously provided for, scraped and saved her pin money to invest behind his back, when he'd gladly have given her anything she wanted. She loved her cousin and would hate to disappoint him with her scandalous behavior. Fane did not understand her passion, or need, to take charge of her destiny. Relying on the charity of others rankled.

So here she was at Capel Court for the first time. The London Stock Exchange, the center of her world. She stood on the cobblestones, undecided, knowing she had to enter and speak with Sprat. Where were her latest investment statements? Tiffany could not tell if she was shaking from excitement at the prospect of entering the institution, or from nerves at the risk of being caught.

Who on earth would recognize her in this disguise?

She adjusted her veil and walked forward. For some reason her last missive to Mr. Sprat had gone unanswered, and her quarterly return statements were late. She had a lot of money invested with Sprat; her plan for financial freedom was at stake should something go wrong. While she appreciated Fane's generosity, she was determined that, by the end of this year, she'd never again have to rely on his charity, or anyone else's for that matter. Financial security was what she craved. Never would she be in the position of having to marry, like most of her fellow debutantes were.

Besides, she wanted to make her father proud. He had recognized her ability with numbers early on, and because he'd never had a son, he'd taken the time to nourish her skills and helped her learn the intricacies of an investment portfolio.

Always spread the risk.

Her father must be turning in his grave at the risk she'd taken, having her money with only one stockjobber. But needs must. Besides, she trusted Sprat. When her father's investments had turned belly up, he'd given her parents a thousand pounds out of the goodness of his heart. It wasn't Sprat's fault the money was stolen and her parents killed shortly thereafter.

With a deep breath she entered the building, and the noisy chatter of men near the entrance dimmed as they noticed her. Before she lost her nerve, she asked the nearest man where she could find Mr. Sprat.

He pointed to a row of offices along the far wall, and with a nod of thanks she moved on. When she reached the bank of doors, the third one along flew open and she recognized the man who emerged.

"Mr. Sprat," she called to him.

He looked toward her, then to those staring at them. His attention came back to Tiffany. "Would you care to step into my office?" He followed her in and left the door open. "How can I help you, Madam?"

She lifted her veil and noted a flash of panic on his face before he smoothly sat down behind his desk. "Miss Deveraux. What a lovely surprise."

"I doubt that. I'm sorry to call on you unannounced, but I'm worried. You have not responded to several of my recent missives, and my latest statements are late."

His mouth firmed slightly. "One of my clerks is sick, and I am running behind in drafting the statements."

"Well, you could have let me know. I was most concerned."

"I thought I had left instructions to do just that. I hope my other clients have not been treated thusly." He rose from his chair.

"If you'll excuse me for one moment, I shall inquire if your statements are ready now."

"Thank you. I would greatly appreciate that."

In Sprat's absence, the noise from the trading floor was too much to ignore. She rose and walked to the door and watched, fascinated, as the men crowding the floor shouted out the sales. The atmosphere was loud and exciting, the tension in the air palpable.

Tiffany's body hummed. Oh, how different her life might have been if she were born a man. She could have come here every day and witnessed commerce in action. She continued to watch, mesmerized, until an all too familiar voice boomed like a cannon in her ear.

"Miss Deveraux, what on earth are you doing here? Tell me you are not alone."

Her heart sank to her feet when usually it would have jumped in excitement upon hearing Wolf's voice. Her hand flew to her face as she realized, too late, that her veil was still up.

The Marquess of Wolfarth towered over her in all his majestic male beauty. She imagined his darkened gaze was very much like the wolf's before he caught the rabbit.

Tiffany offered him a polite smile. "How lucky to see you two days in a row."

His hands moved to his hips. "Don't take that sarcastic tone with me. What are you doing here? And why in widow's weeds?"

It was too late to pull down her veil and pretend he'd made a mistake. Her traitorous body went weak-kneed, her skin tingled, and her mouth dried. If she were to ask any group of women to look over the men in this establishment and pick out the one most like a wolf, not a single woman would select any other man but him. Wolf's hair, dark as a starless sky, showcased the light hypnotic blue of his eyes. His lips could seduce with a hint of a smile, or make you shake in your shoes with a twisted snarl. Tall, broad-shouldered, he wore his clothes with effortless grace, yet the coiled strength hidden beneath was clearly evident. The picture of a man in excellent condition. The leader of the pack. It was ironic how this man's name and title so perfectly fitted his nature.

As much as she appreciated and was tempted by the man and his wolf-like nature, she had chosen not to become one of the willing pack of females who followed him around and hung on his every word. She had her future to consider, a life to build. Even so, it was difficult to ignore the fact his mere presence made her heart dance a jig in her chest.

Bravely she faced him. "If you must know, I'm here for my quarterly statements. My stockjobber is behind in sending them out."

Before Wolf could respond, Mr. Sprat arrived and handed her a file. He looked at Lord Wolfarth. "My lord, I was just fetching papers for Miss Deveraux."

Wolf looked between Mr. Sprat and herself, then took her by the elbow and said, "If Miss Deveraux has everything she needs, I shall escort her home as I promised her guardian I would."

Liar. Wolf had not even known she was here.

They had drawn quite a crowd. Wolf, in his overbearing manner, was trying to save her reputation. If he had simply ignored her, however, no one would have noticed her. His grip tight on her elbow, he said through gritted teeth, "Shall we? And pull down your veil."

Instead of leaving, he drew her further into the building, to a plush office near the main trading floor. The outer office contained over a dozen clerks. Whoever it belonged to, he was obviously a very successful stockjobber. Wolf guided her through the clerks to a large office at the back. He did not even knock. He simply entered.

"Jacob, please excuse me, but our meeting will have to be quick. I have a lady with me today. She was curious to see the Exchange."

Oh, her heart was really hammering now, and not because Wolf had been touching her. This was the office of Mr. Jacob Lane, the biggest and most successful stockjobber in England.

She'd longed to meet him and discuss his investment strategies. She'd studied him for years.

Wolf indicated the chair at the back of the room, and his eyes begged her to lower her veil. Both unspoken commands she ignored, taking the chair next to his in front of Mr. Lane's mahogany desk.

"Refreshments for the lady?"

"I don't think that is necessary, we won't be staying long," Wolf replied. "You said you had a new investment I should consider. We can go over the rest of my portfolio tomorrow at our regular meeting."

Mr. Lane took his seat and lifted a file. "Park Mill, in Leeds, is looking for more capital to expand. As you can see, Mr. Park has very little competition and his profits continue to climb each year."

"Then why does he need outside capital?"

"He wants to more than triple his processing capacity, but still leave a sound cash flow to ensure they can meet the larger wage and coal bills caused by the expansion."

"Do you recommend a loan, or should I buy shares?"

Tiffany waited for Lane's reply, her breath lodged in her throat.

"I would suggest shares."

No. Absolutely not. Tiffany's mind roared. She cleared her throat.

The men ignored her, and Mr. Lane continued, suggesting shares would be the viable option because of the capital gains and tax position.

Finally, she could take no more. "If you'll pardon the interruption, gentlemen, I believe a loan secured against the machinery would be the wisest move—"

Wolf spoke over her. "My estate's tax position is worrying," he said to Lane. "Have you any background on Park Mill that I may take with me to read?"

His ignoring her was to be expected, she supposed, given the reputation of Mr. Lane. It was enough to keep her silent.

He really should listen to her. She'd already done her research on Park Mill. Yes, Mr. Park currently had little competition and it would seem his expansion was well advised. But more mills were planned for the area and, in particular, a small expansion of Armley Mill should be of concern.

Her opinion of Mr. Lane diminished the more the men talked.

Wolf did not address a single word to her as he said his good-byes to Mr. Lane, and with his hand firmly on her elbow, and her veil dutifully lowered, he escorted her from the Exchange.

Not until the carriage door closed behind them and he banged the roof did he speak—though not to her. "A slight diversion, Jones. A detour to Lord Marlowe's, if you please, to deliver Miss Deveraux back where she belongs."

The silence lengthened, and now she was getting cross. He was being boorishly rude. He was not her guardian. Why had she let him bundle her out of the Exchange as if she were a criminal?

"I would prefer if you did not mention my activities to Fane."

She watched him curse under his breath. "I'm sure you would. Marlowe will not be pleased. He is responsible for you."

"I'm a grown woman quite capable of surviving a trip to Capel Court."

"Does Marlowe know you are investing?"

She bit her lip. Delicacy is required, she told herself. "Not exactly, and I'd like it to stay that way until I have a chance to inform him myself. I don't want him to think I'm ungrateful for the charity he bestows on me."

"Charity? It's not charity. You are his family."

She swallowed a retort. Wolf would never understand what it was like to be reliant on someone in order to live. His family was as rich as colossus. They owned half of the midland counties. He saw it as his responsibility to provide for his extended family. She hated being anyone's responsibility.

He turned to look out of the window and in profile he looked like a statue of a Greek god. The planes of his face were sharp-edged, his nose regal, and she could not help naughty thoughts about his lips racing through her head. How would it feel to kiss a man such as Wolf?

As if sensing her scrutiny, he turned and asked, "How is it that you come to be investing? Have you been doing it long?"

"Since I came to live with the Marlowes. Mr. Sprat was my father's stockjobber and he kindly invests for me. I save some of my pin money and use that. I made over a ten percent return for the last three years."

Surprise swept across Wolf's handsome face. "So Mr. Sprat tells you what to invest in?"

She scoffed. "Hardly. I study the market and the economy. I make my own investments. If anything, Sprat uses my research for his clients."

Like most men, he looked at her in disbelief.

She could not help herself. "Take that investment you are going to make in Park Mill. You shouldn't. There is only one way for Park Mill's revenue to go and that is down."

His beautiful mouth firmed before he said, "Mr. Lane does not seem to think so."

"It's obvious that Mr. Lane has not investigated thoroughly."

His lips twitched. "What do you know that Mr. Lane, the most successful stockjobber in England, does not?"

Smugness, thy name is Wolf. "Park Mill *has* had very little competition. There are two new mills being built that will be ready to produce in eight months. But it's Armley Mill that should interest you. It's small and has been operating for about three years. They are very forward thinking and they are the only mill to begin processing merino. Some of their textile designs are so in demand there is a twelve month waiting list for their product. Armley Mill is seeking investors so as to expand. With their design skills and foresight on textiles, I've calculated their profit will outstrip Park Mill's within eighteen months. With the other mills also opening in the area, Park Mill will struggle to sell its extra capacity."

Wolf sat in stunned silence, staring at her as if she were from another world. Tiffany could have laughed at the look on his face. Instead, feeling emboldened, she clicked her fingers in front of his nose to snap him out of his stupor.

His gaze narrowed, and he stared harder now, as if seeing her for the first time. His eyes moved over her face and then traveled down, stopping at her breasts. Heat seeped along Tiffany's skin. If not for the respectable mourning gown, which left not an inch of skin showing, she'd have sworn he was seeing her naked.

His gaze returned to hers. "What's stopping Park Mill from copying Armley Mill's strategy?"

"Mr. Park. It's a family business and he won't modernize."

"How on earth do you know that?"

Her face flushed. She'd be in real trouble now. "I went to the London meeting of textile businesses and listened to him talk."

"Christ. I bet Marlowe knows nothing of this—you running around London unescorted. Do you know what could have happened to you if—"

"I dress as a widow. No one pays me any attention." In a small voice she said to herself, "I'm mostly invisible."

Wolf's head snapped round as if he'd heard that last utterance. "Well, Marlowe has to know. If it became common knowledge that you—that you behave in this manner, your chances of finding a decent husband would diminish and Marlowe would blame himself."

Stay calm. Don't get angry. He's a man who does not know any better. "I don't need a husband. I will soon have enough money to be financially secure, and if I eventually marry, it will be to a man who accepts me as I am." The fact that no man had ever even looked at her in a romantic way was her embarrassing secret. What lord wanted a bluestocking, plain Jane orphan with a small dowry for a wife?

He looked at her as if he finally understood her problem—she was mad. His eyes narrowed. "And this investment in Armley Mill is going to fund this ridiculousness?"

"I shall double my profit and have an annual income of close to five thousand pounds if Armley meets my projections." A sudden thought slammed into her head. "I'll wager you that the share price of Armley Mill will have the biggest percentage rise, more than Park Mill's share price, over the next month. If it does you will say nothing to Marlowe about my investing or my odd unaccompanied excursions. This little excursion will remain our secret."

Wolf stretched his legs out and rested his polished Hessians on the squab next to her, as if he meant to intimidate. He studied her until her nerves stretched and she squirmed in her seat. "You are an interesting young lady."

Interesting. Not *beautiful*. Not *lovely*. *Interesting*. Her heart hurt. Tiffany understood that she'd never be a great beauty. She was an orphan, not a diamond of the first water. But it still hurt to not have the admiration of this man. So she said nothing. She certainly didn't voice her thoughts about how she found him devastatingly handsome, desirable, clever, pompous and arrogant —yet still the only man who made her heart skip in her chest.

He smiled in a manner that reminded her why he was called Wolf. He rested his hands behind his head and stared her in the eye. His gaze was so intense it felt as if he were seeing into her soul. The moment his lips curled slightly at the corner and the hungry challenge filled his eyes, Tiffany shivered. She'd made a dreadful mistake. One did not provoke a wolf.

"I accept your challenge."

Had the carriage not been moving, she might have leaped out and run as far from this unsettling man as she could. Instead, she raised her chin. "So, you will keep my investing secret from Fane until we see who wins?"

"Yes." His fingers tapped his muscled thigh, and for one moment she began to doubt herself. The feeling grew when he uttered, "What shall I ask for when I win this wager?"

She held her breath, not daring to move. He could ask for practically anything and he knew it. She'd revealed her hand, because Wolf knew how much she loved both Fane and Claire.

He leaned across the carriage and tapped her nose with his finger. She wanted to swat it away like an annoying bee, but she was frozen where she sat. "I'll keep your secret if you win, but if I win... Let's see. What do I desire?"

Chapter Three

Desire? Wolf's finger moved from the tip of Tiffany's nose to her lips, gently sweeping over them, and she could not get her brain to function. He couldn't possibly be suggesting he desired—her? Just the idea sent her body into panic mode. Yes, she'd fantasized about Wolf's kisses, but her innocent heart was not sophisticated enough to tryst with Wolf and survive.

"Please move back," she squeaked out.

Wolf ignored her. He merely stared at her lips as if he wanted to taste them. For one wild moment she almost said, "*Yes, please.*"

Softly he whispered, "So innocent. You think you're so worldly, yet the touch of my finger on your lips makes you tremble."

Tiffany noticed her legs were shaking. She licked her lips and his eyes drank in the movement. She felt her face heat. How gauche he must think her.

Finally, just as she thought she might swoon, he took pity on her and sat back on his squab.

"If the share price of Park Mill increases at a greater percentage return than Armley Mill's share price, you will agree to a marriage of convenience—with me, that is."

She gasped. *What on earth...?* No. She could not have heard correctly. Why would a man who could have any woman as his wife want her?

"It would suit my needs," he continued, "and will be a coup for your social standing. A woman who is so obviously sensible, intelligent, and strategic will see the benefit to such an arrangement."

Arrangement—not marriage. While her head wanted to scream yes, her heart threw up a fortress. "No. I will not accept that deal. Thank you for your kind...offer, but I'd rather you told Fane about my investing."

Wolf's eyes narrowed and his nostrils flared. Perhaps she could have turned him down in a more polite manner, but something about his cool delivery of the offer, the way he seemed to think she should be grateful, hurt. Besides, her whole reason for investing was so she would *not* have to accept a loveless marriage.

∼

Did Tiffany just decline his offer? Wolf's hands curled into fists by his side. *Unbelievable!* His first proposal since Margo and it was a "no." If not for the fact women threw themselves at him almost daily, his pride would be dented.

He'd never even considered the possibility she'd refuse him. His title and wealth saw most women do everything in their power to force a proposal from him.

He cleared his throat, refusing to show that perhaps his pride was a *little* wounded. "I thought you intelligent. May I ask why you won't accept my offer?"

"I believe you are looking for a woman who will stay in the background and bear your children while you go about your life much unchanged from what it is now."

His temper, already at the burning embers stage, flared a little. Wasn't that what marriages among the *ton* were? She would have his money, social standing, children, the house to manage and he would... He would do as he always did. "Your point being?"

"I thought *you* were intelligent. I'm investing so I do not have to consider a marriage of convenience. I will only marry a man who loves me." Her face flushed a pretty pink as she said the words.

"Love is for the poets and lower classes. *We* marry for alliances and money." He would never let his heart love again. The pain of loss was beyond imagining.

She frowned. "You do not need money." She considered him for a few moments. "I'd hardly say you need me for an alliance, either."

There she was wrong. While he appeared to be a very successful investor, his was mostly good luck. Take this investment Jacob had suggested with Park Mill. He had no idea if the investment would show a return. He relied on Jacob's advice, and if Tiffany was right, well, then he could suffer a huge loss. A few large losses, coupled with covering his uncle's increasing gambling debts, and his family's situation could be reversed. He did not have his father's natural ability with numbers. His younger brother did, but when Rockwell was on one of his many travels round the globe, Wolf's investments always suffered.

If Tiffany was as skilled as she professed, she would be a huge asset to his family.

Plus, if he married Tiffany, Fane would owe him. And if the scandal surrounding his sister Ashleigh did prevent her finding a suitable match, Wolf knew Fane would offer for her in return for his marriage to Tiffany. Hell, it was Fane who had drunkenly backed his brother's suggestion of a reciprocal arrangement.

Ashleigh could do a lot worse than marrying Marlowe—a fact he did not intend to share with Tiffany. She and Ashleigh were friends, and Ashleigh...well, she was a tad strong willed—hence the scandal she'd walked into.

"Marlowe is like a brother to me. It would bring our families closer."

She sat back and placed her hands in her lap. "My answer is still no."

"I'd let you continue to invest. In fact, you could invest to your heart's content. My assets would be at your disposal."

A glow entered her eyes. *Yes.* Finally, an offer she couldn't refuse. Satisfaction stirred, though he couldn't deny it was a touch demoralizing to learn the idea of freedom to invest excited her more than marriage to him. He waited for her to accept, but then, to his surprise—and annoyance—the glow in her eyes dimmed.

"Tempting as that may be, the answer is still no," and her chin lifted.

He held her gaze and noted her bottom lip tremble. She'd trembled when he'd touched her earlier too. From innocence, or something else? Was she affected by him, as most women were? Did he stir her desires? Her passions? Perhaps there was another way to get what he wanted.

"Have you ever been kissed, Tiffany?"

Her eyes rounded, and she darted a look at his mouth then licked those luscious pink lips, and for the second time in minutes he wanted to taste her. Not just to seduce her into agreeing to this marriage, but because...because he wanted to kiss her. He wanted to be the first man to ever kiss her. He had no idea why that was so important.

"Have you?" he insisted.

She shook her head, her eyes returning to his mouth.

"Would you like me to kiss you now?" He didn't move a muscle, scared he'd frighten her. He waited and watched, almost laughing at the internal battle discernable on her face. Her eyes were so expressive; brilliantly cut emeralds didn't sparkle brighter. She was very pretty in her own way, especially without her glasses perched on her cute upturned nose. If only she'd wear her auburn hair in a less matronly style, flowing a little loose around those defined cheekbones instead of wound up tight in a bun.

He wondered why he'd never noticed her in this way before—her womanly curves drew his eye and stirred his desire, despite the hideous black gown. She was certainly not a tree stick. Tiffany was more like Ruben's voluptuously shaped women, one who would fill his hands with her sensual curves.

He shifted on the squab as his body stirred.

Tiffany was his sisters' friend, so he'd never really noticed her. He had certainly never seriously considered marriage to one of his sisters' friends, and marriage would be the only time he'd ever consider dallying with—

He caught himself mid-thought. Dallying with? When did he dally with respectable debutantes? Never. That was what a mistress was for.

Hell, he bloody wanted to dally with Tiffany Deveraux.

He wanted to ruffle that composure and unleash the passion coiled so tight underneath her prim exterior. She was passionate; he'd seen the fire in her eyes when she talked about investing. Oh, to have all that passion and interest reserved for him alone.

This little mouse was suddenly out of hiding, and for some reason she stirred the animal in him. He sat up straight, honest enough to admit that her rejection of his marriage offer also stirred the competitiveness within him too.

"I *have* never been kissed, and while the idea of being kissed by a man such as you stirs something within me, I'm pretty sure the offer to kiss me is your way of trying to change my mind about a marriage of convenience. So I regretfully decline."

She was clever.

That stirred him too. He should simply let the matter drop, but the idea of nudging Marlowe to offer for Ashleigh in return for him marrying Tiffany was too attractive. It would be the answer to all his and Ashleigh's prayers.

He nodded at her response and refused to let her see she'd gotten under his skin. "Fine. I have a new wager for you then." Her eyebrow rose and her lips firmed. He barely stopped his own from twitching. "If I win, I'll keep your secret from Marlowe, if you allow me to court you and show you how a marriage between us could work."

Her mouth dropped open, then snapped shut. He read suspicion on her face as clearly as if the word was painted on her forehead. "Why this sudden need to have me as your wife?"

He shrugged. "As I said before, marrying would align our families, and I think you and I would be well suited." She scoffed. "Truly. You are intelligent, outspoken, and passionate. I'm pretty sure our marriage would never bore me. Marriage is for a lifetime."

"Absolutely. That is why it's so important to ensure my husband is one I would want to spend a lifetime with."

He moved and sat on the squab next to her. Taking her hand, he pressed his lips to her palm and noted her shiver. She wasn't immune to him.

"I'm simply asking for a chance to prove to you our marriage would make you happy. We could be content. Besides, why are you worrying so much about the wager? I thought you were positive Armley Mill's shares would increase more than Park Mill's."

She pulled her hand out of his grasp and tucked it beside her hip. "I *am* confident." She watched him with those calculating eyes and said the words he'd known she would utter the moment he'd suggested the second wager. "I shall allow you to court me, but you will do so in a way that protects my reputation. No behavior that would see me forced to accept your offer."

Yes. She was very clever.

"I would never do anything to dishonor you or my family."

She nodded. "I believe you. If anything, I know you to be a man of your word. All right. I accept your wager," and she held out her hand for him to shake.

He seized his opportunity, and instead of shaking her hand, he gently turned it over and pressed his lips to the soft skin of her wrist between her glove and her sleeve. He felt her shiver again and wanted to holler with victory. She was most definitely not immune to him.

That would make this easier. He was a man who was no stranger to seduction, and a young innocent lady such as Tiffany

—he should easily be able to turn her head, especially as she seemed in no hurry to withdraw her hand from his grasp. He rubbed his thumb across her palm, and her breath hitched as her eyes tracked the small movement. The moment was broken only when the carriage drew to a halt.

Wolf sat back on the opposite squab and lifted the window covering. "We have arrived at your home."

"Could you ask the carriage to go around the back, please?"

"So you can sneak in?"

"If I don't, our wager might be over before it begins. If Fane sees me with you, he will ask questions and he may learn of my activities. If so, there would be no need for me to allow you to court me."

He laughed. He couldn't help it. Her mind was as sharp as an arrowhead and he loved how she challenged him at every turn.

He banged on the roof. The hatch opened and Wolf told the tiger to drive around to the stables.

"I believe you are attending the opera tonight. You will let me escort you?"

Alarm flashed across her face before she turned away to exit the carriage. "This is all too soon. Marlowe will want to know why you are escorting me tonight. I suggest a more gradual society introduction to our courtship. You could visit the box."

"I shall look forward to the pleasure of conversing," he said to her rapidly departing back.

As his carriage trundled home, Wolf couldn't help but smile. He was very much looking forward to courting Miss Tiffany Deveraux and matching wits with her.

The more he considered the wager and all he had to gain from winning, the more he decided he needed to rethink his strategy. Having had the time to talk with Tiffany, one thing was clear. He didn't doubt she could win the wager with Armley Mill. Therefore, he had best make Tiffany fall in love with him so if he lost, he'd still win.

Pulling out his pocket watch, Wolf noted he still had plenty of time before he met the others at White's. He'd promised to escort his two sisters to the opera tonight, so fortunately he wouldn't have to make any excuses to his mother as to why he suddenly wanted to attend the event. But there was someone he needed to talk to—Delia, his mistress.

He was not crass enough to keep a mistress when he was trying to win a young lady's heart. That knowledge would most likely see Miss Tiffany Deveraux avoid matrimony like the plague.

Once again, he banged on the roof of the carriage. "To Garrard's the jewelers, in Mayfair, and quick about it."

Chapter Four

T he servants paid her little attention as she snuck in through the back stairs. They were used to her antics. She hurriedly changed. She was back much later than she'd envisioned, and the Sisterhood was meeting here this afternoon. Soon Claire would come looking for her.

While she dressed she couldn't stop her hands from shaking. What the hell was Wolf up to? Why this sudden interest in her—and marriage? As a girl she'd dreamed of a man like Wolf offering her marriage, but in her dreams the man had loved her—and Wolf wasn't promising love.

And she understood why. He'd changed after his fiancée, Margo, had died. Just like Tiffany's parents, he and Margo had been travelling by carriage when they were held up by highwaymen, and Margo had died not long after.

She pushed away the sad memories just as the door opened and in walked Valora.

"Oh, please save me from domineering brothers."

Tiffany had not expected Valora to arrive so early, but then Valora liked any excuse to escape her house.

She tried to hide a yawn as she watched her friend pace the

room. This galivanting around London after a sleepless night was taxing.

"What has the mighty Viscount Vale done now?"

Valora moved to look out the window. The shards of sunlight made her beauty almost ethereal. Tiffany's bedchamber overlooked the back garden of her cousin's London residence in Mayfair. Her desk was positioned under the window because she loved the view of the flowerbeds, but mostly because she loved how the early morning sunlight streamed in. Unlike the rest of her household, she was usually an early riser.

"Bloody Vale. My stuffy brother has declared that it is not proper for me to attend Mrs. Buchanan's afternoon fete—"

Tiffany didn't even pretend to stifle her gasp. She quickly sat up. "How on earth did you manage an invitation?"

"I flirted outrageously with young Mr. Turnbull at Lady Temple's ball the other night, and talked him into taking me. When Vale found out, I'm afraid poor Mr. Turnbull got more of a tongue lashing than I. He's also sporting a black eye, Courtney told me last night."

"I should think so. Mrs. Buchanan is an actress and Fane's mistress. You know it would ruin your reputation if you attended one of her soirees."

"It's so unfair." Valora sat on the bed and rolled onto her back, flinging an arm dramatically across her forehead, shielding her eyes from a shaft of sunlight. "Aren't you the least bit curious about women such as Mrs. Buchanan? Vale keeps a mistress too. Mother informs me that most men keep mistresses. I want to know why. What can a mistress do for a man that a wife cannot? Why would my husband want such a woman instead of me?"

Probably because men marry for many reasons, none of which are love. But she did not say this. Instead, she said, "You don't have a husband. And if you frequent soirees such as Mrs. Buchanan's, you'll not likely get one—or not one you'd want anyway."

But Tiffany too was interested in the subject of mistresses, immensely interested. Wolf was also rumored to have a mistress, a Lady Delia. Would she be attending Mrs. Buchanan's fete with Wolf?

And would she be at the opera tonight? Why did the idea of Wolf's mistress inflame her so?

"What do you think Mrs. Buchanan looks like? And why do the men like her so?"

Tiffany felt terribly out of sorts with this line of questioning. Give her a set of accounts or a company's annual report and she could analyze the likely risk and return. But the nuances of human interactions? No. She'd leave those to her friends.

She reached for her spectacles on the side table. "I have no idea."

Valora pouted. "Well, when I do select a husband, I definitely do not want him having any other women. He must love me madly, you see."

Tiffany thought such a thing was quite possible. Valora was such a fair-haired beauty, she could wrap a man around her little finger, as young Mr. Turnbull had found out to his detriment. Since Valora's come-out, many of the *ton's* eligible bachelors, and some not so eligible, had fallen at her feet professing love. A large dowry probably contributed to the attraction.

Financial logic Tiffany could understand. Money was the key to freedom in the world. Many sins were forgiven if a person had well-stocked coffers.

"Can't we wait until after refreshments to have this conversation?" She'd skipped breakfast in her haste to visit Capel Court. "The rest of the Sisterhood will be here soon for an update on the status of our investments. The quarterly payments are in."

The Sisterhood was not, strictly speaking, comprised of siblings, but the eight girls had grown up in each other's homes and were almost as close as sisters. The group comprised sisters, cousins, and friends, all focused on one thing—making money. All of the women had varied reasons as to why making money was important to them.

Valora sat up. "I knew I should have gone to Claire's room first. She'd understand."

"Claire would have thrown something at your head for such a harebrained idea."

"It is so unfair that our brothers get to do whatever they like in this world while we embroider and plan charity luncheons." Valora stood and looked wistfully out of the window. "Don't you want to know the mysteries of the world before you are bartered off to the most sensible man in the most sensible match? I'm sick of being sensible."

Tiffany thought perhaps it wasn't the right time to say that Valora was rarely sensible.

"Your brother is not bartering you off. In fact, Vale has been very patient. You keep refusing offers. You're getting a reputation for it."

Tiffany tried not to be jealous. Unlike Valora, she'd not had a single offer. No man had fallen at *her* feet professing love.

Wolf's image invaded her head. His lips on her skin...his offering her what she secretly wanted—to become his wife. She couldn't believe how strong she was to have turned him down.

However, she did secretly agree with Valora on one thing. Unless a man wanted her for herself, she would never marry. She had a brain and her investments were doing well. She could already afford a small cottage in the country with a small staff. She'd prefer to live as a spinster than be locked in an unhappy marriage.

Besides, you're madly in love with Wolf—but he has to love you back...

Valora pouted. "I'm waiting for the right man."

It wasn't what her friend said but the way she said it that made Tiffany give her a probing look. Valora would not meet her eye. Tiffany gave an excited squeal, and she jumped off the bed. "Goodness, you have a particular man in mind. That's why you are refusing so many offers."

"Don't be silly."

Tiffany clapped her hands. "I'm right. Who is he?" For the first time in her life Valora looked flustered. "Is he someone we know?" When color filled Valora's face she added, "It is someone we know." She prayed it wasn't Wolf. She'd never stand a chance against Valora in a competition for Wolf's affections.

"Whom do we know?" a cheery voice asked, and Claire entered Tiffany's bedchamber through the connecting door. "I could hear your shriek through the walls, Tiffany. I thought you'd found another spider."

"Valora is enamored of a gentleman and he is someone we know. He must be, or she'd have shared her secret."

Claire flopped down on the bed next to Valora and yawned. "There is no secret. Valora's been in love with Fane since the summer we spied on him, Vale and Wolf swimming in the pond on our estate."

Swimming naked. Tiffany's face heated. What a sight that had been. Wolf emerging from the pond like a Greek god, bronzed and glistening. His masculinity had caused her body to heat, and all she'd wanted was to run her hand over every inch of him...

"Goodness," Valora cried out, "please tell me Fane does not know."

Fane? Tiffany shook away the vision of perfection lodged in her head. Her mouth fell open as she stared at the two young ladies lying on her bed. "Fane?" She shook her head. "Our Fane?"

Claire nodded. "Don't worry. He has no idea."

"So that's why you want to go to Mrs. Buchanan's soiree, Valora." Suddenly, Tiffany did not envy her beautiful friend at all. Fane had many ladies, including the type she was supposed to know nothing about, throwing themselves at him. Rich and incredibly handsome, he was renowned for the mistresses and pretty actresses under his protection. In his younger days he'd left a trail of broken hearts in his wake. As he'd gotten older, he'd become more discreet.

Claire reached out and took Valora's hand. "He has to marry one day, but I truly hope you don't waste your life waiting for him. If he cannot see the treasure you are right under his nose, he's not good enough for you."

When tears welled in Valora's eyes, Tiffany did not know what to say. At eight and twenty years of age, it was past time that Fane thought about marrying and filled a nursery, but Fane was in no hurry; he had his younger brother, Dayton, as the spare.

It was time to change this dangerous subject lest Claire and Valora look too closely at Tiffany and ferret out where *her* affections lay. They would call her the worst of fools to have fallen for Wolf. She was waiting for them to ask about Wolf's attentions last night.

Tiffany walked to the bell and pulled it. "Could you take Miss Valora to the drawing room and pour her a strong cup of tea," she told the maid who entered.

Valora rose from the bed and smoothed her dress before walking past her to the door.

Tiffany said, "Claire and I will be down shortly after we have discussed a private matter. We won't be long and the others will be arriving soon."

Luckily Valora was too upset to ask what private matter. Before she left the room she said, "You won't tell the others will you? I couldn't bear it. It's bad enough you two pity me let alone the others."

With that she slipped from the room and followed the maid downstairs.

As Milly, their lady's maid, arrived to sort out their dresses for the day, Tiffany turned to Claire. "You've known all this time?"

"It was not my place to tell. But I think her moping after my brother has gone on long enough. I wish I could make Valora see what a perfect bore he really is. Then perhaps she'd move on. Lord Northbrook is very keen on her."

Lord Northbrook was young and very handsome, and rich, and an Earl with a large estate. Valora could do much worse. "Fane is not a bore," Tiffany said, "and that's the problem. He's charismatic, witty and intelligent. Every debutante falls in love with him. He could have his pick. *And* he's just as handsome as Northbrook."

Just like Wolf.

"I fear that's the truth of it. Valora will risk all if she waits for my brother." Claire paused in the doorway.

Tiffany cleared her throat. "Speaking of risk... I bumped into Wolf at Capel Court."

"Did he recognize you?"

"He escorted me home," she hurriedly added. "But he's promised not to tell Marlowe."

Claire eyed her suspiciously. "That doesn't sound like any friend of Fane's." Her eyes narrowed further. "What did you have to promise him?"

She wanted to tell Claire the truth but she couldn't. "Nothing, I swear. Something about helping him with a painting he's working on."

"How strange. Normally he'd be straight to Marlowe's door." She sat silently for a moment, looking at Tiffany. "Something is up. I want to know what Wolf's sudden interest in you is all about. Dancing with you last night..." At Tiffany's silence, Claire added, "Just remember our French lessons and what happened to Little Red Riding Hood when she played with the big bad wolf. Whatever you are up to, be careful."

Claire left to gather her papers for their meeting. She had not believed Tiffany for a minute. That's what came from being as close as sisters. Tiffany sat at her dressing table and brushed her hair. Her heart hurt. Claire knew there was something afoot because she could not see a man like Wolf taking an interest in Tiffany otherwise. She gave herself a stern talking to. After just one short interval of Wolf's attentions, she had already forgotten this was but a game to him. She had to protect her heart and not lose it to Wolf completely, or she'd be crushed by bitter disappointment. Wolf would never love a woman like her.

Now Valora... A man could definitely lose his heart to a woman as beautiful as she was. Tiffany would love to see her friend happy and she'd love to see her married to Fane. Valora would be the perfect sister-in-law. Surely, if they all put their heads together, the Sisterhood could find a way to bring two of her favorite people in the world together.

They could do it.

She was sure they could.

The afternoon meeting of the Sisterhood would take on a different bent today. For once Tiffany wasn't thinking of her precious investments. They had other fish to fry—but first they had to catch Fane, who would be as slippery as an eel.

Chapter Five

By the time Tiffany arrived in the drawing room, all the members of the Sisterhood, except newly married Serena, were present—Courtney, Ashleigh, Farah, Ivy, Valora, Lauren, plus Claire and herself. She had each of their investment records in her hand, thanks to her visit to Mr. Sprat this morning, and she walked round the table giving each woman her copy.

Last year they had set up the Sisterhood as an investment group, after Serena and Claire discovered Tiffany had been investing a portion of her allowance each quarter for years so she could have a better future. Claire had laughed at her in the beginning, while Serena loved the idea of a woman having financial freedom. Then they saw the returns Tiffany was making and asked her to invest some of their allowance too. Claire mentioned Tiffany's skills to Valora, Serena mentioned it to Lauren, and soon all the girls wanted Tiffany's help, and the Sisterhood was born. To most of them it was a bit of fun. A secret scandalous pastime.

"Oh, my goodness! Look at my balance. You really are a miracle worker, Tiffany. Thank you, darling."

Tiffany beamed at Courtney's praise. Lady Courtney Montague was the sister of Lord Ashley Montague, Viscount Milburn, eldest son and heir to the Marquess of Lorne. At four and twenty, Courtney, an auburn-haired beauty, was the eldest of the Sisterhood. Five years ago, her fiancé, an officer in the army, had gone missing after the Irish Rebellion. As theirs had been a love match, Courtney refused to marry anyone else. She still loved her fiancé deeply, and was investing money for the same reason as Tiffany. They both wanted the freedom from their family to live as they pleased.

Valora barely glanced at her sheet, but then she had no reason to worry about money. Tiffany squeezed her shoulder as she went past.

Lady Farah Perrin also barely looked at the sheet. Tiffany suspected the sister of the Duke of Blackstone had no need to worry about money or marriage either. She was a shy girl with a ghostly complexion. At one and twenty she simply loved being part of the group because Farah was an only daughter and valued the other girls' friendships. Her brother, His Grace, was also a very formidable man. Farah struggled to assert her own wants within his household.

Ivy jumped to her feet and hugged her. "Thank you, Tiffany. I can finally hire an additional woman to teach at the orphanage."

Tiffany loved Lady Ivy Ware, Wolf's youngest sister. It was such a shame Tiffany was in love with her brother. That's the reason she rarely visited Ivy at her home. Two years younger than Tiffany, Ivy was one of those women who always thought of others before herself. Tall, dark-haired, with a creamy complexion, she surely would not remain unmarried for long. She was the patron of an orphanage on the outskirts of London. Wolf had tried to stop her, saying she was too young and naïve, but for once she'd stood up to her "know-it-all-brother". The orphanage was doing a fabulous job and Tiffany often went with her on her calls.

"You can have my dividends this quarter if you need them, sister dear," Ashleigh said to Ivy. "Think of it as my contribution."

Ivy blew her sister a kiss across the table. Ashleigh was the complete opposite of Ivy. Fair-haired like her mother, and somewhat cynical about life, but then she had a reason to be. She was three years older than Ivy, and just as beautiful, and she was officially on the shelf. There was some scandal in her past that none of the girls were privy to, or if they were they'd never said a word. None of them cared. They loved Ashleigh even if she did not mix in society as much as the debutantes. Ashleigh had joined the Sisterhood last. Tiffany suspected it was because she was bored. She always gave her money to Ivy. Perhaps she wanted to atone for her past lack of judgment.

Claire was busy issuing instructions for more tea and to keep her brother out of the drawing room. It was unlikely Fane would disturb them; Tiffany had heard him come in early this morning after carousing all night. He'd almost caught her slipping out. He'd unlikely rise before three.

Lady Lauren Cavanaugh, the eldest daughter of the Earl of Danvers, flashed Tiffany a pretty smile as she took her seat next to Lauren at the head of the table. Lauren's red hair matched her temper, but Lauren rarely raised her voice within the Sisterhood. At home, to her father—that was a different story.

"Do you want to spend your dividend or reinvest it this quarter?" Tiffany asked her.

An expression of pain flashed so quickly across Lauren's face Tiffany almost missed it. "I will take my dividend, thank you."

When her friend did not say more, Tiffany knew it meant her father had been gambling again. Her brother was Courtney's lost fiancé. Lucien had been his father's only son and Lord Danvers had not gotten over his death. He'd taken to drink and gambling. She patted Lauren's hand.

At four and twenty, Lauren had resigned herself to spinsterhood. She had to hold the house together for her sister, Madeline, and their father. Madeline had just turned seventeen, and Lauren had pinned her hopes on next season making a good match for her sister. She was investing as much as she could to have the coin to give Madeline an appropriate come-out next season.

A servant placed food in front of Tiffany. Since she'd missed breakfast she had to eat. Tiffany loved food and she was hungry. She wasn't the thinnest of women and so she made an effort to never overindulge. For one, if she put on weight, she'd need a whole new wardrobe, and she hated wasting her money on frivolous things such as clothes when what she had was more than adequate. She could wear the same gown to every ball for a week and no one would even notice.

Wolf had changed all of that. Bother.

Ashleigh spoke up. "I'd like to skin that brother of yours, Valora. Do you know that at the ball last night he thought it was so funny to introduce Horace Roberts to me, and I had to dance with the man."

Oh, no. Lord Horace had four left feet and most women's toes were bruised and battered by the time he'd finished.

"On top of the fact he bruised my feet, Horace insisted on walking me back to my mother's side and he did not leave all night. Vale was laughing and waving at me as if it was a huge joke, while I had to behave like a proper lady and pretend to enjoy his company. I bet Horace turns up at my house today." She slammed her hand on the table. "It was cruel. They both know I have to behave spotlessly."

Claire piped up. "You'll have to wait your turn. Valora wants to skin Vale too." Claire elbowed Valora in her side. "Go on, tell them."

Valora gave Tiffany a panicked look.

"Valora was telling us that she wanted to go to Mrs. Buchanan's soiree. But Vale has forbidden her from attending."

If a hatpin had fallen on the rug, you would have heard it.

"I can top that," Farah said. "His Grace has issued an order. I'm to allow Lord Franklin to take me for a turn in the park on Friday." She looked at their confused faces. "If I go for a turn with Lord Franklin everyone will assume I favor his attentions. My brother will not listen when I say we are not suited. He thinks I don't know my own mind."

"Sometimes I think I'm lucky that my father drowns his

sorrows in a bottle and barely remembers I exist," Lauren stated, and Tiffany had to agree. It was why she did not particularly want a husband. Children would be nice but not in a loveless marriage where she had no say in her life.

"You are lucky," Farah enthused.

"I must admit I'm starting to get very tired of men thinking they know what is best for us," Courtney said.

Valora spoke over the murmur of agreement. "I think we should bring them down a peg or two. Or at least make them understand we are perfectly capable of making our own decisions. If I want to go to Mrs. Buchanan's famous afternoon soiree, why shouldn't I? What could be so scandalous about a garden party in the middle of the day?"

The silence indicated Valora's question was one they all wanted answered. What were they missing out on?

"We need a plan for how to attend." Claire looked at Courtney and leaned back in her chair with a huge grin. "Courtney Montague, you have a plan."

Courtney mirrored her friend's smile. "Not really, just a germ of an idea."

Ivy giggled. "Share it."

"I think we should make a game of it. Let's each of us select one of our male tormentors' names out of a hat, and in another hat we will place ideas for how we could torment them and teach them a bit of humility. Then we each select one piece of parchment from each hat, giving us the deed and the name of the man to target. At the end we can reveal what we have done. That should make them realize we are women to be reckoned with."

Lauren laughed. "Ooh, I like the sound of that. But what on earth could we do to them that would bring them to their knees?"

Claire sat forward. "I know for a fact that Fane is very vain. Perhaps we could place an order for the most ridiculous colored and decorated waistcoat, tell Prinny what it looks like and that Fane was getting it designed especially for his ball. Fane would be forced to wear it by royal command."

"Forced to? I can't see Fane being forced to do anything," Tiffany said.

"What about making Vale take a swim in the pond in Hyde park?"

"How would you do that?" Farah asked.

"That's up to the person who draws his name from the hat," Courtney replied. "The person who draws the deed must work out how to achieve it."

"Oh, His Grace has a reputation for the finest French brandy," Farah said. "We could send a bottle to all his stuffy friends as a gift but water it down. He'd be mortified."

Ashleigh seemed less than enthused. "How are these pranks supposed to make them take us seriously? We would be better doing something they respect."

They all began to nod in agreement.

Tiffany spoke up. "I was thinking we should concentrate on our investments. I think we should issue the men a challenge. We make a higher return over the next twelve months and they leave us to make our own decisions in all aspects of our lives."

"How can we help with that?" Valora wailed.

"You're the investment brain," added Lauren.

"You will all need to keep tabs on your brothers. What are they investing in? Who are they meeting with? We will have to work the social engagements and the lords in positions of power. We have to keep our eyes and ears open, searching for information and any investment that might give the men an advantage."

"Are we not overlooking something? They have to agree. Why would they bother with us?"

All heads swiveled Ashleigh's way.

Tiffany thought hard for a moment and considered her current wager with Wolf—only the two of them were privy to the bet. "They won't know it is us. We shall issue an anonymous challenge. The winner takes all of what either party earned that year. If I know Fane, Vale, and Wolf, which I do, they won't be able to resist, nor will the others."

"I love this idea." Claire laughed and clapped her hands. "Can you imagine. The men will hate not knowing who their challenger is."

Tiffany gave a sly smile. "They may spend more time on finding out who has challenged them, than on the investing. The men would never suspect a group of young debutantes who are so helpless they can't even choose who they should allow to escort them for a turn in the park."

"Brilliant," Farah said, clapping her hands. "And, if we do all the pranks as well, they'll never connect us to the brilliant investor. I really would love to see my brother embarrassed."

"It all sounds heavenly," Ashleigh stated. She looked directly at Tiffany. "But can we beat them?"

There was the rub. Tiffany was good but so were the men. They had paid investment advisers too. She had Mr. Sprat, and she could call on him as well. She wanted to do this. She wanted to prove herself. Plus, if they won, her share would give her financial security for the rest of her life. She would gain her independence and not have to rely on charity any more, nor would she be forced into a marriage of convenience with Wolf.

It was about time the men in their lives realized that the Sisterhood was a force to be reckoned with. Some ladies wanted more in life than to flutter their fans and bat their eyelashes to attract a man.

She already had a wager with Wolf. Could she out-earn him on one investment in a month? She'd wager her life on the fact that she could make more money in twelve months than he could. But could she make more than all of them combined? Even the brilliant Fane?

"They will be hard to beat. But even if we lose, won't they be impressed at what we did achieve and that we fooled them?"

"Impressed? Maybe. Angry and humiliated, definitely," Claire said.

"Well, that means I'm in," said Ivy.

One by one the eight Sisterhood members agreed to the plan.

"I'm doing the investing," Tiffany said, "so you ladies can think up the pranks. Remember, this is not only about the pranks. You have to learn what is going on in your brothers' investments as well as anyone else's. Most men don't remember to hold their tongues around women. We are brainless idiots who cannot possibly understand what they are talking about."

Before anyone could answer, a loud masculine voice came from the entrance hall. Tiffany looked across at Claire, who frowned and began to rise just as the door flew open.

A man stepped into the room, and Tiffany's heart did that annoying little flip it always did whenever she clapped eyes on Wolf.

His deep burgundy jacket fitted him like a new glove and showed off his broad shoulders to perfection. He was dressed for riding and his Hessians somehow emphasized his powerful thighs.

She noted every inch of him, and her skin prickled with heat as she realized his gaze was taking in every inch of her.

"I see Lady Claire has rallied her troops once more. What on earth are you ladies discussing with such vigor? The latest French fashions perhaps?" His gaze swept across the group.. "A few new dresses might not go amiss."

As usual in Wolf's presence, Tiffany's tongue would not function and she could not think of a scathing retort.

Valora did it for her. "We were discussing what we would wear to Mrs. Buchanan's soiree. Perhaps a different wardrobe would make us blend in better."

For one fleeting moment, the big bad wolf's face showed fear. "Very funny, Miss Valora. Vale has forbidden you from attending. I'm sure once I reveal this ridiculous plan to Marlowe, he'll do the same to you two," he said, pointing at Tiffany and Claire.

"Then run along and tattle to Marlowe. Don't let the door hit your conceited arse on the way out," his sister Ashleigh said.

His face looked like thunder. "You and Ivy are forbidden to attend." When they simply looked at him with angelic faces, Wolf added, "I'm warning you."

At that ridiculous edict the eight women burst into giggles, and Wolf turned his angry gaze on Tiffany. "I'm sure Miss Tiffany won't want to attend. She has more sense. In fact, I've come to request her company for a carriage ride tomorrow afternoon."

The giggling stopped and all eyes swung her way. Tiffany's blood boiled in her veins. The cheek of the man. She'd said a slow courtship. This wasn't slow. How to answer? "If the weather is fine, the outing would be acceptable. I'll bring Milly, our lady's maid."

"Perfect. If you'll excuse me, ladies, I shall find Marlowe and leave you to your, er...leave you."

Chapter Six

"I told you," Valora said. "He danced with her last night at the ball. Two dances. He danced the second waltz. Have you ever known Wolfarth to dance, let alone a waltz?"

The ladies all started talking at once, until Tiffany clapped her hands. "Please, ladies. I have no idea what his intentions are. Like you, I shall just have to wait and see. But we have investments to discuss and a challenge to organize." There was no way she was confessing about her arrangement with Wolf.

"Perhaps one of our male relatives has come to their senses," Courtney said. "Perhaps he realizes what a catch Tiffany would be." Tiffany wanted to hug her.

"Let's see how they react when we go to Mrs. Buchanan's soiree," Ashleigh added. "I can't wait to see the look on Wolf's face when he sees us there."

Once the ladies had wiped the tears of laughter from their eyes, Ivy said, "We have to go now. The look on their faces will be priceless. The gossip sheets will have a field day but I don't care. Safety in numbers. We should call ourselves the Sisterhood of Scandal."

The women began talking over each other in excitement. Claire approached Tiffany. "I'll get the hats."

Tiffany stopped her and whispered in her ear, "Leave Valora until last and keep Fane's name out of the hat until then." She winked to drive her message home.

"Oh, I intend to, don't you worry. I know exactly what I'm doing."

"Good. I'm going to run upstairs and get the latest stock sheets. Then we can divide up the companies to research."

"You do that while we draw our opponents' names."

Tiffany caught Claire's odd smile, but thought nothing of it until she arrived back in the room ten minutes later and learned the man she was to torment was Wolf. She looked at the knowing smiles around the table. It was obvious her secret crush was no secret.

Her face flooded with heat as she sank onto her chair.

"I for one cannot wait to learn how you propose to torment Wolf," Ivy said. "Ashleigh and I are happy to help. It's about time my brother met his match."

Tiffany didn't know what to say, but at the same time excitement skittered along her veins. She now had to pit her wits against one of London's most intelligent, handsome and irritating men. While they privately had their own wager, she wasn't about to tell him of the Sisterhood's other challenge.

As ideas swarmed through her head, a feeling of euphoria warmed every inch of her body.

She now had a reason to study Wolf, even after she won their month-long wager. Her excitement grew. She had the perfect excuse to purposely bump into him, to talk to him, to seek out his company.

Given Wolf's agenda she should not be so excited. But at least this gave her an excuse to find out why he'd offered marriage.

She couldn't wait.

"Who shall draft the note? If it's to Fane it needs to be in a script he won't recognize."

"I'll do it," Courtney volunteered. She readied herself with quill and parchment. "Who's going to dictate?"

Claire took charge. "How about—My Lords Marlowe, Wolfarth, Vale, Lorne and His Grace the Duke Blackstone.

"It is said in the clubs that you are skilled investors, the best in all England, and that everything you touch returns you a healthy profit. It is also known that you are men who love—"

"Would men use the word 'love'?" Ashleigh asked.

"Good point," Tiffany said. "What about—it is also known that you are men who never say no to a wager, and as such I issue a challenge. I offer you a wager—"

"No. Men are more direct," Claire said. "Instead of 'I offer you a wager', say—we each invest one thousand pounds, and in twelve months to this day, we meet at White's—"

There were loud gasps and they all started talking at once.

"We cannot meet at White's," Farah said. "Ladies cannot enter."

Claire nodded. "Quite right. What about this?" She started over, and ten minutes later Courtney had the full letter transcribed and ready for the ladies to inspect.

My Lords Marlowe, Wolfarth, Vale, Lorne and His Grace the Duke of Blackstone

This day, 1 April, 1808

It is said in the clubs that you are skilled investors, the best in all England, and that everything you touch returns you a healthy profit. It is also known that you are men who never say no to a wager, and as such I issue a challenge.

We each invest one thousand pounds, and in twelve months to this day, we meet in His Grace's study with our investment ledgers, where we will determine who has accumulated the largest return from the individual one-thousand-pound investments, and who can claim the title of the most astute investor in all England.

What is the prize, other than the esteemed title? The winner takes the total amount earned, six thousand pounds (one thousand pounds each) plus any capital growth. If you agree to these terms, place the wager in the betting book at White's. The name of your challenger? Well, that is over to you to find out—if you can.

Yours faithfully
  The Most Skilled Investor

"I like it. Especially if we win the esteemed title." Ashleigh was certainly taking this seriously. "How do we deliver the notes to each of the men?"

Ivy spoke up. "I shall ask one of the street urchins near the orphanage to deliver the missives to each house early in the morning before any of the men arise."

~

By the time the ladies had departed, their tasks allocated, Tiffany needed a rest before the opera that night. She collected a plate of food and made her way upstairs. Sneaky, early morning trips led to tiredness. But before she reached her bedchamber, the butler, Booth, presented a silver tray with a missive on it. To her surprise it was from Mr. Sprat. She quickly took the note, hoping Fane had not seen it.

When her mother was alive, she would often scold Tiffany's father for encouraging her investing. Her mother had taken great pains to inform Tiffany that men did not like a wife who was smarter than they were.

But Tiffany worried more about hurting Fane than offending his male sensibilities. Fane, Dayton, and Claire were the only family she had left. She could not lose them, for then she *would* truly be alone. Dayton would probably applaud her initiative, but he was in India. Fane might not be so understanding.

How could she explain to Fane why she invested? He would never understand her feelings on charity. Or the fact he continually tried to marry her off. She wanted to be able to repay his kindness but gain her independence. She had overheard him one night telling Lady Marlowe that he despaired of ever finding a man who would marry her because her dowry was so small, and she was not a beauty. He said the only way to find her a husband was to offer a huge dowry.

Her pride had withered and died. Fane had thought to barter her off his hands. She had politely declined his offer of a larger dowry. That had hurt Fane but he had accepted her refusal.

Never would she allow herself to be married out of pity, or because she was an inconvenience to Fane. Her skills with numbers meant she could marry whom she chose—or, if she chose, no one at all. A good income gave her choices.

She lay on her bed exhausted. Anger at the memory of both Wolf and Fane thinking to manipulate her made her rip Mr. Sprat's missive open a bit roughly. Inside, there weren't the normal company papers. Instead, there was a letter and many sheets of parchment detailing purchase notes made on behalf of a Lord Melville. Before she could read the letter, the door opened.

"That went well," Claire said as she breezed into the room. "Don't forget the opera tonight. Ivy said Wolf is escorting them. Perhaps he'll pay us a visit in our box." Tiffany yawned. "All that dancing *will* make you tired, you know," and Claire winked.

Last night, after the other men attending the ball had witnessed Wolf's interest in her, Tiffany's dance card had filled rapidly. She'd practically danced into the early hours of the morning. "It was fun, but I don't know how the *ton's* diamonds do that almost every night. I'd be exhausted. No wonder they say yes to the first man who proposes—just to be able to rest."

Claire giggled. "Speaking of proposals, you've kept Booth busy answering the door this morning. The foyer is full of flowers. You best be presentable come three. I suspect there will be many gentlemen callers."

Tiffany's heart sped up. Would Wolf be one of them? Suddenly the idea of letting Wolf court her seemed magical, even if it was all a game. "I hope not. I wanted some sleep before the opera tonight or I'm likely to fall asleep during the second act and snore."

"Who is your letter from?" Claire asked.

"It's nothing of importance, just some correspondence from Mr. Sprat."

"We can win this wager?" Claire asked. "You're not having second thoughts."

"We have just as good a chance as the men." Tiffany paused. "Of course, if we get caught before the twelve months are up, we will all be in a lot of trouble. Sisterhood of Scandal will be right. I'm worried for Ashleigh. She can't be involved in another scandal."

"I wish I understood more of the first, but she won't say a word." The clock on the mantle struck two. "Best you freshen up. I suspect it's going to be a long afternoon. The doorbell will be ringing soon."

When Claire made to leave, Tiffany asked, "You'll come downstairs with me, won't you?"

"Of course. I wouldn't leave you to face this mob alone. May I suggest leaving your glasses in your pocket this afternoon? Don't remind your suitors that you are a bluestocking."

"I can't see without my glasses. Although that might be handy depending on who calls," Tiffany joked. "Besides, what is wrong with being a bluestocking?"

Claire's smile died. "Nothing. Absolutely nothing. I'll let you rest."

She could have kissed Claire. Not once had she mentioned Wolf, and Tiffany hadn't because she was too embarrassed to speak his name. Her cousin was pretty cagey about who she might favor, if anyone, this season. Claire was younger than Tiffany by a year. Yet at two and twenty she seemed in no hurry to marry. She had received a few offers, but for some reason none of the men appealed to her. Fane seemed unconcerned, and since Lady Marlowe's death almost two years ago, the girls had mostly been left to themselves.

"I'm going for a walk in the garden to clear a slight headache," Claire added. "We have the opera this evening and I want to go to support Valora. Lady Vale is pushing her at Lord Dingleby, and I said I'd sit in her box for the second act."

"Her mother will soon run out of suitors. Can't we invite Valora to our box? Fane is attending?"

"Good idea. If Wolf is at the opera, Fane will be too. For some of it at least. I'll dash off a note to Lady Vale inviting them to our box. I shall leave you to your correspondence, then. See you at three in the drawing room. Fane is supposed to be acting as chaperon but most likely he'll sleep until late, so we shall have to keep the door open and Mrs. Gibbs will have to join us once again. She hates giving up her time when she's so busy running the house for us." With that Claire departed.

Tiffany turned to the letter from Mr. Sprat. She picked up a piece of bread with cheese and was just about to pop it in her mouth when she read the first paragraph. The bread dropped from her fingers onto the floor and her heart almost stopped beating in her chest.

The letter told her that the purchase notes detailed on the sheets of parchment—all of them from a Lord Melville—had been reneged on. She could barely breathe. She understood what Mr. Sprat was telling her. All the money she had given him to invest on her behalf—and it was just about all she owned—was now in jeopardy. If he went bankrupt, his assets, including her money, would be seized.

Like all stockjobbers, Mr. Sprat used his own money to buy shares on behalf of a lord via a purchase order. Once the shares were bought, the lord would then make good his money and the shares ownership passed to the peer. Most men had enough honor to pay their debts if, between purchase and settlement, the shares decreased in value.

Except Lord Melville, it would seem.

What made this unbearable was that, because she was a woman, Mr. Sprat made her pay upfront, before he purchased the shares. She'd had to agree to that stipulation, but given he'd been her father's stockjobber and had helped him when he was almost made bankrupt, she trusted Mr. Sprat.

She crumpled his letter in her shaking hand. Who was this Lord Melville, that he held no honor? She could not let him do this to Mr. Sprat, especially as Sprat had been good enough to forgo the remnants of her father's last purchase order upon hearing of his death and subsequent bankruptcy, leaving her with a few precious hundred pounds. Plus, he allowed her to trade.

Without Mr. Sprat the Sisterhood of Scandal had no way to win or even begin the challenge they were just in the process of issuing. Ivy already had the notes prepared for delivery to the men.

Tiffany unclenched her fist and read the rest of the letter. Mr. Sprat was asking for her help. Her eyes widened. Lord Melville was Lord Wolfarth's uncle on his mother's side. Mr. Sprat wanted her to persuade Wolf to intervene in the honoring of the debt. Since he'd seen them together at the Stock Exchange this morning, he presumed they were on familiar terms.

She slumped back on her bed. How on earth was she to get Wolf to do that? She could hardly say, oh, by the way, your uncle is forcing my stockjobber into dun territory and it might mean I lose all my money. And the Sisterhood's money!

She slapped her forehead. If she lost her money she lost the bet with him.

Poor Mr. Sprat. Poor her. She had to do something. She would have to think of a way to elicit Wolf's help without revealing her true interest in the matter.

And blow it all, she now had to sit for a couple of hours and prattle inanely with gentlemen about the weather and the latest on-dits when really she needed time to think.

As her lady's maid, Milly, helped make her presentable for her callers, she hoped Wolf might be among them so she could talk with him alone.

Chapter Seven

To Tiffany's dismay, Wolf had not called on her this afternoon. Still, there was always the opera, although how she'd have time to speak with him privately at the theater, she had no idea. But he had promised a carriage ride in the park tomorrow afternoon. That would surely be the perfect time to talk about his uncle. No one would overhear.

She had managed to snatch some sleep before dinner, and now Milly was finishing her hair for the excursion to the theater. She usually hated the theater. Everyone attending simply to be seen. Since no one particularly cared whether she was present or not, the evening usually dragged. But tonight would be different. Valora would be in the box. Claire was determined to make Fane take note of their beautiful friend.

Wolf might pay her a visit also, and she wanted to see if he did, and how he behaved. Would he declare to the *ton* his intentions to court her?

It was not very surprising that the Marlowes' carriage arrived directly behind Wolf's. They only lived a few houses apart and had left at about the same time.

She watched Wolf help his sisters from the carriage. Their party made their way over to where she stood with Fane, Claire and Valora. She took a few deep breaths. In evening attire, Wolf could outshine a full moon. Several women descending from their carriages almost stumbled at the sight of him.

"Good evening, ladies. Marlowe."

"Your box or mine this evening?" Fane replied.

"Ours I'm afraid, we invited Valora," Claire replied.

"I'm happy to join your party, Lady Claire," Wolf said, then moved to talk with Marlowe as they made their way into the Theatre Royal. Tiffany overheard Fane ask, "Can you see the ladies home? I wish to stay after the performance."

She could not hear Wolf's reply but obviously Fane wished to visit backstage to see his mistress, Mrs. Buchanan. She looked at Valora, who didn't appear to have heard Fane's comment, thank goodness.

The ladies took the seats at the front of the box. Claire placed Valora between her and Tiffany, knowing that Wolf would sit behind her. That meant Fane would be right behind Valora. Ashleigh automatically sat on the side almost hidden by the curtain, still not happy to be the object of gossip given the *ton* had not forgotten her scandal almost two years ago now.

One day Tiffany would ascertain what had occurred. Not because she was nosey, but so as to help Ashleigh find her own worth and make her not care what society thought of her.

Heat hit the back of her neck as Wolf leaned forward and whispered in her ear, "You look very pretty tonight, Miss Deveraux. No glasses this evening."

"Luckily the opera is more about hearing than seeing as I'm almost blind without them." She did not care what this man thought of her. Besides, it was the truth. She was very short-sighted. He may as well learn her flaws now.

"I always found the opera is more about feeling than seeing or hearing," and she could have sworn his lips brushed the skin of her neck. Her body heated immediately and she was pleased he could not see her face. Wolf had decided fairness was a word he did not know the meaning of.

"Claire, would you mind swapping seats with me so I can talk to Ashleigh?" That should fix him. Wolf wouldn't be able to switch or it would be commented upon. She couldn't help giving him a snarky smile as she rose to move.

She turned her attention to Ashleigh and drew her into a conversation, hoping the opera would start soon.

~

Wolf had meant it when he'd said you feel rather than hear the music. He loved opera; maybe it was his artistic nature. The music swirled around him, but for once he couldn't appreciate it because all he could focus on was the shape of Tiffany's neck and how her skin had tasted.

The little minx bested him this evening. She'd moved on purpose. He sat back and let the music flood his senses. Closing his eyes, he pictured his lips dancing over her creamy skin in time to the music.

Her neck was long and slender and he'd love to draw it. He'd love to draw her. She was all womanly curves and bristling passion. He wondered if she actually understood her nature. He was confident it would not take him long to make her soften to his advances. The way she'd shivered as he'd tasted her skin was evidence enough. Plus, why move if he had not affected her?

So lost in thought was he, he had not noticed the first act had ended. "Shall I organize some refreshments?" he asked Marlowe.

"I want to go for a cheroot. Can you see to the ladies?"

"Can't you wait until the opera finishes to see her? I can't chaperon all five ladies. What if one wishes to use the retiring room?"

Marlowe was already on his feet. "I'm sure if they go in pairs they will be perfectly fine." He left before Wolf could object.

Lady Claire watched her brother depart and shook her head. She rose and approached Wolf. "Could you organize some refreshments?" In a louder voice she added, "Tiffany can help you."

Tiffany didn't look pleased, but she could hardly object.

The corridors were crowded and Wolf tucked her arm in his as they made their way toward the rear of the theater.

"I'm very much looking forward to our ride in the park tomorrow."

She flashed a look at him. "I am too. I have a matter to discuss with you."

That sounded ominous. "Can we not discuss it now?"

She shook her pretty head. "No. It must wait until tomorrow."

Even more puzzling. Tiffany seemed to be searching the crowd for someone, her head turning left and right. "Are you enjoying the opera?" She kept looking around. He cleared his throat.

"Oh, I'm sorry. Did you say something?"

"I was asking if you were enjoying the opera."

She looked over her shoulder. "Yes. Do you know where Marlowe disappeared to?"

He was not about to tell her the truth. That her guardian had raced off to see his mistress. "I think he had business with Lord Tyler. Can I help you with anything?"

She swung to face him. "No. I hoped he wouldn't be too long. Miss Valora is a guest and I thought he might have conversed with her."

A smile broke over his lips. So that was why Valora was in their box while her mother was with friends in their family box across from them. How did he explain to Tiffany that Marlowe was not even considering marriage?

His smile quickly vanished as he noticed who was determinedly walking his way.

"Lord Wolfarth, how lovely to see you tonight."

Delia, on the arm of Lord Wilton. Wolf had broken off their arrangement only yesterday, so this was Delia showing him how quickly she could move on. And he didn't care. Since Margo, his relationships never involved feelings. Sex and mutual pleasure—a physical release only. And it had taken many years before he could face even that, but a man did have needs. He still felt guilty and often had to drink in order to relax enough to enjoy sex.

"Lady Delia and Lord Wilton, I hope you're enjoying the opera. May I present Miss Tiffany Deveraux?"

Delia's eyebrow rose. She hadn't recognized Tiffany but obviously knew the name. "Marlowe's ward?" Lord Wilton offered. "Good of you to escort her since Marlowe has disappeared backstage," and Wilton laughed.

Tiffany turned accusing eyes his way, while he, had ladies not been present, would have punched Wilton in the face for his crude behavior. Instead, he drew himself up to his full height. "I'm sure I have no idea what you mean."

Wilton took the hint, clearing his throat and turning to talk with Lord Milburn, who had stopped at his side.

Lady Delia, however, looked like the cat about to lick the cream. She looked Tiffany up and down and dismissed her as of no consequence. It was true that Delia was an exceptional beauty to whom few other women compared. After all, her looks were how she made a living. But on the inside, she couldn't hold a candle to Tiffany. Delia had been a mistake the minute he'd formed their arrangement. Far too demanding of his time and wanting more than money and sex from him. Lady Delia had fallen on hard times upon her husband's death. With no widow's portion, she needed an arrangement, but she was also looking for marriage and he would prefer someone less scheming.

Delia sidled up to him and whispered loud enough for Tiffany to hear. "I hope you were not too late to your engagement yesterday, after spending the afternoon with me."

Tiffany's fingers dug into his arm. "I was in your house for barely five minutes, if you recall, so I was not late to my meeting, but thank you for your concern." Delia's smile dimmed slightly.

"Well, I look forward to a longer visit soon."

Sometimes he wished he could slap a woman. Delia new damn well he would never be back. "I'm afraid I'm likely to be very busy for quite some time. Lord Wilton looks happy enough to keep you company. Come, Tiffany, refreshments await," and he almost dragged her away.

"Slow down, Wolf. My gown will not allow long strides. Your mistress seems to have upset you. Is it because she was with Lord Milton?"

His mouth almost dropped open. He stopped and swung Tiffany around to face him. "How do you know... No. Don't answer that. Lady Delia is no longer my mistress and she is a tad unhappy with the situation."

"Oh," was all Tiffany said, and he could see her mind working.

"And no, I do not have need of a replacement. It would not be honorable when courting you."

"I do not require such a sacrifice," she hissed.

He drew them into the shadows. "I do not consider it a sacrifice. You promised me that you would allow me to court you and I have too much honor to court a woman while in the bed of another." At her gasp, he reached up and brushed his finger down the soft skin of her cheek. "I swear, it is no hardship at all. I find you infinitely more interesting." And he pressed a kiss to her forehead before drawing them back in to the crowd.

"You are serious, aren't you?"

"Serious?"

"Your offer of marriage. A marriage of convenience. You were actually serious."

He leaned closer as they walked so only she could hear. "Of course. I would never be flippant with the woman whom I wish to align my life with. Or whom I choose to be the mother of my children."

His words were true. Tiffany's sharp wit and intelligence thrilled him in ways Delia's bountiful breasts couldn't.

With refreshments organized, they made their way back to

Marlowe's box. Many of his contemporaries stopped to converse and it was very noticeable that none of the ladies bothered with Tiffany. It was as if she were invisible, just like she'd mentioned on the carriage ride home from Capel Court. By the time they arrived back in the box, Wolf was decided. Even if he could not convince Tiffany to become his countess—something he refused to believe he could not achieve—he would ensure Tiffany became the *ton* diamond, or at least ensure that no one ignored her ever again.

To his delight, this time she stayed sitting in the seat in front of him. He leaned forward. "Be warned. You should take my courtship seriously, because I intend to win your hand."

Tiffany peered over her shoulder and met Wolf's smoldering eyes, and for the first time she was unsure whether she should continue their wager. Perhaps confessing all to Fane would be the best course of action.

Why? Why did Wolf wish to marry her?

Surely her investing skills were not the only reason? There had to be something else.

He didn't love her. How could he? He barely knew her. Besides, she'd seen how he acted when he was in love.

He had been madly in love with Lady Margo, but she had died before they could wed. The exact cause of Margo's death she'd not heard the full details of, but the pair had been set upon by highwaymen, like her father and mother had. Margo had survived but died shortly after. Maybe she'd been wounded in the attack?

Tiffany and Claire had been so envious of Lady Margo. Her and Wolf's engagement was six years ago, just after Tiffany had arrived to live with Lord Marlowe. Tiffany's heart had broken as she was infatuated with the young Wolfarth. But he'd only had eyes for Lady Margo.

At two and twenty, Wolf had swept Margo off her feet. Theirs had been the match of the season, more so because it was obvious to all that they were madly in love.

Perhaps Wolf was still in love with her memory, and did not

wish to find a love match again. Much like Courtney and her fiancé, who'd died in the Irish Rebellion.

She would speak to Courtney about her love for Lucien. Did he still fill her heart? Did Courtney think she could forget him and marry another?

She risked a glimpse behind her and shivered as she realized Wolf wasn't watching the stage, but watching her. She was too intelligent to believe she was so desirable that he just had to marry her. The only reason they'd even conversed about such a topic was because he'd caught her at the Stock Exchange. He suspected her skills but had no proof. Was this courtship a way to ascertain her skills?

She slumped in her seat. So it must be her investing proficiency that attracted him. She wasn't sure how she felt about that. Her mother's words—*men don't like wives to be smarter than they are*—rang in her head. Wolf didn't seem to care, though. He obviously saw it as an advantage. She'd give him points for that. But would she be happy in a marriage that was more a business arrangement? Or should she stick to her original plan to remain a spinster? A life on her terms.

There were distinct advantages to such a marriage with Wolf. She'd no longer be a charity case and she'd contribute to her new family's wealth. She'd belong. Having Ivy and Ashleigh as sisters would be lovely. And then there was the idea of children. She'd never let herself consider her chances of becoming a mother. Now his offer threw the possibility in her face. And she found it very appealing.

But not as appealing as the man.

She looked over her shoulder once more and straight into Wolf's handsome face. He was so tempting. Sharing his bed would be...most likely a dream come true. But would he promise to share her bed and no one else's? Love could hurt her. Destroy her. Because her infatuation with the man hadn't waned since the day he'd carried her into her new home all those years ago.

She glanced at Ashleigh sitting quietly in the corner as she usually did when out in public. Tiffany's heart bled for the woman, who was so beautiful she'd tempt a priest. Ashleigh was also one of the cleverest women she'd had the pleasure to meet. So it puzzled Tiffany greatly as to what Ashleigh could have done. She seemed too smart to fall for any rogue.

She would talk to Ashleigh about her brother and his offer. Claire had suggested that she also confess to the Sisterhood that Wolf had learned her secret and knew that she invested in the stock market. Would this mean he'd guess who was challenging him and the other men?

Perhaps she should have told the girls today.

Chapter Eight

Given Wolf had to drive the carriage only a few houses down their street to collect her, Tiffany wasn't surprised he was on time. She liked punctuality in a man. It demonstrated he was considerate of others.

The drawing room windows gave her a perfect view of the sight he made. He drew up in a glamorous phaeton drawn by a matching set of chestnut geldings. If he wanted the *ton* to take notice, this conveyance would do it. She and Wolf would be the talk of the *ton* by supper.

She wished her nerves would calm. She ran her hands down the front of her gown. Her gloves were clean, her hat fashionable, and hopefully it was large enough to hide her identity.

Awake and pacing her room late last night, or into the early morning really, she'd spied Wolf and Fane arriving home only a few hours before sunrise. She wondered what the men had been up to.

She'd followed Claire's instructions and not worn her glasses today, but her eyes were red with tiredness and worry. She carried Mr. Sprat's papers in her muff. Thinking of them made her stomach churn once again. She prayed Wolf would help her.

She stood in the drawing room, watching his approach. He

looked up and saw her. His smile made her worries lift for a moment as he drew level with their door.

"Make him wait," Claire advised.

"The sooner I go, the sooner I'm back and can rest before another ball tonight." She turned just as Booth entered.

"Lord Wolfarth is below for Miss Deveraux."

"Tell him I'll be down shortly," Tiffany said while smiling at Claire.

"Of course," Booth replied.

"Talk to him about his investments. See what you can learn," Claire called as she made her way from the room.

Even from the top of the stairs, she could see that after very little sleep he still, to her annoyance, looked incredibly handsome. It was not fair. She was already nervous enough without being reminded of how gorgeous he was. He'd recently shaved, revealing the sharp lines of his face. The seductive smile upon his lips when he spotted her added to his allure. He made every woman want to touch him to see if he was real. Maybe that's why she'd decided Milly could stay behind.

The touch of his hand on her arm and the small of her back as he helped her into the carriage made her body catch fire. He took his seat beside her and let his thigh brush her leg. But she was not moving away. He'd only take that as a sign he affected her. It was a lie to say he didn't, but Wolf didn't need to have that confirmed.

"I've been looking forward to this ride since last night."

A flash of surprise crossed his features. "Are you coming around to the idea of a proper courtship and marriage?"

"Good gracious, no." She shook her head. "I have business of a personal nature to discuss. This will allow us the privacy to conduct such a discussion without raising the *ton's* interest."

"That sounds rather dramatic. I was hoping for a pleasant drive in the park to get to know you better."

She rolled her eyes. "You are trying to alert the *ton* to our courtship, which I believe was not part of our arrangement. I have no idea why you are doing so. I will not be forced into a marriage. What will you tell Fane when this comes to his attention?"

His mouth tightened. "The truth. I wish to court you."

She almost pulled her glasses out of her muff and put them on. She wanted to read his face, only it was a mere a blur of handsome masculinity. "I don't think you'll want what I'm about to share made public, even to Fane."

At his raised eyebrow she knew the time had come, and a cold sweat ran down her spine, which she held ramrod straight.

"Well? How can I assist you?"

She drew in a deep breath. "It's more how I can assist you in a matter regarding your uncle. It appears Lord Melville is refusing to make up his losses to his stockjobber, Mr. Sprat."

She leaned as close to Wolf as she dared, squinting to make out his expression.. His handsome features displayed a myriad of emotions: a frown, followed by disbelief, then anger, and lastly embarrassment. "What on earth has this situation got to do with you? Ah, Mr. Sprat. That name is familiar. Your stockjobber?"

"Mr. Sprat was my late father's stockjobber and a family friend. He has tried to gain an interview with you, and has been consistently turned away. He approached me knowing I had a connection as he saw us together at Capel Court."

She did not add that if he were declared bankrupt because of the huge losses he'd incurred on behalf of Lord Melville, her ability to invest would be hindered. Wolf would no doubt think her stupid for paying for her share transactions upfront.

His face took on the arrogant, look-down-thy-nose expression of a Marquess. "I still do not see what it has to do with me."

Her legs began to shake under her gown. Her mouth was dry, as if filled with sand, and she couldn't swallow. "Mr. Sprat has said that unless the account is settled by the week's end, Lord Melville will be posted as a defaulter. I'm sure you would not want your family connections disgraced in public."

He slowed the carriage to a walk, seemingly blind to the curious looks thrown their way. "Is Mr. Sprat threatening me?"

"I would not call it threaten, precisely."

"Then what would you call it, *precisely*?"

She licked her lips, which were suddenly sticking together. "I'd call it a desperate move brought on by self-preservation. All of Mr. Sprat's clients may be affected too if Lord Melville does not pay up, as Mr. Sprat won't have the money to pay for trades, and if he doesn't stand up for himself others might follow suit."

Wolf's jaw tightened. "Why is it you are so passionate in your appeal for a man who all but saw your father bankrupted? I might agree to see Mr. Sprat simply so I can berate his use of a young lady to gain entry to my house."

Now she was angry. As if she would be stupid enough to let any man fool her into pleading his case. "I am not doing this for Mr. Sprat." Well, she was. And herself too, but also to save Wolf's family from embarrassment. Ashleigh was already the talk of society. If the family were too, that would hurt Ivy as well. "If I were you I'd meet with him. Your family name will be disgraced next Friday if this situation is not rectified. Please think of your mother and sisters."

He stared at her as if she were a mouse with two heads. Finally he said in a tone that was definitely verging on anger, "Does Mr. Sprat think I will simply hand money over on his word alone by sending a woman?" The horses jerked as his hands tightened on the reins. "How do I know this is not a lie, and in fact my uncle never asked for those shares to be bought?"

The muscles in her neck and shoulders seized so tightly her head pounded, but too much was at stake to turn back now. She had lived all her life on charity. Her cousin Fane, and his father before him, had paid for everything, dictating what she wore, what she ate, and where she lived.

All she wanted was to be able to financially keep herself without being forced to marry in order to survive. To marry without love was not an option for her; the thought of a lonely, loveless match for the rest of her life made her want to throw herself off a cliff. She was sick of feeling like a bird in a gilded cage

—trapped and flightless. She knew her thoughts were ungrateful; she loved her cousins, and that's why she'd originally kept her investment activities secret, not even telling Claire, whom she considered a sister. She had the skills to make her own money, but since it was deemed scandalous for women to directly invest, or trade in shares, she needed Mr. Sprat to do it on her behalf, to keep Marlowe and the family from scandal due to her.

Wolf's eyes narrowed, and he placed a finger under her chin so she had to look into his gorgeous blue eyes. "I remember Mr. Sprat well, as should you. He helped your father lose everything on one deal."

Wolf's words made her cringe. "That is not fair. My father made the investment decision against Mr. Sprat's advice."

Wolf gave an incredulous laugh. "You are far too naïve if you think that. What should I expect from an inexperienced young lady?" He turned away and concentrated on avoiding the other carriages in the park. "Ladies are too trusting."

In case he should look too closely at why she was trying to ensure her stockjobber did not go out of business, Tiffany bit the inside of her cheek to stop from robustly disputing his words. When this was over, she would somehow make Wolf eat his words. She was not sure how, or when, but she would. Winning the investment challenge would be a good start. They had yet to hear any gossip regarding the challenge. Maybe tonight at Lady Skye's ball...

She looked up to see steely eyes watching her—and remembered that unless Lord Melville paid up, she'd have no way to invest.

"Will you at least meet with Mr. Sprat and listen to what he has to say before you dismiss his claims?"

Wolf slowly nodded. "It seems I have no choice. How much money does he say my uncle owes him?"

She took a deep breath. "Just over ten thousand pounds, I believe."

Curses issued forth from Wolf's mouth. "I now understand

why you have brought this to my attention. It is a considerable sum. Mr. Sprat has some explaining to do."

His tone indicated how much he hated having to have this conversation with her. "You will be civil with Mr. Sprat, won't you?" Oh goodness. Wolf didn't look as if he knew what "civil" meant.

"I assure you I know exactly how to deal with Mr. Sprat."

That didn't sound good. Would he intimidate the man? What if Mr. Sprat spilled the fact the ladies had just given him two thousand pounds to invest? Wolf might work out they were the challengers. "Perhaps I should be there when you meet with him."

"I beg your pardon?"

She noticed a few people peering their way. "Keep your voice down. As I said, Mr. Sprat is a friend—"

"He is your stockjobber. If these nice people driving in the park learned that secret, Fane would have you married off before you could say no."

She couldn't look at him. "Mr. Sprat left my father with one thousand pounds when he should have left him with nothing. He covered that loss himself so my family would not be in debtors' prison. I owe Mr. Sprat, and this small task repays his kindness." She didn't intend to tell Wolf that the money from Mr. Sprat had then been stolen by the highwaymen who killed her parents on the road from London to Yorkshire.

The hardness around Wolf's mouth softened at her confession. "I give you my word that I shall give Mr. Sprat a fair hearing. Thank you for bringing this to my attention, but I shall take care of the situation. There is nothing for you to worry about, Miss Tiffany."

Miss Tiffany. That wasn't a good sign. He only used "Miss" before her name when irked. On an inward sigh she realized it would be hopeless to argue with Wolf. She was being dismissed. She would just have to hope that the big bad wolf did not consume Mr. Sprat. Wolf may be a man with a core of steel but he was fair, honorable, and she trusted him. "I have the papers in my muff. I shall give them to you when you take me home."

Wolf nodded at a couple passing by before saying, "Make sure you stay away from Sprat until I have ascertained what he is about."

She hesitated, before, with fingers crossed in her muff, she nodded. "I also wanted to thank you for the dance the other night. It had the desired effect. Suitors have been calling."

She wondered what had made her blurt that out, but she looked for a reaction to her words, something to indicate that Wolf had not merely danced with her to prove a point. His blank look said it all, and she felt her face flush with color. What had she expected? That he would be jealous?

His grim features softened and he actually smiled. "You deserve to be seen. I was honored to be of service. However, I don't wish for competition to win your hand."

Competition. No other man could compete with Wolf. She would learn what this sudden courtship was all about. It wasn't about love, of that she was sure. Until her meeting with him at Capel Court he'd rarely spoken with her. She wished she could tell him to go away and leave her alone, but the Sisterhood needed her to keep her secret if they were to win the wager. And the men were not stupid. If everyone learned about her investments...well, the scandal that would cause... The wager would be off before it even began.

She lived in a man's world and until she could financially survive on her own, she had to live by the constraints that society placed on women.

Mr. Sprat was the key to her achieving her dream and she wasn't about to let Lord Melville destroy her plans.

~

Wolf had to control his desire to slam the door behind him as he walked back into Wolfarth House. That had been the most frustrating ride in the park he'd ever had. He rarely took a lady out in a carriage in the park, and he'd hoped the *ton* would see this as a sign he was courting Miss Tiffany Deveraux.

However, *bloody Melville.* For the most part, those partaking of the park had seen the two of them engaging in a heated conversation. It was clear to all that Miss Tiffany Deveraux wasn't enamored of his company, and now the *ton* was more confused than he was. Why wasn't Tiffany overcome by his attempt to court her? Most ladies would be swooning at his attentions.

His uncle had ruined what was supposed to be his first attempt at thawing Miss. Tiffany's frosty demeanor. Helping Mr. Sprat now seemed the obvious way to defrost her feelings toward a marriage.

Melville was a problem Wolf had put off for too long. If it wasn't persistent gambling it was risky investments. Melville trying to make back all the money he'd lost on stupid wagers. He could well believe the story Tiffany had told him.

He sat down at his desk and tried to let the worry gripping his innards ease. He was tired from being out all night, and sick to death of having to manage his uncle's affairs as well as his own. His uncle was old enough to know better, but then he had Wolf to pay his debts. Once again he cursed at being the eldest son. Rockwell would have made a much better Marquess. He had a head for numbers and business. All Wolf had ever wanted to do was paint.

On a long sigh, he quickly penned a missive to be sent to Sprat. He'd meet with him tomorrow. Next Friday was not long off. He needed to think and he needed to find Rockwell and decide a course of action.

He picked up a pencil and, as usual, lines and shapes appeared on the parchment that lay on his desk, as if an unseen force was guiding his hand.

A strong chin, cute dimples and button nose took shape. He was drawing Tiffany. Only he began to draw her as he saw her in his mind. Instead of the severe bun she wore, her glorious auburn hair was cascading in thick waves over naked shoulders. Her glasses were nowhere to be seen and it gave her face a younger, softer look. Her luscious lips were slightly parted, and her emerald eyes glinted with sensual heat. His pencil drew her looking alive and voluptuous.

When he'd finished, he sat back and grinned like a schoolboy. He wondered what she'd think if he had the balls to show her his sketch. Would she recognize the woman deep inside, the woman she tried so hard to keep at bay? No woman with eyes that sparkled with fire could possibly be so cold and stiff. She was afraid to be herself and he longed to learn why she kept herself so contained.

He couldn't bring himself to throw the etching in the fire, so he put it in his top drawer and turned his attention to his duty. Duty stopped the bad memories eating him from the inside out.

The love of his life—Margo—had taken her own life because he'd not saved her. Now he focused on duty and family, to make up for his inadequacies. Hence, he knew Miss Tiffany Deveraux, if he married her, would also help him protect his family—from financial ruin at least.

Once he'd organized Donaldson, his man of business, to send the note to Sprat, he made his way to his room. He needed some sleep before the ball tonight. He was sick of bailing Melville out of his messes. Two thousand pounds of gambling debt was a lot of money and he had to take a stand at some point. He had no idea how much Melville actually owed at Capel Court. Was Sprat the only stockjobber he'd used?

This time Melville had gone too far, but Wolf did not know what to do. He hoped his brother did. If he covered the loss it would happen again. If he told Sprat not to take any further investments from his uncle, Melville would simply find another stockjobber.

As he sunk into a hot bath he tried to think of a way to cut off Melville's gambling and risky investing, but the only solution he could think of was to banish him to the country or, worse, to the

Americas, and that would hurt his mother. Perhaps she could talk some sense into her brother. Make him see that Wolf *would* banish Melville to protect the family. He would not fail again.

For some reason, as he climbed into bed, the prim and proper Tiffany popped into his head. She could be a very beautiful woman if she didn't dress so severely, and if she smiled more. A bluestocking of the first water. Even her glasses were quite lovely, especially the way she kept pushing them up her cute button nose.

As he drifted into sleep his artist's eye tried to imagine what lay beneath Tiffany's clothes, and for one moment, as he entered dreamland, he forgot her guardian was his best friend, forgot his promise not to compromise her, forgot that he was a gentleman, and gave into the temptation to seduce her and find out.

Chapter Nine

Lady Skye's ball was crowded, as usual, and tonight Tiffany had barely had the chance to catch her breath. Men she'd rarely spoken to all season had filled her dance card, except the one man who mattered—Wolf. He appeared to be absent this evening. Perhaps he was seeking out Mr. Sprat. Surely not at night?

"He's not here," Claire muttered. "So stop searching the room, it's being noted."

Before she could respond, an excited Valora appeared at her side. "Julian told Serena about a curious wager posted in the betting book at White's."

"Is it our wager?" Tiffany asked excitedly.

Valora looked like a preening peahen. "Yes, and apparently it's the talk of the clubs. Who would dare challenge these four men."

Lord Julian Montague, the second son of the Marquess of Lorne, had married Valora's sister a few months ago. Serena had been instrumental in bringing the Sisterhood together. It was her idea to form the Sisterhood investment club. She didn't come to the meetings as often now, too content in matrimonial bliss with the love of her life. However, as a married woman, Serena was extremely helpful in gathering information that young unmarried ladies were not party to.

"And, I have initiated my first prank on Vale. I told Lady Dourest that Lord Vale thought he could commission a more flamboyant waistcoat then Prinny. I may have suggested that Prinny challenge him to a reveal." Lady Dourest was rumored to be Prinny's latest mistress, and while Prinny wore the most outlandish waistcoats, Vale preferred the elegance of plainness. "Lady Dourest loved the idea and she's already whispered in Prinny's ear. I expect a challenge may be issued this very night." Valora could hardly hide her glee.

"Vale's going to have to make a waistcoat of many colors and wear it in public," Farah said in delight. "He'll hate that and I want to be there to witness his embarrassment."

"And loss," Valora added. "There is no way he'll make the most flamboyant waistcoat to outshine Prinny. He can't win. It's not done to wager with the future King of England and win."

The giggling grew louder until a hush fell over the ballroom. Standing at the top of the stairs, very late in his attendance, was the Marquess of Wolfarth, searching the crowd, and everyone knew when he'd found his prey, because a seductive smile spread over his face. The crowd turned to see whom he was seeking out and all eyes fell on Tiffany.

He made his way down the stairs, guests parting in his wake as he strode purposefully toward Tiffany. She stood on the edge of the ballroom with her friends, her face heating. Soon, every fan was fluttering with women twittering behind them. Lady Vale, Valora's mother, moved to hover over the young ladies.

"My, Tiffany. You have collected quite the suitor. Has he talked with Marlowe?"

Tiffany choked back the words *I hope not*. "I have no idea what you mean, Lady Vale."

Valora's mother looked quizzically at her. "But Valora mentioned Wolfarth had also taken you for a ride in the park.

Plus, I remember he danced with you at the ball the other night and was in your box at the opera. He is courting you, dear girl."

She could hardly argue with the lady. Most of the *ton* had made the connection. There was a courtship in play and the Marquess of Wolfarth was finally hunting a wife. What most of them were probably thinking was why Miss Tiffany? *She* was.

Valora's mother addressed Claire. "He is best friends with Marlowe so it would seem natural to align the families, but I did think it might have been Claire. Has Marlowe got other plans for you?"

"I don't believe my brother is aware of any formal courtship with Lord Wolfarth," Claire said.

This was the exact talk Tiffany hated. Women were to be shoved off into marriage by fathers, brothers and guardians. Why couldn't a woman make up her own mind as to whom to marry? There'd likely be much happier marriages and fewer mistresses.

Lady Vale stepped forward. "Oh, since your mother's death, Fane has been most neglectful of you young ladies. I shall handle the situation and talk to him immediately. It's high time all you ladies found husbands. My daughter is becoming known for her refusals. Vale is too lenient. Lord Marlowe should be aware that his friend is courting Miss Tiffany."

Tiffany wanted to run. And fast, but it was too late.

"Lady Vale, how lovely to see you looking as beautiful as ever this evening," Wolf said as he bowed low over her hand.

"You flatter me, my lord. Which of these lovely ladies are you really here to see?"

"My apologies for my late attendance, but I was hoping Miss Tiffany had a dance left on her card?"

Before she could say that he was the last man she'd dance with this evening, and that her card was full, Lord Templeton appeared at her elbow. "My dance, I believe, Miss Tiffany."

She beamed at Templeton as if he were her savior. "Oh, lovely," and she slipped her hand through his arm and let him lead her onto the floor. She tried to ignore the vision that was Wolfarth, but to her horror he was deep in conversation with Lady Vale, who was gesturing wildly with her fan. Tiffany couldn't bear to think what she might be saying. If Fane learned of Wolf's courtship, he would pressure her to accept.

"You seem decidedly preoccupied this evening," Lord Templeton said in passing as they twirled. "Please don't shatter my heart and confirm Wolfarth's suit is in your favor."

She thought to laugh before she saw the serious look on Templeton's face. "I had no idea you cared, my lord. I think this is the first evening we have danced together let alone conversed."

His mouth dropped open at her rudeness. "It would seem Wolfarth will have to teach you your place."

"I'm quite sure I am well aware of my place." And it would not be married to a man like Lord Templeton. But could it be married to a man like Lord Wolfarth?

Templeton snorted. "Why he's interested in you is beyond imagining."

"Perhaps you lack imagination?" She could barely hide her grin at the shock on his face. *Please let the music end.*

She peered over her shoulder once again and saw the man himself leaning against the wall, watching her with hooded eyes. Lady Vale was still talking to him but his sole focus was on Tiffany, and then, she noted to her horror, on Lord Templeton. She expected flames to burst from the top of Wolf's head, such was the dangerous look he was giving her dance partner.

The dance finally ended and Wolf was at her side before she could blink.

"Templeton, I do hope you have not upset Miss Tiffany, for I may have to seek retribution."

Oh, please. Tiffany rolled her eyes. She could most certainly handle anything Lord Templeton said to her. He'd not said anything that the whole *ton* were not thinking. To her surprise, Templeton began to splutter.

"I-I-I am a gent-gentleman." He bowed to Tiffany and fled.

This time Tiffany wished to scoff, but with Wolf so on edge it would be best to not cause a scene. Or more of a scene. Already most eyes were pointed in their direction.

Wolf led her back toward Lady Vale and her friends at the edge of the ballroom. "Did you need to do that?" she said. "You are making it very obvious what you are about, and I thought our agreement was that you would not put me in a position such that I could not decline your offer without ruining my reputation."

"He insulted you."

"How do you know?"

"I could see it on your face, in your eyes and the way you held your body. You stood straighter after one comment he made, your spine stiff as a ramrod. What did he say to you?" Wolf demanded.

Luckily they had reached the others and she didn't have to answer.

"Goodness, Lord Wolfarth, that was quite the performance." Lady Vale indicated the interest in the room. "I assume you will be seeking a meeting with Lord Marlowe tomorrow."

Before Tiffany could protest, Wolf answered. "I assure you I will be paying a call on His Lordship as discussed."

This would never do. She was being talked about, her future was being talked about, as if she had no voice. Tiffany wished she could leave, but one glance at her dance card...suddenly she felt a headache coming on. "Lady Claire and Miss Valora, I'm suddenly not feeling very well. I need to retire for the evening."

"It's obviously been an overwhelming evening for you, dear. I shall call for our carriage and Valora and I shall escort you both home." With that, Lady Vale led her and Claire away, leaving Wolf alone. As she made the top of the stairs she couldn't stop herself from looking back, and Wolf was no longer alone. Serve him right. Mothers with daughters in tow crowded around him, and for the first time since he'd entered the ballroom she giggled.

Chapter Ten

The following morning, Mr. Sprat stood in Wolf's study. His demeanor was polite but firm. However, the evidence he laid on Wolf's desk was hardly damning. They were purchase orders with a signature purportedly belonging to Lord Melville, but Wolf couldn't make out the name. It certainly held no seal. But then Melville might not use a seal.

Wolf gestured to the purchase orders. "Of course, I will need to discuss these with my uncle."

"That is his signature," Sprat said.

"The sum is quite considerable, and I wish to discuss with my uncle how the money should be paid."

Sprat shifted on his feet. "I do not wish to appear ungrateful, my lord, but when will you confirm payment? I have creditors of my own to pay and I am conscious that if word about this gets out I could lose my customers. Or worse, others will try to withhold payment if I'm seen to be an easy mark." He looked Wolf in the eye. "Plus, if word gets out that Lord Melville has not paid, he may find no one will take his purchase orders."

Good. Wolf hoped that would happen, but not publicly of course. Melville's name was attached to his. "You have my permission to quietly let it be known I will no longer be honoring my uncle's share trades."

"And this debt?" Sprat asked. "It could sully the Wolfarth name too if a scandal erupted."

"Are you threatening me?" Wolf rose from behind his desk. Something about this man did not sit right with Wolf. Why use Tiffany to get an audience with him? If he'd contacted Wolf directly about Melville's debts, he'd have met with Sprat. He didn't need Tiffany to be a conduit.a

"I was merely pointing out that my situation may not be the only situation regarding Lord Melville, and word could get out."

"Thank you for bringing this to my attention. I shall discuss the situation with my uncle and send word when the purchase orders will be honored."

Sprat's expression was almost a sneer. "Once paid, I will have no further need to bother you, for I shall not be acting on Lord Melville's behalf again. I shall also make it known that he is a bad risk."

Wolf nodded. With that, Sprat took his leave. Wolf knew it would be the last time he would see the man, but who else could, or would, come walking through the door asking him to cover Melville's debts? He'd asked Melville to call but the bastard hadn't even had the decency to show his face.

He had to find Melville and soon.

He swiped up the brandy bottle sitting on his desk. He needed a drink. He stopped himself from pouring though. He needed to call on Fane before word of his pursuit of Tiffany reached his friend's ears and he drew the wrong conclusion. Plus, he was supposed to be drawing this afternoon. He still had not decided what he would paint for the Academy. He needed some inspiration and soon.

Before he painted he'd visit Fane. He would of course honor Tiffany's agreement and not disclose her investing. He could also take the opportunity to ask Fane to discreetly make it known within the investment community that Melville had no money to pay for any purchases. That should slow Melville's debt collection down somewhat.

Tonight he'd call off any social engagements and spend his night hunting down his uncle. Melville would be in some gambling den somewhere. He could not hide from Wolf forever.

∼

By the time Tiffany arrived in the drawing room, all the other ladies were present—Courtney, Ashleigh, Farah, Ivy, Valora, Lauren, Serena, and Claire and herself.

A servant placed her breakfast in front of her. She had the same thing every morning—eggs, ham and toast. She found a good breakfast kept her hunger at bay during the day. She had other, more important things to do during the day than eat—analyzing the financial pages for one.

Courtney clapped her hands. "Ladies, please. Ivy needs us to have a successful fundraising event. We need some ideas. Something different so we can stand out from Lady Ashby's group of ladies."

Tiffany knew she was going to hell for what she was about to propose, but it would aid them and help Valora to slip into Mrs. Buchanan's soiree. "I was thinking about having a clothing stall. We could sell gowns we no longer wear, shoes, reticules, gloves etcetera. Women who could perhaps not afford such gowns and items could buy them at near giveaway prices."

Courtney frowned. "Where would we sell them? No lady who lives in Mayfair would stoop to purchasing used items."

She flashed a look at Valora. "I rather thought we could ask the Reverend Smith if we could use the hall next to his church near Russell Square. The women in that area would probably like to buy such items to wear, and if we also position it as fundraising to help the orphans, well I suspect we could raise a lot."

Valora's mouth dropped open, as if she was about to laugh, but Tiffany shook her head. The church was very close to Mrs.

Buchanan's house and they could slip away for half an hour while the fete was being held. Russell Square was just at the edge of Mayfair. An area where the up and coming, or ladies on the fringe of society like Mrs. Buchanan, lived. She was sure the stall would make a lot of money if they could collect enough clothes to sell.

Ivy stood up. "Bravo, Tiffany. A splendid idea."

"At least it's not selling lemon drinks," Valora whispered under her breath, and Ivy chose to ignore her.

Ashleigh laughed. "Finally a place where I might even be able to help out on the stall."

"Courtney and Farah can be responsible for collecting donated items," Tiffany said. "Nothing like a duke's daughter to open closets. Claire and I will approach Reverend Smith."

They discussed the operation of such a charity event. Afterwards, Claire sidled up to her. "Very clever. The church is near Mrs. Buchanan's townhouse."

"Shh."

"If any of us get caught there..."

"What can they do? We could pretend ignorance as to why we shouldn't be there. It would be an embarrassment to try and explain it to us. If anything, Fane will be blamed for his lack of forethought since your mother died."

Before Claire could answer, Ashleigh called out from near the window. "Wolf's just pulled up outside. It's a bit early for him, isn't it?"

Tiffany slumped into her seat, her nerves fizzing. Surely he hadn't come to...

"Oh, Lady Vale spent several minutes chastising Wolf for not having spoken to my brother about his intentions regarding Tiffany," Claire said, as if it was nothing of note.

"Well, I never. He was at Lady Skye's ball? And he's come to call?"

"Hardly a call," Ivy muttered. "I don't believe he asked for your hand last night, did he? What is going on Tiffany?"

"I have no idea what your brother is up to, but I swear I have done nothing to encourage him. I have no idea what has brought on this sudden interest in me." Just a little white lie. Wolf thought to form a marriage of convenience, but he could ask any woman for that. Why her?

"Men. They really are quite arrogant. Are you saying he hasn't formally asked for your hand? Then why speak to Fane?" Ivy asked.

Tiffany nodded. "It's as if I'm supposed to be grateful for his attention. As if there is no doubt I'll say yes."

"Is Lord Wolfarth wife hunting?" Lauren asked.

Ashleigh scoffed. "Not that I was aware of. I think he is still with his mistress, Lady Delia. She sent a note to the house this morning. I recognized her handwriting on the card."

Tiffany looked across at Valora, suddenly understanding why her friend wanted to attend Mrs. Buchanan's afternoon fete. "I was informed she is no longer his mistress." Tiffany wished she could take back the words as soon as she'd spoken. Mouths hung open. But really, she did have some pride.

"You've discussed his mistress with him?" Ashleigh sunk into a chair. "I say, it sounds to me like Wolf is serious. Tiffany, how are you feeling about all of this? It would be lovely to have you as our sister."

Courtney sat next to her and patted her arm. "This is rather sudden. But Wolf is a clever man, and he's proved it by selecting an absolute treasure of a woman to be his wife." She paused. "But we will all stand by you should you not wish to accept his offer. No matter what scandal ensues."

"Yes. We will," Claire said. "We all know you want a love match or to remain a spinster. You have the financial means to do so, but it could be lonely. Maybe Wolf has developed feelings for you. He seems most set on his pursuit and I've never seen him work so hard to impress. Not since Margo..."

The girls were being so kind but she could see their looks of concern and pity. None of them believed a man like Wolf would suddenly develop a tendre for her.

"I can highly recommend married life but only if it's to the right man. I am so lucky Julian loves me." Serena's quiet words made Tiffany think. If Wolf was the right man for her, if he could love her, she'd marry him in a flash.

Just then they heard male voices in the hall. A knock on the door, and the butler was there summoning her to Fane's study. "Would you like me to come with you?" Claire offered.

She shook her head. "This shouldn't take long." She would not be rushed into anything, and until she understood why Wolf wanted this marriage she would never agree. Her plan was still the same—marry for love or not at all. She hadn't spent the past four years investing and risking scandal so that this choice was not hers to make. No man, or men as the case may be, were going to corner her into giving up her dream.

Yet, as she drew closer to Fane's study and heard the two men laughing, her bravery felt as strong as a piece of parchment trying to hold water. At the door she took a deep breath. *Be polite. Don't lose your temper and don't give in!*

Shoulders squared, she entered the room without knocking. She needed her defiant manner to send a message, but the two men didn't even seem perturbed. Both rose swiftly to their feet.

"Tiffany, do come in and sit. Aren't you a sly one. Why did you not tell me Wolf was courting you?"

Fane looked immensely pleased with himself, as if Wolf was the answer to all his problems. "He may be courting me, but I'm yet to decide if I am interested in his attentions," she answered politely but firmly. Honest, at least.

Fane's smile dimmed. "There is no need to be rude, Tiffany."

Wolf merely grinned. "She's not being rude, Fane. Just truthful. I did tell you she was not enamored of my pursuit."

Fane shook his head. "Women. I'll never understand them. Most are throwing themselves at Wolf and yet you are not sure?"

"I wonder if he'd want me as his wife if I were like the other women, and throwing myself at him?" She hadn't realized she'd spoken aloud until the two men burst out laughing. At least her stupid question broke the tension.

"Let no one say Miss Tiffany Deveraux isn't one of a kind." It surprised Tiffany to hear what sounded like pride in Wolf's voice.

"If that is all, the ladies are waiting for me. We are planning another charity event for Ivy's orphanage."

"No, that's not all. I would like you to know that I have given Wolf permission to court you and that I would welcome the match. I am happy to support his suit." Fane looked at Wolf and smiled.

Tiffany rose and softly replied, "I thank you for the support, Fane, but the decision to accept his suit, or decline, is mine and mine alone."

Fane opened his mouth, but Wolf shook his head then stood and addressed her. "Of course, the decision is yours. I would not wish to marry a woman who did not welcome the arrangement. But I felt that to protect your reputation, society should see that I am pursuing you honorably."

Arrangement.

The unspoken meaning was that a man like him pursuing a woman like her could be construed as dishonorable, because why would Wolf want to marry her? Well, that had clearly put her in her place.

"I'm pleased my wishes are now apparent," Tiffany answered more firmly. "Who I marry, or if I marry, will be my decision alone. If you'll excuse me, gentlemen. I have other duties to attend to."

"Before you go, I wonder if I could impose on you for a favor?" Wolf hesitantly asked. She eyed him warily. "I am contracted to provide a painting to the Royal Academy and I was hoping that you would allow me to paint your portrait. It will be auctioned by the Academy to raise funds for a scholarship."

Tiffany couldn't hide her enthusiasm. She loved art. "I don't know how you find the time to paint now that you are the Marquess. You must be busy. But to be commissioned to paint for the Academy, what an honor, Lord Wolfarth. However, I'm not sure my portrait will raise much money."

"I assure you the painting will be in much demand."

It probably would, considering Wolf was the artist. "If you are sure, I'd be flattered and delighted."

"I was thinking of painting you as you sit reading under the large oak tree in my garden. I'll call it 'Lady Tranquility'. I do admit there is a time constraint, so I'd need to get started almost straight away, and it will unfortunately take up a large amount of your time. Three to four mornings per week."

Was this simply another ploy to spend time with her? To make it difficult for her to face the *ton* should she decline his proposal? "I'm assuming your mother would be chaperon and Ivy and Ashleigh will be there too?"

"We shall adhere to all proprieties."

"I have your word?"

"Indeed."

As she closed the door behind her, she resisted the temptation to press her ear against the wood to hear what the men were now discussing. Instead, spotting Booth hovering nearby, she walked away, her fists clenched and hidden in the folds of her gown. Wolf was taking this agreement much further than she'd thought he would. She must contact Mr. Sprat and see how strongly her Armley Mill shares were performing. She needed to win. To give her choices.

Shivers of anticipation and fear settled over her skin. A part of her wished she could simply relax and see where his courtship might take them, but the voice screaming loudest in her head was self-doubt. Why on earth did he want her? Until she had the answer, she couldn't let herself fall in love with him.

Unfortunately, her heart was falling faster than her brain could cope with.

But as she walked determinedly back to the drawing room, real pleasure at the idea of being painted by Wolf engulfed her.

Fancy being immortalized in a painting. Never had she imagined a man would wish to paint her portrait.

Plus, sitting for Wolf would give her an excuse to be in his company without society's eyes upon them. She could begin her investigation of his motives. With Wolf's sisters there too, maybe they could gain an insight into his sudden interest.

❧

"You are right. She is definitely not thrilled at your interest. Women..." Marlowe shook his head as he poured them both a drink. "You told me you like Tiffany, but what is really behind your plan to marry my cousin? I would have thought Claire was more to your taste. Tiffany's rather bookish."

Wolf couldn't tell Marlowe why, because that would reveal Tiffany's secret, and if Marlowe learned of her investing, there would be trouble and he'd lose his wager. He'd never get near enough to win Tiffany's hand if she were at odds with him. In fact, the more he discovered about Tiffany Deveraux, the more he believed the only way to win her approval would be to make her fall in love with him. However, he knew that road led to danger. He would not allow himself to love again. Not after losing Margo. Besides, he didn't deserve to find love and happiness. He hadn't saved her.

"Tiffany will suit me just fine." As long as it was only her that fell in love.

"And you're sure you don't wish me to offer for Ashleigh in exchange should this marriage go ahead?"

"Quite sure. I must admit that I did think on the idea we discussed. However, upon consideration, Ashleigh probably wouldn't have you. In fact, most of the ladies presently in this house wouldn't have you. Your reputation with lovers precedes you. They know about your Mrs. Buchanan. Tiffany even knew I had a mistress. We underestimate how much these ladies overhear.

I know I will be more circumspect around Ashleigh and Ivy in future."

"Speaking of my lovely Mrs. Buchanan, it's Pip's soiree in a few days. Will you be escorting Lady Delia?"

"I thought I'd told you I'd put an end to our arrangement. I cannot court Tiffany with a mistress underfoot. I don't wish to embarrass Tiffany. Besides, if she got wind of a mistress the answer would be no."

"Why is it so important that she accept you? You could have any woman you wanted. I must say, although I like Tiffany, she's always presented herself as a true bluestocking, humorless, remote, and unapproachable. I hardly see the appeal."

Wolf wondered why the hairs on his arms rose. In the years since Margo, he'd never been provoked to anger over a woman he was interested in. Tiffany, however, was a different story. More than once he'd felt his ire rise in her defense. Anger was a new emotion where a woman he was interested in was concerned. "That is my future wife you are talking about. I suggest you refrain from such comments. I have my reasons for wanting to wed Tiffany. I hope you'll respect my choice as I will respect yours, when you finally make it."

Marlowe scoffed. "I'm in no hurry. However, your marriage will certainly put the pressure on me. Mothers will assume I'll follow suit."

"Maybe you should. It will stop mothers and daughters chasing you."

Marlowe slapped the desk with his hand. "By Jove, you're right. I should marry and then I can continue my life without being hunted."

"Still have your mistresses? That doesn't always make for a happy marriage. Alternatively, you could look for a woman who might make the need for other dalliances obsolete. It makes for a sound marriage and a happy family."

His friend sat back in his chair with his mouth hanging open. Wolf merely shrugged.

"Are you telling me you won't keep a mistress once you marry?"

"That's exactly what I'm telling you."

Marlowe looked as if he'd rather die than entertain that thought. His eyes narrowed. "Is this because of what happened with Margo? Rockwell told me you had a problem—"

"No." The sound he made, half human, half wolf, was so loud it almost rattled the windows.

Marlowe looked at him skeptically. "I can perfectly understand how—how what happened to Margo in front of you and her subsequent death would affect you. But you're over that now. Aren't you?"

Wolf's vision narrowed to one black spot. Bloody Rockwell and his big mouth. But he knew his younger brother had been scared by how Wolf had fallen to pieces after Margo's death. Memories, nightmares actually, still invaded occasionally, especially on still, starry nights—he could still hear her screams. What ate him up inside is that they'd never caught the men who'd attacked them. He'd lived with that every day for years.

He'd tried for months to find some leads on his attackers. Their ambush had been well planned. Wolf had never believed it was arbitrary, as the magistrate and Bow Street Runners had believed. He'd been targeted. Young, arrogant...stupid in the extreme. He'd thought nothing could touch him. They'd preyed on his egotism.

He'd just got engaged to the most sought after debutante of the season; he was a Marquess and had the world at his feet. He hadn't thought twice about driving unescorted, alone with Margo. He'd planned a romantic picnic in Richmond Park, where his staff had awaited his arrival. They had a lovely afternoon, and as the sun dimmed he left the staff to pack up and turned for home.

The carriage had barely made it out of the park before the attack and...

He swallowed back the bile that always rose from his stomach as the memories rushed in.

"Wolf, you are...that is. Hell, have a brandy," and Marlowe shoved a glass at him.

And he hated how he needed it. The heat and taste of the alcohol drowned his bile. He drank the glass dry.

Wolf ignored his friend's inquiring eyes and got to his feet. "Let's be on our way. You know how Blackstone hates to be kept waiting."

Marlowe stood and put the brandy decanter back on the sideboard. "Blackstone is on the rampage. He's livid that someone has the audacity to challenge him, or us, anonymously. He's ranting about the coward and he's already called for the Bow Street Runners to find him."

"That's a bit heavy handed. It's probably some new buck who wants to prove himself. What I can't understand is how this silly investment challenge made the betting book at White's." Wolf thought the challenger had to be a member. "It's not even an interesting challenge. The result is twelve months off."

Marlowe sniffed. "I think it was Julian Montague. He was there when his father received the missive. He thought it was a great lark. The elder Lord Lorne challenged along with the young bucks of the *ton*."

"Lord Lorne is a shrewd investor so I'm glad his name is on the challenge too. He might also keep hothead Blackstone in check." Wolf needed to marry Tiffany quickly. She could help him win this wager. He'd have to wait a month to tell the men about her skills, though, and then only if she said yes to his proposal. "Do you really think it could be Montague?"

Marlowe considered. "Perhaps not. He hasn't got a head for numbers. It might be Viscount Timmings. The young buck is renowned for his way with numbers. He's always thought to best me."

Wolf nodded. "You could be right. But if he wants to take your crown as the investment king, then why challenge all of us?"

"Arrogance, perhaps. I'm not worried about losing. I have a couple of investments underway that will earn me a fortune. It's a nice day. Let's walk to Blackstone's townhouse. I'm off to the club afterwards."

They walked down the steps to the street and it was pleasant in the sun. "Nothing of note for me this evening. Rockwell and I are spending tonight on a hunting trip. Bloody Melville's creditors are coming knocking and I mean to put a stop to his spending."

"I had heard a rumor. I saw him being thrown out of the Gloucester Club the other night for an unpaid debt. He's not allowed back until it's paid."

Wolf was glad to hear that. If more clubs stopped men gambling they wouldn't lose everything they owned. "At least I know I don't have to look there."

A few minutes later they were ushered into the Duke of Blackstone's library. All the other men were already present. "Tardy as usual, Marlowe. I expected more of you, Wolfarth. I thought you'd ensure he was here on time."

"Nice to see you too, Blackstone," Wolf responded dryly while he nodded greetings to the other men. Lord Lorne had brought his eldest son, Tarquin Montague, Earl of Milburn, with him.

"Gentlemen," Lord Lorne said. "I'm not sure why anyone would issue such a challenge, but I for one suggest we ignore it. The wager is not worth bothering with. I say we do not accept the challenge."

"Of course we will accept the challenge. I've already done so." Blackstone wore his ducal glare, daring anyone to disagree. Lord Lorne merely sighed.

"I think that is a mistake. It will make the result public too, and I for one do not wish society to know what we earn from our investments, and what if we lose?"

Wolf could sympathize with Lord Lorne's privacy concerns. As to losing...

"Then best we don't lose," replied Blackstone as he thumped his desk. Lord Lorne hmphed.

"The first point of business," Marlowe said, "would be to hold a meeting with our investment advisers to ascertain how to pool our money, and ensure we make the biggest return from this small investment." There was one thing Marlowe took seriously in life and that was money. It was his father's legacy; for the previous Lord Marlowe, money had been all that mattered. Maybe that was why Marlowe took his pleasures a little too far at times. Being responsible for a huge family, lands and tenants did weigh on a man, and Marlowe broke free from those shackles occasionally. Wolf understood the burden of responsibility and this was one of the reasons Tiffany would be such an asset.

"Yes, instead of investing individually, we should pool our money," Vale enthused.

"But would that be in the spirit of the challenge? Since we have already accepted—" Lord Lorne pointedly looked at Blackstone "—perhaps we should act like true gentlemen and invest separately as indicated."

Vale looked around the table. "The challenge doesn't specify we have to invest separately, it merely indicates each sum of one thousand pounds should show an individual return. Therefore, there is nothing stopping us all investing in the same thing."

Wolf shook his head. "I agree with Lord Lorne. Our challenger is only investing one thousand pounds. If this challenge is to prove who is the best investor then surely we must follow suit or victory could be hollow."

"Or at least questioned," added Tarquin.

"I certainly do not wish my honor to be questioned. I believe the intent of the challenge is that we must each show the return we make on our own one-thousand-pound investment. An apple is only an apple if it's off the same tree," Blackstone said.

"Are you saying we cannot compare unless we do exactly the same?" Vale asked.

"Absolutely. I for one would think it a hollow victory if we pooled our money *or* our knowledge," Lord Lorne agreed. "We need to each invest our money with no help from each other."

Marlowe cleared his throat. "You make a good point. Individually investing will also spread the risk of losing. We are all likely to invest in different things. I don't care who wins, as long as it is one of us."

Wolf said, "So let us be clear in regard to the rules. We will each individually invest one thousand pounds, and keep a separate ledger. We will not confer as to what investments we have made. And may the best man win."

The men all raised their glasses and drank to the wager. Soon discussion turned to the latest bill before the House of Lords. Wolf looked at the clock and rose to his feet. "Please excuse me, I have a meeting with Rockwell."

As he made his way back up the street to his townhouse, Wolf pondered on how he should invest his one thousand pounds. He longed to win the six-thousand-pound prize. It would go a long way to making up for the losses he had to cover for Melville. In a month's time he hoped he could ascertain Tiffany's advice; she would surely want to help her husband win.

As he entered his home, Wolf turned his thoughts to finding Melville. Surely between Rockwell and himself, they could find one elderly gentleman.

Chapter Eleven

Tiffany had hoped Wolf would be at home when she and Farah called on Ivy and Ashleigh. She'd planned to get an update on the Lord Melville situation. But he was out. Her spirits lifted when Ashleigh informed them he'd been summoned to His Grace's house. All the men they had challenged were attending. The ladies laughed so hard... The challenge was underway.

Tiffany and Farah were there to collect items for their charity sale. Ivy said they could go through some of the ladies' clothes. Valora had suggested they also offer some men's clothing, as the ladies who were likely to buy at the stall might also buy for their husbands.

They spent over an hour in Ivy's room, selecting all sorts, from gowns to petticoats, to gloves and hats. They then added the selection to Ashleigh's pile.

Now they were in Rockwell's wardrobe. Well, a very scant wardrobe as Rockwell had taken bachelor accommodations, away from the family townhouse.

"Are you sure Rockwell won't mind us raiding his attire?" Farah asked. "These Hessians look as if they've never been worn."

"He's probably forgotten he even owns them," Ivy responded.

Soon the pile of men's gloves, cravats, waistcoats and boots had grown considerably large. Ivy left Tiffany and Farah to go in search of a trunk to put everything into.

"Look." Farah kicked off a slipper and lifted her skirt to slide her foot into one of the Hessians. "Gosh, he has very large feet, and the boot comes all the way up my thigh," and she pulled her gown almost to her waist.

Tiffany was about to comment when a deep voice said from the doorway, "But they don't look nearly as good on me."

Startled, Farah tried to step out of the Hessian and instead began to fall backward. Before Tiffany could move, Rockwell sprang across the room and caught Farah before she could hit the floor. He slowly set Farah on her feet, and just like the prince in the French fairy tale *Cendrillon*, he reached for her slipper and, after pulling the Hessian off her leg, placed the slipper back on her foot. Tiffany couldn't help noting Rockwell's hands lingered longer than necessary, while Farah appeared motionless as if under his spell.

Just then Ivy appeared in the doorway. "Rockwell, what are you doing here?"

He rose slowly, all six feet of him. Farah's face had flushed a pretty pink, while Tiffany had started breathing again.

"Silly me. I was under the impression this was still my room. And—" he gestured to the pile of his belongings "—these were my clothes."

Ivy crossed the room and embraced her brother. "We didn't think you'd miss a few items. We're having a charity sale to raise money for my orphanage. You don't mind, do you?"

Three sets of ladies' eyes turned his way and he took a step back. "I would have preferred to have been asked, but as it's for a good cause... But you know, Ivy, I'm happy to donate actual money if you need it."

She pressed a kiss to his cheek. "I know, but I do like to try and do it without my two wonderful brothers' help."

"And when and where is this charity sale to take place?" The question Tiffany had been dreading.

Ivy, without a slip, said, "Thursday next at Reverend Smith's hall, next to his church near Russell Square. He will be there to supervise, so don't get all brotherly concerned."

Tiffany waited to see if Rockwell thought the location or date odd, but he merely smiled and said, "If you ladies wish to raid Wolfarth's room, I suggest you do it soon. He's due home any minute to meet with me. I'd say I'll be able to keep his attention away from his bedchamber for a good hour."

"Any tricks on how we can get past his valet, Simpson?"

Rockwell headed for the door. "Where would be the fun in that? Good day, ladies."

Once Rockwell had exited, silence reigned. Farah stood where she was—staring after him.

"He didn't even blink at the date or place", Ivy said. "I don't think he realized it's the same day as Mrs. Buchanan's soiree, or that our location is very near to said event. So that's a relief. I don't want Wolf or any of the men putting two and two together."

Tiffany nodded. "They will be so surprised, or appalled, when Valora and I turn up." The Sisterhood had decided that only two of them would attend, and as Valora was the one who most wanted this, and she was loved by the *ton* so might be easily forgiven, it was agreed she would go and Tiffany would accompany her. Tiffany had the least to lose if caught. Most of the *ton* didn't even know who she was, although Wolf's attentions were changing that rather too quickly for her liking.

When the ladies kept standing in the middle of the room, Ivy said, "What is the matter with you two? Come on, we have an hour to raid Wolf's things."

"We need the trunk," Tiffany reminded her, barely able to hide her excitement at getting to explore the wolf's den.

Just then a footman arrived with said trunk, and the ladies filled it with Rockwell's things. Tiffany looked up and caught Farah sniffing one of his fine linen shirts, and she smiled. It would seem Claire knew a bit more than she let on in regard to whom each of the ladies had set their sights on. Farah and Rockwell? Farah was a timid mouse and Rockwell was larger than life. Claire couldn't possibly imagine they were suited. Or that Rockwell would pay any attention to a woman scared to have any part of her hair out of place.

But then again, the way he'd looked at Farah when she wore his boot... Tiffany shook her head to clear the images of romance. Why was romance filling her head when she should be thinking about their investments? Wolf's handsome face swam into her mind's eye.

She stood just inside the door of the Marquess's bedchamber and although calm on the outside, inside she shook. The room was vast and the huge four-poster bed drew her attention like a quill to parchment. Before she could stop herself, she moved to the bed and ran her hand over the quilt. If she married him... She swallowed hard, though whether from fear or thrill at the idea of having to lie with him in this very bed, she wasn't sure.

"We're not here for quilts, although they might sell well too."

Tiffany pulled herself together at Farah's comment and made her way into Wolf's dressing room, where Ivy was rifling through shirts. Tiffany wanted to copy Farah and smell one. She'd just picked up a shirt made of the finest linen when a voice said, "Ladies, is there something I can help you with?"

Ivy swung to face Wolf's valet, Simpson, who stood in the doorway. "Well timed, Simpson. I'd like some of Wolf's clothes for my charity auction."

Simpson walked in and removed the shirt from Tiffany's hands. "I shall talk with His Lordship and see what he is happy to donate."

Ivy's smile dimmed. "I'm sure we do not need to disturb him."

"Disturb who?" And there he was, filling the doorway. "Ivy,

what is going on? Simpson, perhaps you could excuse us for a moment."

"Yes, my lord."

"I was hoping you'd donate some items to my charity sale."

Wolf looked at each of the ladies in turn, then said, "Miss Tiffany and Lady Farah, perhaps you could wait for Ivy in the drawing room while we have a conversation."

"May I have a talk with you afterward?" Tiffany asked. She wanted to learn about Melville.

Wolf nodded. "Of course. We should also discuss our painting schedule. Taylor will show you to the drawing room."

Tiffany looked at Farah, and the two ladies sent Ivy a sympathetic look before following Wolf's butler downstairs to the drawing room. "I'll organize some refreshments for you," Taylor said, and shut the door as he left.

"I hope Ivy's not in too much trouble," Farah said, just as Ashleigh breezed into the room. With the door open, they could hear Wolf's raised voice from above.

"Oh dear. It would seem Wolf is not in the best of moods. It's nothing to do with any of us, it's my Uncle Melville. He's apparently been gambling all around town and his creditors are asking Wolf to cover his debts."

Tiffany sat forward. "Gambling? Debts? That goes a long way to explain..." She broke off, remembering she didn't want the others to know of her predicament with Mr. Sprat just yet.

"What does it explain?" Ivy asked.

"Why Wolf seemed preoccupied today. I thought he'd seek me out for the painting earlier than this." The other girls simply nodded in agreement. Shortly after, Wolf arrived with Lady Wolfarth on his arm. As his mother swanned into the room he stayed in the doorway.

"My son says he's going to paint Miss Tiffany. How exciting for you, my dear. Of course, I shall chaperon so it's totally respectable."

Oh dear, thought Tiffany. That would not allow her to discuss Lord Melville with Wolf, or their wager.

"What will be the setting for the painting?" Ashleigh asked.

Wolf smiled at Tiffany. "I would like to paint Tiffany under the oak tree in the back garden. I may need your help, Ashleigh, in regards to Tiffany's dress and—positioning. Is tomorrow at ten agreeable? It will have to be the same time every third day, I'm afraid. Can you commit to that?"

"Absolutely. Although I have no idea why you would want me as your subject. Farah or even Ivy would be more suitable."

Wolf leaned against the drawing room door, as if too scared to enter the room full of women. He smiled as though he was keeping a secret. "I have the artist's eye, so believe me when I say you're exactly who I wish to paint." Tiffany's mouth went dry. What was he trying to tell her? "If you'll excuse me, ladies. Rockwell is waiting for me in my study. Until tomorrow—"

"Are you not attending Lady Carthor's ball tonight?" Ivy asked.

"Probably not." He looked at Tiffany. "I have a business matter I need to take care of."

Melville, Tiffany thought.

"Business at night?" Ashleigh added, but Wolf was already walking down the hall.

"Your brother works too hard," Lady Wolfarth said.

Under her breath, Ashleigh said, "More like business with a female companion." She looked at Tiffany. "Sorry, that was rude of me."

Tiffany remained silent. Wolf had told her he'd broken off his arrangement with Lady Delia, and one thing she respected about Wolf was his honor. He would never lie. He didn't need to. A wealthy, handsome Marquess could do as he pleased.

Most likely he and Rockwell would go looking for Melville tonight. Tiffany tamped down her frustration. She wanted to speak to Wolf alone—before tomorrow's painting session. Although it was risky, she would have to pay him a private visit..

She just hoped she didn't get caught, or Wolf wouldn't need to win their share wager. She'd be forced to marry him.

Blow it. That thought didn't upset her at all!

~

Wolf entered the study, and Rockwell rose to pour him a drink. "Were they in your dressing room?"

"Yes. Ivy even let Tiffany and Farah rifle through my clothes. The cheek... I'd hate to think I now have to lock my bedchamber door every time I leave the house. Poor Simpson was mortified."

"They are determined. Speaking of which, you do know the day and time and place of this charity stall? It's Reverend Smith's church hall in Russell Square."

Wolf didn't even glance up from the notes he was looking through. "And?"

"It's the same day as Mrs. Buchanan's soiree."

This time his head snapped up. "I beg your pardon?"

Rockwell laughed. "It's the same day. I hardly think it's a coincidence, do you? They have all threatened to attend."

"They would not dare." But Wolf then swore under his breath. They absolutely would dare. "It would be the end for Ashleigh. Her reputation could not stand another scandal."

Rockwell's smile died. "Is Ashleigh the reason you are pursuing Tiffany? Did you decide to accept Marlowe's ridiculous proposition. I cannot see Ashleigh being happy married to Fane."

"It had crossed my mind. But no. I am not pursuing Tiffany for that reason."

Rockwell's smile was back. "But you are pursuing her. This new interest is a tad strange. Care to share why? Not that she isn't a lovely young lady but... Well, she is a bluestocking. I would have thought Valora more to your taste. She reminds me of—"

"Don't say her name." Rockwell shook his head, a worried frown on his face. Wolf sighed. "Don't worry about me. I will tell you the reason when I can. At the moment I am honor bound to simply say, trust me. Miss Tiffany Deveraux will suit me perfectly and will make a fine countess."

His brother stood looking at him for a few moments. "I just want you to be happy. You deserve to be happy. Margo's death wasn't your fault. I know you blame yourself, but there was nothing you could have done. You were lucky to both get away with your lives."

Margo hadn't thought so. She'd killed herself two months after the incident, on their intended wedding day. And it *was* his fault. Changing the topic, he asked Rockwell, "I'm thinking of investing in some shares. Have you heard anything about an Armley Mill or a Park Mill?"

Rockwell cocked his head in thought. "I've just invested in Armley Mill. The owner is quite progressive and has been using this new merino wool. Park Mill is a sound investment too, but probably not in the long run as the owner needs to modernize and I've heard he's refusing to look to the future."

"So, in the short term Park Mill would be the better share to buy."

"How short term?"

"Say a month from today?"

Rockwell sipped his drink. "I'm not sure, but there is more demand for Armley shares, so that might increase the price over the coming month. Investors will want to get in before the price rises if the mill's profit forecast is met. Why this sudden interest in mills?"

"Park Mill was a recommendation from Mr. Lane."

"Well, to ensure you spread your risk I'd also buy Armley Mill shares too."

"Thank you." Damn. Wolf took a long gulp of his brandy. If Tiffany won the wager... He'd have to gain her hand in marriage the old-fashioned way—seduction. He would have to make her want to become his countess. Painting her portrait should allow him the time to turn her head.

First, he needed to take care of Melville. "Have you managed to learn Melville's habits and where he's likely to be tonight?"

Rockwell nodded and settled back into his chair. "He's been staying at Lord Lincoln's townhouse. The two old codgers have been gambling like the world is about to end. I have some young urchins watching the house and they will follow the men should they leave."

Wolf rose to his feet. "Then let's pay Melville a visit before they leave for the night. I'd prefer to have this conversation in private."

"And if they've already left?"

Wolf made for the door. "Then we drag him home and have a none too pleasant conversation with our uncle."

Chapter Twelve

Thank goodness Rockwell had the sense to stand at the servant's entrance, because when Melville learned who was at the door of Lord Lincoln's townhouse, he tried to make a run for it.

Rockwell marched him back inside, and Wolf said, "Lord Lincoln, may we borrow your library? I need a word with my uncle regarding family matters."

"Of course, dear boy," was Lord Lincoln's response. "Shall I send in some refreshments?"

Rockwell laughed. "We may need some brandy."

Melville walked with his head down into the room and took a seat by the fire. He looked older than Wolf remembered, yet he was younger than Wolf's mother. His uncle hadn't had it easy in life. A second son, he'd never really found his path. Wolf was thankful Rockwell seemed to know exactly what he wanted. Rockwell traveled far and wide. Exploring new places seemed to soothe his restless personality. His allowance was all he needed to live off because he invested well and sold treasures from abroad when he found them. Most importantly, and thankfully, Rockwell seemed content with his lot in life.

Melville was a man who had nothing left in his life except his sister. His wife had died a few years ago and they had never been blessed with children. Upon Dorothy's death his uncle had fallen to pieces. He'd stayed with them for quite some time before returning to his hunting lodge in Sussex. That was when the drinking and gambling began. He'd lost his home within twelve months, in a game of whist.

Melville's elder brother, the Marquess of Durith, was dead and his eldest son, the current Marquess, had refused to contemplate paying Melville's debts. The family had turned their backs on him. But Lady Wolfarth had not. She loved her younger brother. Only, Wolf's family coffers might pay the price for her love.

Once the brandy was delivered and poured, and the servant had closed the door behind him, Melville finally looked at Wolf. "I promise—"

"Don't make promises you know you won't keep." Wolf almost growled.

Rockwell sat next to his uncle. "This can't go on, Melville. Do you want to see the Wolfarth family destroyed? Your sister with no money?"

Melville gaped like a fish out of water. "But...but the Wolfarth family coffers hold plenty."

It suddenly struck Wolf that maybe Melville had no idea what he owed. "You do realize your gambling debts total almost two thousand pounds. And then there are the share deals you've reneged on. They—"

"Shares? What shares?"

Rockwell's eyes met his, and a look of worry entered his gaze. "A stockjobber named Sprat came to see me, holding notes for shares he claims you asked him to purchase. He's claiming you refused to pay for them once the prices dropped."

"I have never even heard of the man, and I certainly have not bought any shares. I've had no money to do so."

Rockwell leaned forward. "Sprat indicated you'd ask him to

buy the shares to try and earn money to pay your gambling debts."

Melville's face turned purple. He spluttered. "I tell you I have never asked anyone to buy shares on my behalf. I swear on your mother's life—on my late wife's grave." He looked at the floor. "I may gamble a bit—" At Wolf's scoff he added, "Gamble a lot. But that is my only vice in this life."

"There is no reason to lie to me, Uncle. I'll find out the truth soon enough." Wolf watched him closely.

Melville thumped the arm of his chair. "I have never met a man named Sprat and I have not bought any shares."

"I tend to believe him, Wolf," Rockwell stated.

Wolf nodded in agreement. He paced the room, trying to understand what the hell was going on. Why would Sprat bring him this tale? Why accuse a man like his uncle, a man of such high rank, the younger son of a Marquess? What was going on? Had Sprat thought Wolf would pay up without proof? That was the thing. There was no proof, just Melville's word against Sprat's. Melville was a lord, but then Sprat could point out Melville owed money everywhere. Would society believe a degenerate gambler, a man desperate for money?

Wolf snarled. "Sprat's hoping to keep this quiet and that I'll pay up to do so. I'm not such an easy mark."

Rockwell spoke up. "Scandal will erupt if you don't. But hell, we can weather a bit of scandal."

"We first have to prove Sprat is a cheat and a liar."

Melville looked as if he was about to cry. "How will you do that?"

He swung around to face Melville. "I have no idea. Not yet. But I will." He moved and took the chair next to his uncle. "This is what we will do. Melville, I will clear your current gambling debts." He held up his hand as Melville tried to thank him. "But you will retire to my country estate tonight. I'll send some of my men and a couple of Bow Street Runners with you, and you must stay there until this all settles down."

"Bow Street Runners? That's not necessary. Besides, I don't want to leave London."

Wolf looked him in the eye. "Until I understand what Sprat is about, or how far he'll take this obvious swindle, I want you out of London. If you turn up dead, I'll have absolutely no choice but to pay him, as you won't be alive to deny the purchase. It's a lot of money. With regards to Mr. Sprat, I am not taking any chances."

Melville's face paled. "Dead." He covered his face with his hands and wailed. "How did it come to this?"

"Dorothy would be appalled. I'm being cruel to be kind, Uncle. This gambling has to stop or Wolf will do something drastic like send you to the Americas," Rockwell uttered.

"The Americas? You wouldn't do that to an old man?"

"I'd have no choice. Family comes first and your debts put us in jeopardy." Wolf wasn't inclined to be nice. The debts would cut a hole in his finances and if these shares had to be honored too— well, he'd need Tiffany even more. "Gambling is a fool's game if you cannot control it. I'm making it clear tonight to all the gambling dens in London that I will not be responsible for any future debts you incur, and some of the places you frequent are known to be brutal if debts are not paid. So I suggest you take the time at the country estate to find another 'hobby'."

Rockwell stood. "I'll summon the Bow Street Runners and send a note to the house to organize some men and a carriage."

"While Rockwell is organizing your travel arrangements, you will tell me who you owe money to and how much. All of it. I want this over." When Melville merely shrugged, Wolf added, "And if I see or hear of any other gambling, I will be talking to mother. I will tell her exactly what you have been doing and how much you have cost this family and that we have to send you away. So, if you don't want to break your sister's heart, I suggest you do as I say."

~

It was close to six in the morning when Wolf finally made it home. Stepping down tiredly from his carriage, he was pleased with the night's endeavors. Melville and his armed guard had gotten away just before dusk and then, with Rockwell beside him, Wolf visited all the gambling dens in greater London and told them to send their notes to him. He also warned them he knew the exact amounts owed and would pay no more.

His carriage had dropped Rockwell off at his lodgings, and Wolf was looking forward to getting some sleep. Tomorrow he'd start talking to his stockjobber, Jacob Lane, about Sprat. What did he know of the man? He'd also ask at the club if anyone used Mr. Sprat and then talk to those who did. This swindle was well organized and targeted. He wondered if Sprat had done this to another family before.

He'd just started up the steps when out of the shadows stepped Tiffany, dressed in her widow's weeds. "What on earth are you doing here?" he demanded with a frown. "Quickly, inside." Grabbing her hand, he ushered her across the threshold and literally dragged her down the corridor.

Tiffany didn't speak until they reached his study. With much agitation in her voice, she said, "I want an update on Lord Melville. When is he going to pay his debt to Mr. Sprat?"

"I'm tired, hungry and in need of sleep. Surely this discussion could have waited until later? I'm supposed to start my portrait of you at ten, and that's only four hours away. And you should *not* be here." Damn it to hell, the staff would soon be up. What if one of them saw her?

"Well, perhaps you should have thought about that before staying out all night doing God knows what."

He was too tired to even smile at the jealousy in Tiffany's words. "I was out dealing with Melville and our Sprat problem, if you must know." He was not about to inform her he thought her stockjobber a liar and a thief. He wondered exactly how her father had lost all his money, and why he'd come down to London to meet with Sprat in person. Had Lord Deveraux also been concerned with what Sprat was doing? Had Sprat pulled the same swindle on Tiffany's father? Or perhaps purposely placed bids without Deveraux's permission on bad shares?

Her face lit up. "You've spoken to Lord Melville. When will his debt be settled?"

"I have a little more information to wade through, but soon." Not exactly a lie.

"Lovely. I shall leave you to your sleep and be back at ten," she calmly replied.

"In future, please do not wait outside on the street like a poor urchin. These widow's weeds won't hide you for very long and also, it doesn't look good if I am seen escorting a widow into my house early in the morning with my sisters here. Ashleigh does not have the best standing in society as it is." He put his grumpiness down to exhaustion.

Bowing her head, Tiffany agreed. "You are right. I'm sorry. I should be able to speak with you when I sit for the portrait, so I won't have to sneak another interview."

Wolf walked toward her, and to her credit she held her ground. He ran a finger down her cheek then pushed her glasses back up her nose. "As I'm courting you, all you need do is send for me and I shall come."

She looked at him, those green eyes open wide. "But...but you have so many responsibilities, I wouldn't want to interrupt you."

He cupped her chin in his hand and bent closer. "I'm never too busy for the woman I want to marry," and he pressed a kiss to her sweet lips and felt them tremble beneath his. He knew he should pull away. She'd come here to talk, but he'd been dying to taste her and when she didn't retreat he deepened the kiss. She tasted of innocence and desire. She didn't try to stop him and when her mouth opened to admit him, his tongue swept in. Her arms rose to wrap around his neck and he pulled her hard against him.

This was what he knew lay underneath Tiffany's bluestocking exterior. Passion. He intended to make her understand that a marriage with him would suit her very well. They had friendship, respect and, most importantly, passion. They didn't need anything else. He didn't want anything else.

Her delightfully delicious moans inflamed his need and were he not a gentleman, he'd have taken her right there in his study. Luckily, he understood she wasn't ready for more—yet. So with a groan he pulled back and rested his forehead on hers, trying to bring his body and breathing under control.

Tiffany was the one to step back first. "That was interesting," she whispered dazedly, her fingers pressed to her lips.

"That was passion. Don't be scared of it."

She looked at him as if he had two heads. "Scared? I wasn't scared, merely curious. That was my first proper kiss. It was— indescribable. Wonderful. Sensual. Stirring. Captivating. Addictive..."

"Not so indescribable then. I'm happy to oblige any time." Wolf smiled brazenly.

"I wonder if every kiss is like that." Worrying her lip between her dainty teeth, she turned to leave. "I'll sneak out the servant's entrance and see you back here at ten." Before she closed the door behind her, she smiled to herself and demurely said, "And I liked it. I liked it a lot."

Wolf was still grinning as he walked to his bedchamber to grab a few precious hours of sleep. It was no wonder he dreamed of Tiffany laid out in his bed like a gift. How could one innocent kiss stir him so?

He fell asleep trying not to think too closely about the answer to that question.

～

Wolf had only been asleep for two hours when Rockwell was beside his bed, poking him awake.

"You were right. There is definitely more to this. The carriage was attacked near St. Albans on the way north. They didn't try to rob as in 'stand and deliver', they attacked with pistols firing. It looked as if they simply wanted to kill Melville. And it was as if they knew he was coming."

"Sprat. He must have had men watching Lord Lincoln's house." Wolf threw back the covers and jumped out of bed, calling for Simpson. "Did Melville get away?"

Rockwell nodded. "They have continued north. The Bow Street Runners have contacted some men in York who will ride south to meet them just in case."

Wolf pulled on his shirt, while Simpson found his Hessians. "We need a plan. I need to learn all I can about Sprat as fast as possible. I have Tiffany coming at ten for her first sitting. Can you talk to your stockjobber today? I'll talk to mine later this afternoon."

"I've already instructed the Bow Street Runners to find out where Sprat lives, where he came from, what's his background."

Wolf looked at Rockwell. "I hope they will be discreet. I don't want Sprat learning we are investigating him."

"He'll know that already. He knows we sent Melville home. Why would we do that? He'll know it's because we believe Melville."

"Maybe he thinks I've sent him home in disgrace and to stop his gambling? Our trip around the dens last night would indicate my intentions, surely?"

Rockwell shrugged. "Sprat must know our suspicions have been aroused, because Melville was well protected."

"True. That makes Sprat dangerous. We don't know enough about him and I don't like that either." What he definitely didn't like was the fact Tiffany was dealing with this man. Her outings to meet with him would have to stop. Convincing her to cease her dealings with Sprat would be difficult, like moving heaven and earth. For some reason, Tiffany thought very highly of the man.

"Let's see what Jacob Lane has to say about our Mr. Sprat." The clock on the mantle in Wolf's bedchamber struck half past the hour. "Damn. You'll have to go alone. Tiffany is due in an hour and a half and I won't get back in time. I have to start the painting today if I've any chance of getting the piece ready for the opening."

"Let's meet with Lane this afternoon. I'll visit my stockjobber this morning. Harold Parker has an office away from Capel Court, so Sprat won't see me."

"I suspect he's got men watching this house."

Rockwell shrugged. "I bet he's not watching my lodgings. I'll return home and wait for a period then go see Parker."

"Good idea, but be careful."

Rockwell nodded and as he left, Wolf called for Simpson to find his old painting clothes. He knew exactly how he wanted Tiffany to pose, so now all he had to do was organize the props and ensure the dress he wanted her to wear had been collected from the dressmaker.

The problem now was how to persuade Tiffany to wear it.

Chapter Thirteen

Tiffany's last missive to Mr. Sprat had resulted in no reply. She thought she'd at least get a thank you from him, for Wolf had told her he was working on the Melville problem. She wanted to know if Sprat had received the payment and whether her money was no longer at risk. But the silence was deafening. She'd talk to Wolf again today. Even with his mother in attendance, she'd find a way.

The one bright spark of the morning had been when she'd checked the Armley and Park Mills' share prices in The Times. She was in the lead by quite some margin.

On their short walk to Wolf's townhouse, Claire said, "Farah and Valora heard some interesting gossip at the ball last night. Apparently, the Marquess of Titchfield is building a railroad in Scotland for his coal transport. Blackstone considered investing but decided it was too risky."

Tiffany's mind stopped worrying about Sprat and concentrated on Claire's news. "Railways are risky. It's huge capital investment and the returns are slow to eventuate. I have heard of the Kilmarnock and Troon Railway. I like that the Marquess already has customers lined up to use it, and it will carry passengers as well as coal. That is forward thinking."

Claire looked at Tiffany with admiration. "Your plan is working. The men think nothing of talking business in front of us. They really have no idea who is behind the challenge."

"Let's hope it stays that way." Tiffany chewed her bottom lip. Wolf knew she invested. Would he guess who was behind the challenge? Perhaps he'd be too arrogant to consider that the women would issue such a challenge. "No talking about investing or business or shares in front of the men. We can't have any of them guessing what we are up to."

Claire nodded. "I feel the news about the location of our charity stall will keep the men otherwise engaged. Rockwell will have told Wolf and he's not dumb. He was there when we said we wanted to go. Has he said anything to you?"

"No." Claire looked at her. "I don't think they have guessed. I was at his house after Rockwell asked for the details of the stall, and Wolf didn't say anything to me or his sisters."

"Valora might think her looks, and title of the *ton* diamond, will save her from the scandal of going to Mrs. Buchanan's, but she could destroy her chances with Northbrook. After Northbrook, I can't think of any other gentleman who would be good enough for her."

"Fane," stated Tiffany bluntly.

Claire shook her head. "He'll never notice Valora. When he decides he needs an heir he'll marry the debutante of the season and then treat her as nothing but a glorified baby maker. His wife will lead a lonely life. I wouldn't wish that on my worst enemy."

"I think you're being too hard on Fane. When he meets the right lady—"

"Is that what you think Wolf is doing? He's met his right lady —you? What triggered his sudden interest in you?"

Tiffany wished she knew the answer to that question. Part of her believed that Wolf had suddenly seen her in a different light when he caught her at Capel Court. Maybe he liked the assertive, clever Tiffany. But the other side of her was filled with doubts. She wasn't pretty enough for such a handsome lord. She wasn't desirable. She wasn't wealthy, and an alliance wouldn't benefit Wolf at all.

Tiffany shrugged, "I guess I'll have to wait and see how his courtship goes. He might decide we're not well suited." She hoped not. The minutes in his company were becoming the best parts of her day, and now, because he was painting her, she'd be in his company a lot more.

On that exciting thought, she and Claire made their way inside the house. Ivy met them and dragged them up to her bedchamber.

"Wolf has asked me to help you dress in this," Ivy said, and she pointed to the most glorious emerald green velvet gown on the bed.

Tiffany looked down her person. "What's wrong with my gown?" It was her best and she thought it flattered her figure.

"Nothing. I assume Wolf has an artist's view of what he is trying to deliver in this painting. I think the color will look amazing on you. It will really enhance the green of your eyes."

Claire said, "I agree. Did Wolf pick the gown?" Ivy nodded. "He does have a wonderful artist's eye for color."

Tiffany could feel her face heat. How was she supposed to wear a gown Wolf had selected for her? It was—very personal. Still, before she could think on it for too long, she reached out a hand to stroke the beautiful, seductive fabric. "I did agree to sit for him and if this is his vision then who am I to argue," Tiffany declared, and she began to undress.

Her two friends stood silently in surprise as she turned toward them in the glamorous gown. "You are shining with light, like a gemstone," Ivy said wistfully.

Her reward for her bravery was the stunned look on Wolf's face as she made her way across the grass to where his easel sat waiting. His eyes darkened with heat as he watched her approach. She could see a pile of fur rugs and cushions under the tree.

"You look beautiful," Wolf said as he bowed low and pressed a kiss to her gloved hand. "But we will have these off," and he began to tug at the ends of her gloves. She tried to stop him but he gathered both her wrists in one large hand and said softly, "I know what I am doing. Can you trust the painter in me?"

Tiffany nodded, and he finished sliding the gloves from her hands just as his mother arrived. "You look lovely in that gown, my dear." Lady Wolfarth settled into a large chair and took out her crochet. "I hope the weather stays warm, at least until Wolf has enough of this painting done for us to venture back inside."

Ivy and Claire sat next to Lady Wolfarth, watching Tiffany and Wolf as if they were at the theater.

Wolf led Tiffany to the rugs under the tree. "I want you to curl on your side and look as if you're reading this book," and he handed her a book that when she glanced at the cover made her knees almost buckle. Wolf merely winked. "Educational, I feel."

Memoirs of a Woman of Pleasure by John Cleland. She glanced at Lady Wolfarth and then lay it down next to her on the rugs. Wolf had known she'd accept the book because he understood her very well. Her curiosity made it impossible to turn away.

But she'd hardly gotten over the shock of the book when Wolf's hands went to her hair. "What do you think you are doing?"

"It's rather obvious. I'm taking your hair down." He had her hair unpinned and uncoiled within seconds, and it annoyed her because she realized he'd done this many times before. He ran his fingers through her hair, placing it about her shoulders. Once he was satisfied he stood back to admire his work.

"One more thing," and he stepped forward again and removed her glasses and then casually opened the book to a page. "There. Now try to stay still. I need to get this beginning sketch done quickly before the light changes."

Tiffany wondered how long she could lie still. Ivy and Claire were making the most unusual noises. Whispering and giggles were all she could hear and she couldn't move to look at them.

"Did you manage to take care of the matter we discussed the

other day?" she asked. When he didn't answer, she wondered if he had posed her like this so she couldn't look at him, or anyone else for that matter.

He didn't answer.

Ivy spoke instead. "He won't answer. Once he begins painting, the world could end and he'd not notice. It's very boring. That's why I never agree to sit for him."

"I can't even read as I don't have my glasses." She squinted at the words on the page.

"Don't squint," he barked at her.

"Please talk to me, Claire."

Claire heeded her call while trying to stir the pot. "The Reverend has the tables set up ready for our stall." Was she deliberately trying to scuttle Valora's plan to attend the soiree? Or ruin Wolf's concentration. But Wolf said nothing.

"That's good. Perhaps we could ask the Reverend to spread the word at his service on Sunday."

"I believe he already has. They are expecting quite the crowd. Courtney has organized plenty of grooms and footmen to ensure the day runs smoothly."

"I do think you ladies are marvelous the way you raise money for Ivy's orphanage. In my day, it just wasn't done."

"Oh, Mother. You donated to lots of worthy charities in your day, and you still do."

"But you ladies seem to be having so much fun together. I envy you your youth and the excitement of finding a handsome young man to be your husband. In my day, our fathers had the final say."

"I suspect Wolf will be equally ridiculous when I find my young man," Ivy teased. Again, no reply. Wolf was totally engrossed in his art. "But, Mother, you loved father."

"I was lucky, I admit. Wolfarth was so handsome. But it was his kindness and humor that won me over. A kind heart is worth far more than a handsome face. Just you remember that advice."

"It's very nice when they are handsome and kind," Ivy said.

"And do you have your eye on anyone in particular?" Claire asked.

Tiffany wished she could see Ivy's face. She suspected it was bright red at this moment. Did Claire know Ivy liked her brother Dayton? Tiffany had guessed because Dayton had called one day to visit Rockwell, and Tiffany caught Ivy hiding on the stairs peering over the banister at Dayton. The look on Ivy's face... Tiffany wondered if that's how she looked at Wolf, with love in her eyes.

"I'll share if you share," Ivy challenged her friend.

Claire scoffed. "I am in no rush to wed. The current *ton* bachelors do not have much to recommend them."

Tiffany wished she could give Claire a hug. Fane's behavior had made Claire wary of all men. She thought they all had mistresses, and Claire wanted a husband who would be true to her. So did Tiffany, and that's what worried her. Wolf had given his word he would not have a mistress while courting her, but what if they married? Could he stay true to her—especially if he didn't love her?

Soon the muscles in her back were screaming. Being told not to move only made her want to move every inch of her body. She needed to stretch so badly. Instead, she tried to read the print on the page in front of her. She had just about managed to read the top line, which was something about bare breasts, when Wolf told her she could move.

"That's enough for today. I'll need you again tomorrow morning at the same time if that's convenient for you?"

She stretched her arms up over her head and eased the numbness in her legs. She wanted to say no, but how could she? He needed this painting and she'd agreed to sit for him. "Fine."

"You can change in Ivy's room again, leave the gown here. It can't be damaged." He handed her glasses back to her but, to her dismay, took the book. "Once you've finished posing for me, I may let you read it, or perhaps I'll read it to you," he whispered so only she could hear. *Be still her pounding heart.*

"May I see the painting?"

"Oh, yes, please let us see it, Wolf." Ivy begged.

"Absolutely not. You know no one sees my work until it's finished." And he threw a cloth over the canvas before anyone could approach. "Tiffany, may I have a word in my study once you've changed and before you leave? I know you have an invitation to Lady Fairfax's masquerade costume ball and I'd like to coordinate our outfits."

Thank goodness. She'd bet a gold coin that he didn't wish to talk about a ball. He must have some news regarding Melville. "Of course."

With that he walked off, his canvas safely carried inside by the footmen.

"My son has finally set his sights on a young lady, and I'm very pleased it's you, Tiffany." Lady Wolfarth gave her arm a squeeze.

"You are?"

"Absolutely. Did you know your mother was one of my best friends?"

"Yes, she sometimes shared your letters with me. You wrote such vivid accounts of the season when we were stuck in Yorkshire." Stuck because they'd had no money to come to town. Lady Wolfarth had never deserted her mother.

"Your mother and I had agreed I would sponsor you for your come-out since your father could not afford it...but sadly they had passed by then. I'm not sure Lord Marlowe has afforded you a stellar come-out, but my son was sensible enough to see what a catch you are.

"You have your mother's eyes. You'll make Wolf a fine countess. A woman who is his equal. He needs that. He needs someone to make him forget Lady Margo. She was a mistake in more ways than I can count." With that she pressed a kiss to Tiffany's cheek and retreated inside.

Tiffany turned on Ivy. "What did she mean when she said Lady Margo was a mistake?"

"I have no idea. I can't really remember her. I was only

sixteen, so not out in society. You weren't either. All I can remember is that she was very beautiful. And that she died the day of their wedding. I can remember Wolf going crazy..."

"It must have been dreadful for him. How did she die?" Claire asked.

"We ladies were never told." Ivy's eyes welled with tears. "I never thought Wolf would get over her death. He did, but not for a long time. Everyone was worried about him, especially Rockwell." Ivy hugged Tiffany. "That's why I'm so pleased he's decided to court you. It's a sign he's ready to move on with his life."

Tiffany pondered on Lady Wolfarth's words as she changed out of the vibrant gown. Another mystery. Why were relationships so complex? Was that why Wolf wanted to marry her? Because she wasn't beautiful and so she couldn't remind him of Margo? She wished she had the courage to ask him.

Perhaps she would. But not today. Today all she needed to discuss was Mr. Sprat. She knocked on the door to Wolf's study and he bid her enter.

"Have you news on Lord Melville's debt?"

Wolf's smile faltered. "And it's nice to see you too, Tiffany." He pressed a kiss to her knuckles. "You do know how to bring a man down."

"I've already seen you today." She smiled sweetly at him.

"But not privately. Not in a way in which I can greet you properly," and he pressed a kiss to her lips. She glanced worriedly at the open door.

Feeling out of her depth, she stammered, "Sorry, it's just I'm worried about Mr. Sprat."

"You shouldn't be. Why is this debt of concern to you?" With a smooth nod he elegantly indicated she should sit.

What to tell him? If she revealed too much, the wager in the White's book might well be a lot less anonymous. She wished the door wasn't wide open. She didn't want anyone to overhear. She turned to face Wolf and for a moment her breath faltered. He wore no cravat, allowing her to glimpse tufts of dark hair, and she longed to see him without his shirt on. She knew the sight would be breathtaking.

"Well?" He smiled reassuringly.

"My father helped me invest, but not with my share selection. Instead he helped by telling Mr. Sprat to take my investments. Since the South Sea share debacle over fifty years ago, many stock-jobbers won't touch a female investor. They blamed females investing in the market for the last big bear run and many people lost everything."

"Surely that's not the case now. I'm sure a stockjobber would—"

"Would you take a woman's order and hope she paid up? Many stockjobbers are concerned that a woman has no money of her own. Would her husband approve? Would he honor any debt?"

"But not your Mr. Sprat. He took your orders?" The way Wolf looked at her suggested he had a suspicion about what she would say.

"Not exactly." Tiffany twisted her fingers nervously in her lap.

"Oh, my God. You paid him upfront." Wolf leaped from his chair and began to pace the study. With his long legs, he was turning pretty frequently. Suddenly he stopped and faced her. "How much of your money does he have?"

She swallowed. "I'm not sure that's any of your concern." But what concerned Tiffany was it was no longer just her money he held. It was the Sisterhood's. "Besides, if Melville pays his debt all will be fine."

"Melville insists he never placed any share orders with Sprat, or anyone. Rockwell is asking around at Capel Court right now. If Melville has never dabbled in shares, I'm inclined to believe him."

Was it Wolf's proximity that made her brain so fuddled? "I don't understand, why would Sprat tell this tale... Oh!" The warmth drained from her face and she closed her eyes in disbelief.

"Yes. It's a swindle. I'm also investigating if Sprat has done this before. If he's ever targeted a lord down on his luck and threatened him with bogus purchase orders."

Why did her father's face suddenly swim into view? Surely not?

"What do you know of your father's dealings with Sprat? Were there any problems?"

"Father never mentioned anything. Surely he would have told me to be careful if he had any concerns over his stockjobber?"

"What if he didn't know until it was too late? What if Sprat tried to say your father had invested in shares when he hadn't? Just like he's doing to Melville."

Tiffany's mouth dried and she could hardly swallow. It had always concerned her that her father, who was a shrewd investor, had lost everything. Had Sprat swindled her father? But her father would never have stood for it. She thought back to the last time she'd seen her parents. They were packing hurriedly. Maybe Sprat *had* tried to swindle her father. Whatever had happened, it was enough to see her father suddenly head to London. Is that why he'd urgently needed to see Sprat? Had Sprat's deceit led to her family's downfall and her parents' deaths at the hands of highwaymen?

"I feel sick," she said as the enormity of what Wolf was insinuating hit.

"I don't want you anywhere near Sprat, and I'm going to insist he hand over any shares he holds for you to my stockjobber, Mr. Lane. If you want to trade, I'll ensure Lane honors your orders."

He was dangling a dream in front of her. To work with a stockjobber of Mr. Lane's skill... But would Mr. Lane tell Wolf what she was investing in, and would Lane guess who was challenging the men? How did she keep the secret that the Sisterhood had issued the share challenge? Her next thought was even worse. What if Sprat was swindling her and he'd taken all her money and never bought one share? The room began to spin as she realized the gravity of the situation. She might not have a penny to her name, and the ladies had trusted her with their hard-saved pin money.

She looked anxiously at Wolf. "Have you spoken to Sprat about your concerns?"

A cunning smile curled his lips. "No, but I think he's suspicious. I sent my uncle home to my estate in disgrace and the carriage was waylaid on the way home."

Shivers covered her skin as she whispered, "Was it highwaymen?"

"No. However, I believe they wanted me to think they were, and their target was definitely Melville. All they wanted was to kill him."

"How do you know that?"

"Highwaymen try to make the carriage stop so they can rob it. These men simply shot it up, and then rode away without looking for loot. I know Sprat had someone watching the house where Melville was staying and saw him departing London."

Tiffany clutched her stomach. "My parents..." Wolf had just painted a horrific picture of what could have happened to her parents.

"If my uncle dies, I will be honor bound to pay Sprat because Melville is not here to defend himself. The scandal should I deny the claim... I need proof. I won't have my family name dragged through the mud and Sprat knows that."

"That's his game, isn't it? Did he do this to my father?" She stood up and opened her mouth to request clarification, but Wolf suddenly pulled her into his arms and pressed kisses to her cheek.

"I don't know, but we need to be suspicious given the attack on Melville." She sobbed silently, and tears fell on his shirt. "I'm sorry, sweeting."

"I've been such a naïve, trusting fool." Her world grew dark and the joy of investing escaped like smoke up a chimney. She knew, deep in her soul, that Sprat had killed her parents. And Tiffany vowed there and then: she would have her revenge.

She let Wolf's strong arms support her. "I'm going to ensure he never does this to anyone again. I don't know if I will be able to prove he was complicit in your parents' deaths, but I will get him for fraud and for the attempt on Lord Melville's life. That will likely see him hang."

She pushed out of his hold and wiped the tears from her face. "What can I do to help?"

Wolf's fingers wrapped around her chin, and he tilted her head so he was looking directly into her grieving eyes. "Tomorrow, when you come for the painting session, bring me copies of your purchase orders and a list of the shares you believe Sprat holds for you. I'm going to pressure Sprat to give me the share notes. I suspect he doesn't have them. That will be the start of us uncovering his tangle of lies. But you are not to contact him. He's extremely dangerous."

Her tears continued to fall as reality hit. "He was never going to pay me my money back. He simply fed me some dividends and some sales income to reel me in further. My money is gone, isn't it?"

He let go of her chin and cupped her cheek. "I suspect so, but if we can arrest him before he can dispose of the money we might recover at least some of it."

She took the handkerchief he handed her and wiped her face. She would not waste a single tear on Sprat again. "You've won our wager. I can't get the money off Sprat."

"No, I haven't. We wagered on whose shares would rise in price the most, not on who made the most money in the month. This wager had nothing to do with actually buying the shares. But I'm hoping I don't need to win the wager for you to realize I am courting you because I truly want you to become my wife. Would that be so terrible?" Wolf asked temptingly.

If she didn't get her money back, her bid for financial freedom would take quite a few years as she'd have to start all over again. Thankfully, Wolf had ensured she could earn it back by promising her Mr. Lane's services. Did he realize she'd have less choice if he didn't help her? That it would make her situation untenable and that perhaps she'd be best to marry him? But that wasn't the kind of man Wolf was. He wanted to win her agreement to wed, but honorably. *Or he knows how desirable he is and is confident of you accepting his offer of marriage.* Words were whirling in her head.

Tiffany straightened and held herself stiffly. "I'll consider your suit, my lord, if you can tell me why you want to marry me."

Chapter Fourteen

W hy did he have to select a smart woman? *Because a lifetime of marriage is a long time and you want a partner to challenge you, help you and...* "I'm not having this conversation over and over again. We will suit each other well."

Her eyes widened. "We are nothing alike."

"Of course we are. We both believe in family. We are both honest and kind and want to be happy."

He could see her building up to another question and dreaded what it might be, but then, thankfully, Ivy poked her head in the door. "Claire needs to leave. She's waiting for you." Ivy's smile died as she took in the strained silence. She stepped into the room. "Is everything all right?"

Wolf ignored her question. "So we are agreed. You will attend the ball as a shepherdess and I'll go as a shepherd."

Tiffany blinked at him as if he'd gone mad, then understanding dawned in her eyes and she played along. "I was going to suggest you go as the big bad wolf I have to protect my sheep from."

He laughed. "Perhaps I will, but I'm pretty sure I won't be chasing your sheep."

Ivy giggled. "Come on, Tiffany, you can't stay all day flirting with Wolf, he's far too busy. Besides, Rockwell's just arrived and is looking rather harassed."

Tiffany's eyes met his and he turned away. How had she managed to get under his skin in such a short time? Until this past week, he'd barely paid her any attention since her come-out. "I'll see you this evening at Lady Combes's recital."

The tightness in his throat wasn't from his cravat; he wasn't wearing one. He rubbed his chest and pushed away the thought of how he enjoyed Tiffany's company a little too much.

With Margo he'd fallen for her with one simple smile. She'd been beautiful beyond words, but if he had to find fault, she wasn't very intelligent. That's what surprised him now. He hadn't known he wanted intelligence in a wife until he'd appreciated Tiffany's. Rather than beauty, it was her mind that had captivated him on that carriage ride home from Capel Court.

He heard Rockwell in the hall greeting Tiffany and Claire. He poured himself and Rockwell a drink and handed his brother's to him as he entered.

Rockwell sat and said, "Best you bring the decanter closer. You're going to need more to drink when you hear the information I've gathered." "Harold Parker had lots to say about Sprat. And none of it good. However, he had heard nothing about him faking purchase orders or any other swindle. Parker merely mentioned that Sprat could employ unsavory tactics to gain a man's business, he was slow at paying out dividend or share income, and if the investor was a tad slow in paying up, well, thugs paid the person a visit."

"Well, that's disappointing. I had hoped we could prove a pattern of purchase order swindles should I need to defend my decision not to pay up."

Rockwell smiled. "That's not all I found out. Parker told me to speak to one of Sprat's biggest clients, a Lord Dunmar. But I shall wait to tell you that story as I have summonsed Marlowe and Blackstone. I thought we should update them on the situation.

Having a duke's support will be helpful should Sprat press ahead with his claims."

"I'll go and change out of my painting clothes then. After our conversation with Blackstone, I'll pay Jacob a visit, but I promised to attend Lady Combes's recital, so I want to ensure I don't have to come home and change first."

～

By the time Wolf arrived back in his study, Blackstone and Marlowe had arrived.

"Rockwell has brought us up to speed on the Melville situation. I've never heard of this Sprat character but I know Melville is a man of honor. If he says he didn't purchase anything from Sprat I am inclined to believe him."

"Thank you, Blackstone. I appreciate your confidence in my uncle's honor. If I can uncover unscrupulous behavior on Sprat's part it will help me should I have to publicly defend Melville against Sprat's claims."

Marlowe spoke up. "I might be able to help you with Lord Dunmar. James's father died over twelve months ago. So I think Rockwell's stockjobber, Parker, would have been talking about the late Lord Dunmar. I think the new Lord Dunmar is having a few problems. He's not been to the club for months and rarely attends town. However, he is currently in residence in London."

Rockwell looked at Wolf. "Are you thinking what I'm thinking?"

Wolf nodded. "That Sprat has done something similar to Lord Dunmar. Told the new Lord Dunmar that his father had purchase orders outstanding."

"If we can establish a pattern of such behavior, then we might have enough evidence to at least shut Sprat down."

Wolf looked at Marlowe. "I want to do more than that. Did you know he was your uncle's stockjobber?" The look on

Marlowe's face said it all. "After the attack on Melville last night, I have a suspicion the late Lord Deveraux's run-in with high-waymen and subsequent murder has Sprat's signature all over it."

Marlowe jumped to his feet. "You think he did something to Tiffany's parents?"

"I think he was swindling or blackmailing her father with bogus purchase orders and that Sprat took all his money."

"Has Tiffany said something to you?" Marlowe asked.

How to answer that without revealing her secret? Before he could reply, Rockwell jumped in. "My stockjobber mentioned her father was one of Sprat's clients. Perhaps Wolf and I have jumped to a conclusion, but the similarity to the attack on Melville made us wonder why your uncle died penniless when he was supposedly such a skilled investor. I believe it bears investigation."

"I'll have the man hung if he had any hand in their deaths. If it's true, Tiffany will be devastated. We must keep this from the ladies until we know more."

Rockwell looked at Wolf. "Of course," his brother replied, so Wolf didn't have to lie.

Marlowe moved toward the door. "Let us pay a call on Lord Dunmar."

❧

It didn't take the men long to walk the two blocks to the Dunmar residence. To say the young lord was overcome at the visit was an understatement.

His face paled further when they informed him of the reason for their visit. When he slumped back in his chair it was obvious this was the miracle young Dunmar had been hoping for. He poured out his terrible tale.

"Yes, Sprat appeared a few weeks after my father died, with purchase orders he said my father had placed. The amount was substantial and I didn't have the money to pay. I talked with my father's lawyer but he had no information. When I pointed out I did not have the funds, Sprat got angry and threatened to tell everyone I was in dun territory. I wouldn't have been if not for those notes. Sprat is letting me pay it off but with a hefty interest rate."

"Please tell me you are not using him as your stockjobber?"

"I am not. I began to suspect him when I started asking a few questions about my father's purchases. I just couldn't imagine Father investing in some of those companies. I could see Sprat didn't want to answer them and he got quite aggressive. When I was riding home, someone took a shot at me in the park. If I hadn't ducked under a branch I'm not sure I'd be here today. That is why I'm rarely in town."

Wolf shuddered. He needed to ensure Tiffany was safe. At least she understood how dangerous Sprat could be. She wouldn't be foolish enough to engage him on her own.

Blackstone cleared his throat. "Stop your payments to Sprat and tell him I've picked up your debt obligation. I believe your father never made such purchase orders. I'm happy to deal with Sprat."

Wolf stood. "Take your new wife and family and return to your estate until we have taken care of this. Blackstone's name should protect you for a while, plus the fact Sprat knows we are investigating. An attack on my uncle's carriage is one thing, but a second attack so soon would only give our case ammunition."

As they left a very thankful Lord Dunmar, Wolf considered this was going to get much worse. Blackstone would not pay Sprat, and Wolf was about to call in Tiffany's investments. Sprat's cash flow would be squeezed. What would he do in retaliation?

"We should put a guard on our houses and loved ones."

The men all stopped mid-stride at Wolf's words. "You think he'd risk attacking us personally?"

"I do." They didn't know Wolf was also calling in Tiffany's money. He intended to do that in person tomorrow afternoon, and he'd have Jacob Lane by his side. He'd demand repayment at Capel Court with witnesses. Maybe he'd take Rockwell with him, but then he'd know about Tiffany's foray into investing. He'd promised to keep her secret, so he'd just have to do with Jacob Lane.

"We can't decamp our families back to our estates in the middle of the season. I'm expecting Farah's engagement to be announced soon." Blackstone's words were like a command.

"I agree. How would we explain all of us leaving so suddenly? It would create its own scandal." Marlowe continued walking. "Besides, I want to watch Wolf's courtship of my ward, Tiffany. I've heard she's not exactly falling at your feet, but making you dance a merry dance."

Blackstone frowned. "Really, Marlowe. You should be insisting she accepts Wolf's offer. I already have someone lined up for Farah if she continues to dally in her decision."

"If only all our dependents were as docile and obedient as Farah," Marlowe stated.

By the time they reached Wolf's townhouse the men were ribbing him about Tiffany's reluctance. Wolf didn't mind. He liked that Tiffany had a mind of her own and that she was a challenge. Margo had simply said yes, as if it was expected of her. Perhaps if she'd had Tiffany's strength of mind she would never have killed herself. She could have survived her ordeal.

Margo wouldn't tell him the details of what happened to her during the attack on his carriage, but the screams told Wolf all he needed to know. She'd been raped. Margo never recovered. She couldn't bare him touching her and thought herself unclean. The note she'd left before killing herself on their wedding day said she could not marry him as she was with child. She would not risk his firstborn being a son who was not his. She was a disgrace and her life was over.

Wolf had crumpled the note and dropped to his knees and cried. Blaming himself for her death. It would not have mattered to him if he'd known her secret. He had loved her and would have stood by her. It was his fault she'd been attacked in the first place.

In the weeks following Margo's death, Wolf went on a rampage. Wanting revenge. The only thing her mother had told Wolf was that the man had a birthmark behind his ear. A mark in the shape of a star. Wolf wondered if Margo had seen a tattoo rather than a birthmark, but he'd never found the man.

The idea that a woman he chose to marry was once again under threat of harm put him in a quandary. Marlowe wouldn't understand the danger unless he knew Tiffany's secret. Marlowe needed to be warned, but then Wolf would have to break his promise to Tiffany.

Once they were all seated in his study again, Wolf said, "I have a personal confidence that I have decided to share, but I want all of you to promise me, on your word of honor, not to share this or take any disciplinary or other actions without my knowledge."

"This sounds rather serious."

"It is, brother." He looked directly at Marlowe. "Melville's situation came to my attention via Tiffany." He paused at the shocked gasps. "Tiffany has been investing in shares since her father's death. Her stockjobber is Sprat. Sprat used her connection to me to gain admittance to present Melville's debt."

Rockwell said under his breath, "That explains a lot."

"You should have told me immediately," Marlowe bellowed.

"I couldn't. We made a wager and only if I won could I tell you her secret. My word is my bond. The wager has many days to run, but I can't keep this from you when she's at risk of becoming a target. Her safety means more than my honor."

Marlowe began to pace the room. "A wager with Tiffany? Has this wager got something to do with you courting her?"

He sighed. "If I win, I can tell you her secret. If she wins, she gets to keep her secret. I may have said I'd only agree to this wager if she let me court her. I really do want her to become my wife. She, on the other hand, has this crazy idea that she's financially secure enough to choose to marry only for love."

That made Marlowe quickly sit down. "Love. I shudder to think. Men like us don't marry for love. A suitable young lady, well connected with a good dowry, is all that's required."

"I beg to differ. Wolf almost married for love," Rockwell said softly. He was referring to Margo.

Wolf cleared his throat. He would not lie to Marlowe. "I'm not in love with Tiffany. I just know we're well suited and she will make me a fine countess. However, convincing her of that won't be easy. Especially when she learns I've shared her secret."

"I shall tell her—"

"No, Marlowe. You will say nothing. This is between Tiffany and I."

Blackstone spoke up. "I'm not sure I understand why she is in danger. So, she uses Sprat—but why would he want to hurt her? To get to you? You needn't have shared her secret for that."

"The only way she could get any stockjobber to take her purchase orders was to pay upfront. Tomorrow I am going to confront Sprat and ask for her investment share certificates to be transferred to my stockjobber, Jacob Lane. If my suspicions are true, I suspect there are no shares in Tiffany's name."

"The bastard. He's stolen from Tiffany?" Marlowe looked as if he wanted to hit someone.

Blackstone frowned. "Still, it shouldn't upset Sprat too much. How much money can it be? She must have been investing her pin money, and as a woman what does she know—"

"That's why you were asking about Armley Mill shares," Rockwell interrupted. "She's invested in them rather than Park Mill. If so, she's an astute investor. That's your wager, isn't it? The growth in share price of those two shares. I'm sorry, brother, but you're going to lose."

"I'll find out tomorrow how much she's given to Sprat." Wolf suspected it was a considerable sum, as Tiffany had all but said she was financially secure. This news of Sprat's betrayal must be devastating to her.

Rockwell, as canny as ever, said, "You think it will be a large amount? You think it will put her in danger?"

"I do."

Marlowe issued several curses. "We are going to have to accompany them everywhere. Or have men we trust do so."

"I suggest we ask them to cancel their charity stall as well. There will be too many people there to ensure their safety."

"What charity event?" Blackstone asked Rockwell.

Wolf didn't want to tell Blackstone because the Duke would erupt with anger. Or maybe he'd think Farah was not involved. "They are holding a charity fundraising stall selling old clothes at Reverend Smith's church near Russell Square. The same day as Mrs. Buchanan's soiree."

The significance of the location and date went over Blackstone's head. "We will have to speak with the Reverend and postpone the event. If Sprat reacts the way we expect, the ladies should be confined to home except if we accompany them to a social event."

"I agree," Marlowe added. "What are the ladies supposed to be attending tonight?"

Wolf wasn't surprised that Marlowe didn't know the ladies' social calendars. He really needed to give his friend a kick up the behind. Wolf always knew where his sisters would be and who they would be with, largely because of his mistake with Ashleigh, which had almost cost Ashleigh her life—not literally, but she could have ended up in a marriage from hell. "Mrs. Combes's recital is tonight. It will be a relatively small gathering compared to the masquerade ball. Marlowe, you need to pay more attention since your sister and Tiffany have no mother."

Rockwell stood. "I'll go and talk with Lorne and Vale to apprise them of the situation. Their families may need protection too. I guess I'll be attending the recital now." With that Rockwell took his leave, Blackstone on his heels.

Marlowe poured another drink. He sat down and silently stared at Wolf. Wolf wasn't going to be the first to talk. If

Marlowe had something he wanted to say, let him speak. It was a staring contest until finally Marlowe sighed. "What else are you not telling me about Tiffany? Why your sudden interest in courting her, Wolf? On the back of Dayton's suggestion, I offered you a deal months ago. I'd marry Ashleigh if you married Tiffany. It solved both our problems, but you said no."

"For God's sake. You were drunk. I was drunk. I'd never barter off Ashleigh and especially not to a man who wouldn't care anything for her. Marlowe, you're better than this. Why won't you let yourself feel?"

His face paled, and with shaking hands he tried to light a cheroot. "It was my fault. Margo's death was my fault."

"What the hell are you talking about?" But Wolf's sixth sense made the hairs on his arms rise.

Marlowe threw the flint on the floor. "She came to me the day before your wedding and told me she was with child. She told me it couldn't be yours and I realized what she was saying."

Wolf's fists curled tightly around the arms of his chair.

Marlowe took another large gulp of brandy. "I told her she should postpone the wedding. Wait for the child to be born and then get married to you. If she married you and had a son, he would be your heir. I know you. You'd never have let her secret out. You would have claimed the boy. I told her my father would make it happen. That she could come to our estate for the duration and no one would ever know."

An image flashed in Wolf's head of his hands wrapped around Marlowe's neck, squeezing the life out of him. It was only Marlowe's fist slamming into his stomach which made him realize it wasn't an image in his head. He let go and took a step back, anger roaring through his blood. "It was you. I always wondered why she did it."

"She was so upset and crying and my heart bled. She kept saying everything was ruined, she was ruined. I'm so sorry. I thought I was doing the right thing for you and for her."

"You should have told me. You should have come to me. Surely you must have understood how fragile Margo was."

Tears were rolling down Marlowe's face. "I live with that real-ization every day. The knowledge that I could have prevented her death. The knowledge that I am not a man who deals with people well. Since then, I have kept everyone at arm's length, in case they get too close and I make a dreadful mistake again. I thought if I offered for Ashleigh I'd be righting a wrong done to her, and the wrong I did to Margo."

Wolf understood guilt. He'd lived with his guilt for years. Yet he hadn't felt that dragged-down, gut churning guilt since he'd started courting Tiffany. The thought alone should shock him, but it didn't. He'd never let anything happen to anyone he cared about—that was the vow he'd sworn over Margo's grave. Suddenly the fear was back. Fear that he wouldn't be able to protect Tiffany.

"I'm relying on you to protect Tiffany in a way you didn't do for Margo. Tiffany is under your roof. She's your ward, your responsibility. If anything happens to her... I won't be so forgiving."

"You forgive me? For Margo?"

Wolf looked him in the eye. "You did what you thought was right—for both of us. And if I'm truthful, your solution was one, had she come to me, I probably would have suggested." And the guilt weighed on him again. He would have waited for the child to be born. But he would have protected Margo from gossip and scandal and he would have married her. He would also have bought the child into his household as his bastard if that was what Margo had wanted. Society would have been shocked, but he could have weathered the scandal—for her.

Marlowe slowly rose to his feet. "I will ensure Tiffany's safety. I'll have someone with her, looking out for her every hour of the day and night."

"She won't like it. She'll try and break free of your protection."

"One thing our Tiffany isn't is stupid. If we both point out the danger, she will obey."

"I hope you're right." But Wolf suspected Tiffany would do as she pleased. "Let's talk to Claire and Tiffany. I'll bring Ivy and Ashleigh too. Shall we convene at your house an hour before we are due at the recital? We can talk to the ladies and then attend together. Safety in numbers."

Chapter Fifteen

Tiffany paced her room, trying to decide what to share with the Sisterhood. If Wolf could get Sprat to pay up... But she thought the likelihood of that was nearing zero. She looked in the mirror. *You've lost all their money.*

The only woman who would really be affected by the loss was Lauren. Lauren's father was practically in the poorhouse. It was only Lauren's dividends keeping her father and her afloat. Thank God Sprat had been paying those small amounts. Of course, he did so only to get the larger investment amounts. And most of the ladies simply reinvested the dividends, paying the money right back to Sprat, the thief. What a fool she had been.

She would ask Wolf to take her to meet Jacob Lane as soon as possible. She had some money from her latest quarterly pin payment and some dividend money set aside for emergencies. She would invest it in Armley Mill. All of it. It should make her enough to pay back all of the Sisterhood and keep Lauren and her father from the poorhouse. However, her plans of financial security would be set back several years.

Now it was even more imperative to win the contest with the men. She would need the money.

"Miss. Tiffany, you're next."

Milly indicated the chair Claire had just vacated in front of the dressing table mirror. As Claire rose she said, "I wonder what Fane wants with us. My brother has called us to a meeting in the drawing room before we leave tonight. He's actually accompanying us. I wonder what has happened?"

Tiffany didn't know what to say. She had an idea of what the discussion to come was about, but would not believe it until she heard it with her own ears. Wolf had promised to keep her secret until their share wager was complete. He would never go back on his word. *Unless you were in danger...*

"Miss Tiffany?"

"I'm sorry, Milly. Did you ask me something?"

"Do you want the pearls weaved through your hair or just a simple coil tonight?"

"It's only a recital—"

"But Lord Wolfarth is escorting you. You want to look nice for him." Milly giggled. Claire merely snorted.

Tiffany reluctantly gave in and let Milly thread the pearl string through her hair. She had to admit, the pearls glowed beautifully in her hair and lifted the color from dark auburn to golden. She gave herself a critical look. She'd never been concerned with her appearance. Not being a great beauty, she never thought it mattered. But she did want to look nice for Wolf. And Milly had achieved a miracle. For a moment, before she slipped on her glasses, Tiffany almost didn't recognize herself.

Soon Milly was finished and a footman knocked to say Lord Marlowe was waiting for them downstairs.

Why did Tiffany feel as if she were going to the tower rather than the drawing room? If her secret was revealed...

As soon as she entered the room and looked at Marlowe, she knew Wolf had told him about their wager.

"Claire, Tiffany," her cousin said stiffly. Luckily, Ivy and Ashleigh and their handsome, traitorous brother had yet to arrive. "Please sit."

"What's this about, Fane?" his sister asked.

Fane ignored Claire and asked Tiffany, "Why did you not come to me if you wanted to invest your pin money?" It was hurt, not anger, pouring off Fane. "I would have let you use my stockjobber and you would not be in this position of possibly losing everything."

Claire gasped. "What is he talking about?" she directed at Tiffany.

"It would appear Tiffany's been investing in shares behind my back. Her stockjobber, Mr. Sprat, is a swindler. He is trying to defraud Lord Melville and it looks as if he's done it to others."

Claire turned concerned eyes her way. "And you think he has ou—your money and we—you won't get it back?"

"There is that possibility. I'm sorry, Fane. I didn't come to you, because Mr. Sprat was my father's stockjobber and it never occurred to me not to trust him. I wanted to prove I could make my own money. I wanted to relieve you of the burden of providing for me. And now my pride comes before my fall."

"Burden? You are family. I have never considered you a burden. Is that what you think? Have I ever made you feel as if you were unwanted?" His disappointment speared the room.

She'd insulted him. "Perhaps burden is the wrong word. All of you have made me feel so welcome. I know exactly how lucky I have been to have received your love. I'd never have got through losing my parents without you all. Your father and mother were like second parents to me. But look at it from my position. I have a skill that means I could earn my own money. If you were in my place would you stay beholden to others?"

Fane's mouth firmed but the look of betrayal left his eyes. "But I'm supposed to look after you financially. You have no need to earn your own money. You'll marry, and marry well if I have anything to say about it, and look, you've garnered the attention of a fine man in Lord Wolfarth. You'll have no financial concerns as his wife."

How did she explain that one chance meeting with Wolf had brought this courtship about? She could have gone her whole life and he may never have noticed her. As she moved toward spinster-hood, Fane would try to buy her a husband, and she would never put up with that. So she said nothing, just shrugged her shoulders.

Fane simply shook his head. "Hopefully you've learned your lesson and realize investing is really best left to men. If you wish to invest your pin money in future, come to me and I'll suggest some investments for you. Wolf told me he's going to approach Sprat on your behalf to get your funds back, if he can. I'm sure if Wolf can't pressure Sprat into returning the funds, given the situation with Lord Melville, I can refund you the small amount. How much can it be if it's simply been your pin money?"

Claire sent a concerned look her way. Tiffany wanted to scream at Fane and tell him she was quite capable of selecting her own investments and that, in fact, in twelve months he would see that when they won their wager against the men. But the fact he was asking to know the amount Sprat owed her kept her silent. How did she reveal it was close to five thousand pounds? Her money and the Sisterhood's investments.

Instead she sent Claire a warning look and simply said, "Thank you, Fane. That is most kind of you."

Just then Ivy, Ashleigh and Wolf arrived. Once all the greetings had been observed, Wolf cleared his throat. Tiffany simply sat scowling at him. She knew she shouldn't be that upset, given this was a terrible situation and he'd probably had little choice, but really. He should have talked to her first, so that they could have shaped the reveal. But then he didn't know about the Sister-hood...yet. She'd have to reveal all when she presented him with her purchase orders. How had she invested such a large sum when she had little to begin with?

"Tiffany has brought to my attention that a stockjobber—do you know what that is?" When the girls nodded, he continued. "This Mr. Sprat is insinuating our uncle, Lord Melville, has placed share orders that have not been honored. Melville swears that is not true and I and Rockwell believe him. I've managed to do some investigating and this man is very dangerous. So all of you must ensure you are never alone when out of the house. No more walking between our homes, even if it is only two doors down the street, without at least a footman with you, preferably two, one on each side." He aimed this comment directly at her.

Tiffany wasn't stupid. If her hunch was right, and Sprat had played a hand in her father's death, either from shady share dealings or direct murder, she would not underestimate the man.

"I assume you gentlemen will be sorting this situation out quickly. We have a charity stall to run in a few days' time." Ashleigh's raised eyebrows and the straight line of her mouth indicated she knew what her brother was about to say.

"The stall will have to wait. I've already spoken to Reverend Smith on Ivy's behalf and explained a family emergency has occurred. I shall advise him of a more suitable date shortly."

"But that is not your call to make," Ivy protested before Tiffany could do the same.

"Of course it is. You ladies are my responsibility." Wolf stared them down.

"And what about the money I need for my orphanage?"

Tiffany sucked in her breath. Ivy was pushing the limit of Wolf's temper if his scowl was anything to go by.

"I'm happy to fund you over this period if you need. But your safety comes first." His voice deepened. "I won't have a repeat of Margo..."

Had Tiffany just seen Wolf's hand shake? Ivy's face paled and she nodded. "Of course. You know better than I of the dangers."

"Tiffany, do you concur? You must not meet with Sprat in person, promise me that."

The underlying fear in Wolf's voice made her want to lean in and hug him. What had happened to Margo? Something truly awful, because the look of terror in Wolf's eyes sent a shiver down her spine.

"I will follow your and Marlowe's instructions to the letter. I don't wish to end up like my parents. But I want you to promise you'll get this man and make him pay." Her reward was a wave of relief rolling across Wolf's features.

"I give you my word." There was nothing more to be said.

"Shall we depart?" Marlowe stood. "The carriages are below."

She had disappointed and hurt Fane and she felt sick. She hated that Fane had found out this way. One day, when she was ready, she would have told him about her investing. He'd have found out in twelve months anyway when the truth of the wager was revealed.

The party made their way down the stairs. She could feel Claire's eyes seeking out hers. She would have to call a meeting of the Sisterhood and confess all, but first she would speak to Wolf and meet with Jacob Lane so she could earn enough to repay all they had lost. She needed to talk with Wolf in private. Had he already spoken to Sprat to get her share certificates?

Claire walked next to her and, without looking at her, took Tiffany's hand in hers and squeezed. She whispered, "It will be all right. It's only money."

She wanted to turn and embrace Claire for her kindness and cry. Ivy and Ashleigh hadn't looked at her since Wolf had revealed the situation. Both had invested quite considerable sums. Both for Ivy's orphanage. Ivy must be so worried. She was thankful they hadn't come at her in front of the men, for then Wolf and Fane would know she hadn't just lost her own money. She'd lost everyone's.

However, the weight of their disappointment cloaked her. To be responsible for such a loss for each woman in the Sisterhood—when she'd pridefully boasted how much she'd made—was mortifying. But her profit would have been on paper only, as she doubted Sprat had ever bought any shares in her name. How would they ever forgive her?

And she couldn't talk to them in front of the men for fear of alerting them to the Sisterhood and its wager with them. Tiffany needed to win their wager now more than ever, as she'd need the winnings to repay everyone.

It was a very subdued trip to Lady Combes's recital. As soon as they arrived, the ladies excused themselves and headed to the retiring room. Tiffany's stomach rollicked as she walked to face the music.

They excused the maid and ensured no other ladies were present. Tiffany spoke first, tears welling. "I'm so sorry. I swear I'll earn all your money back. This time I'll use a reputable stockjobber."

Ivy pulled her into her arms. "Please don't cry. You don't want red-rimmed eyes when you sit next to Wolf tonight. There is only one person to blame for this and it's not you."

"That's right," said Ashleigh. "It's bloody Sprat. Men. Honestly, if women ruled the world it would be a much nicer place."

Claire scoffed. "Women rule the world? I doubt that will ever happen. Not in our lifetime anyway. I'll call a meeting with the Sisterhood tomorrow. If some of the ladies are here tonight, tell them to be at my house after midday. I'll send notes to the others in the morning."

"I have a plan to earn the money back. I have two shares that are likely to out-perform the rest this year, and I doubt the men will have invested in them." Except Wolf. He might because she'd alerted him to Armley Mill. She pushed that thought away. "Wolf has offered me his stockjobber, and I'm hoping I can hide the fact we are the challengers by investing only in these two shares. I'm hoping you'll let me wait until after the challenge is won to pay you back, as I'll need what little I have set aside to fund the challenge."

"I can always give you more money," Ashleigh said.

"Absolutely not. You wanted the financial freedom as much as I did because of your—situation. I will earn it all back. Just watch me."

Their plan set for a Sisterhood meeting tomorrow, Tiffany made her way back to the music room. By then she'd have met with Mr. Lane and could place her share purchase.

She stood in the doorway and sought out the man she should be furious with, but deep in her heart she understood it was merely concern for her that saw him betray her secret. The fear in his eyes when he'd talked about keeping the ladies safe. And he mentioned Margo. What had happened to her? How had she died?

The need to know sent her mind into a whirl. It must have been awful if even Ashleigh and Ivy weren't told. Who would tell her? If she wanted to understand Wolf and, in particular, why he wanted to marry her, she needed answers from his past. Why was he happy to marry a woman he didn't love when it was obvious Margo had been a love match? Tiffany wasn't beautiful. She was a woman most of society ignored. Why her?

If she knew the answers to these questions, she might ascertain if she'd ever be able to win Wolf's heart. If she couldn't, then he was not the man for her, no matter how much her heart wanted him to be. You couldn't make someone love you. Love had to be freely given.

Just then his eyes found hers across the room, and the smile curving his lips appeared genuine and only for her. Her heart did a little flip, as it always did when he gave her his full attention. He rose to his feet and, as if she were walking on air, she made her way to his side.

He took her hand and bowed low, placing his lips on her gloves. How she wished his lips touched bare skin instead.

"No longer angry with me?" His words were soft so only she could hear over the conversations going on around them.

"I'm too sensible not to recognize you had no choice." He waited while she took her seat. "I was wondering if you would escort me to meet with your Mr. Lane tomorrow. I'd like to place some share purchase orders. I'd also like to be there when you meet with Mr. Lane to discuss Sprat."

He didn't answer her immediately. He sat looking at her as if trying to see inside her head. Finally, "You would be safe with me, and I did promise you access to Mr. Lane. We shall go to Capel

Court immediately after the painting session so that we can see Lane before the afternoon share trading session. Does that suit you?"

Bother. She hadn't thought this through. She'd also wanted to talk to Lady Wolfarth after the painting session. The one person who would know his past. The question was, would his mother share her son's past with her? Tiffany thought Lady Wolfarth might reveal the family secrets, as she seemed very keen on this match.

"That would be suitable."

"Will you share the names of the stocks you may purchase with me?"

She smiled at him, aware that he was teasing her. "If I didn't know better, I'd think you're only interested in me for my share advice," and he laughed along with her. "I've already given you one share tip—Armley Mill."

"Yes, but have you heard about the challenge?" She tried not to let her face betray anything. "Someone has challenged myself and a few of the *ton* peers to a twelve month investment wager. Each of the men challenged will be investing one thousand pounds, and the winner is the person who achieves the highest return on their individual investment. I did think the woman who will become my wife would help me win such a wager."

"Between your investment skills and Mr. Lane's, you're quite capable of winning that sort of wager. You certainly don't need me."

"I like that you didn't disagree you'd become my wife." With the other guests still chatting and milling around, Wolf leaned closer and slowly put his hand on her knee. Tiffany could feel the strength of his touch right through his glove and her gown, and she shivered. This dream of a marriage with Wolf filled her with longing for it all to be real. His voice dropped to a husky whisper. "I think I do need you. And not just for your investing skills."

She wanted to push his hand away. *No, you don't.* Instead, she got her muddled brain working. He'd expect that revelation about the wager to pique her curiosity. "Do you have any idea who would issue such a challenge? Or why?"

"I did for one moment think it was Sprat, but the bet was placed at White's. How would he get access?"

Tiffany shifted her leg as she couldn't stay still a moment longer. To her disappointment, his hand withdrew from her person. "He could have got someone to place it for him." The Sisterhood had done that. They'd convinced Serena's new husband, Lord Julian Montague—or rather, Serena had seduced him into agreeing—to place the wager on their behalf. Tiffany just hoped Julian would keep their secret. She was pretty sure he'd do anything to keep his new wife happy. Especially now Serena was with child.

Was she a terrible person for sending Wolf's thoughts on the challenger's identity on a wild goose chase? For once, Sprat wasn't the villain in this piece.

"I hadn't considered that. Maybe one of the lords he's black-mailing. I shall share those thoughts with the men. We really need to ensure we win, if it is Sprat."

"Not if he's found guilty of fraud and murder." The last thing she'd meant to do was stir the men up so they took the wager even more seriously. She wanted to win.

"True. I don't think it is Sprat. He'd not want so much atten-tion on himself given the frauds he's perpetrating. I really have no idea who it might be."

"Who are we talking about?" Farah asked as she took her seat next to Tiffany.

"Wolf was trying to determine who the man was who placed the investment wager with the men. Have you heard about it? I've only just found out." Tiffany almost winked. To her surprise, Rockwell took the seat on the other side of Farah.

"Maybe a man whom one of us has caused heartbreak to," said Rockwell with a raised eyebrow at Wolf. "Fane has stepped on a few toes recently."

"I'd suggest any of you could have stepped on toes. You're all favorites with the ladies," Claire stated, seating herself on the other side of Rockwell. "Who is angry at you now, Fane?" she added, as her bother also sat.

"No one. I make it a principle never to anger anyone. It's a waste of emotions."

Tiffany smiled at her cousin. Everyone here was well aware Fane had angered quite a few women. He was known to discard lovers as often as he did waistcoats. "Wolf has told me about the investment wager and we were discussing who the challenger might be. Rockwell thought it might be a man associated with a woman you may have seduced." Had Fane just sunk lower in his chair?

"I'm sure I don't have any idea to what you are referring." His response made everyone laugh.

Soon the music began, and Tiffany's stomach calmed and her shoulders relaxed. Tomorrow she'd begin again. She would not let the Sisterhood down for a second time. And she'd never let Sprat win. She would avenge her father.

Chapter Sixteen

"Why on earth have we arrived for the sitting so early?" Claire complained as the two grooms escorted her and Tiffany only two houses along the street.

Claire hated early mornings.

"I told you, you needn't come. Lady Wolfarth will chaperon. I want to speak to her alone before I sit for Wolf."

"Why?"

"I want to learn what happened to Margo. Wolf seemed most fearful yesterday. Are you not curious as to how she died?"

"Of course. I'm a lady, aren't I? So much of life is hidden from us. If not for you, I'd never know about shares and stockjobbers. I'd never even considered that a stockjobber could be a thief, for instance." Claire shook her head as they walked up the front steps of Wolfarth's townhouse. "Why do you think Lady Wolfarth will tell you?"

"She talked to me the last time I sat for Wolf, and told me she thinks I'm perfect for her son. Perhaps if I point out I want to know him better before I agree to marry him, she might open up and explain why all of sudden he is fixated on me. He's barely noticed me before."

"I do agree his sudden interest is puzzling, but maybe on your trip back from Capel Court he realized what the Sisterhood already knows. That you are a very loveable, kind, generous, honest and loyal person. You'll make Wolf a perfect marchioness."

"I do love you," Tiffany said, hugging her briefly. Taylor, Wolf's butler, bid them enter. She said to the grooms, "You may go, as Lord Wolfarth will see us home." The ladies would go to Capel Court with Wolf after this. To Taylor, she added, "We're early, and I was wondering if Lady Wolfarth would see us?"

A voice called from the landing, "I'm just about to break my fast. Please come and join me. Ivy and Ashleigh are still abed."

They followed Lady Wolfarth to the dining room while she chatted away about the latest gossip within the *ton*. "Lady Vale let slip that Serena and Julian are expecting their first child. Isn't that exciting? I'd always hoped I'd be the first grandmother. I'd almost despaired of Wolf marrying. He has Rockwell as a spare, of course, but that's all changed now he's courting you, Tiffany."

Tiffany couldn't believe that Lady Wolfarth had brought the topic up herself. "I would like children," Tiffany said to soften Wolf's mother up. "I'm still not certain Wolf and I are suited. His sudden interest in me raises questions. Why has he left it so long after his previous engagement to find a wife?"

"My son is older and wiser than the man of his youth. Margo was a darling girl. I don't wish to appear unkind, but as is often the case with a woman of great beauty, she relied on that. I really don't believe Margo knew who she was without her looks, and when faced with...some tough situations, she could not cope. Wolf, in his naïve youth, simply saw what was on the surface. With you he's looked deeper."

Claire choked on her tea. Lady Wolfarth had pretty much implied it certainly wasn't Tiffany's looks that drew Wolf.

"It's obviously taken Wolf a long time to get over Lady Margo. I imagine that would not be the case had his head been turned by beauty alone. He must have loved her very much."

Lady Wolfarth considered Tiffany's words. "I think Wolf's reluctance to face marriage stems from guilt, not love."

Tiffany flashed a look at Claire. *Now they were getting somewhere.* "Guilt? Has this something to do with Lady Margo's death? How did she die?" Tiffany asked innocently.

"She killed herself the day of their wedding."

Claire's butter knife hit the table with a clatter, while Tiffany's gasp echoed around the room. Of all the things she had expected Lady Wolfarth to say, that was not one of them. She took a deep breath. Wolf... No wonder he hadn't recovered very quickly. "Oh my goodness. I can't imagine..."

And then Claire said what Tiffany was thinking. "Why? Why would a beautiful woman, who was madly in love with a handsome Marquess, kill herself?"

"Where's Mother?" A deep male voice came from the stairs. Wolf, on his way down.

Before he arrived, Lady Wolfarth turned to Tiffany and said, "That is not my secret to share. You'll have to ask Wolf."

He stepped into the room and must have noted the tense atmosphere. "Has something happened?"

Lady Wolfarth laughed gaily. "Of course not. I was regaling the ladies with tales of how you and Rockwell used to torture your sisters with dead mice and lizards."

"We weren't that bad. Besides, the girls got their revenge by making us help them with dancing lessons." That made Claire and Tiffany chuckle. "When you're ready we should make a start. The weather looks like it might turn."

Tiffany glanced out the window; it still looked like a fine spring day to her.

"You young people. I envy you the freedoms you have today. In my day, a young lady would never sit for a painting unless she was married and her husband had organized a portrait. But since you are courting, society will assume this might be a wedding present to your bride. How romantic to receive a painting of yourself. An image of how your husband sees you."

Husband? Oh, no. Was this painting a vehicle to force her into marriage? Had Wolf tricked her?

Wolf must have seen her fear, for he quickly intervened. "Now, Mother. No one will recognize who the lady in the painting is. Her features will not be revealed clearly. There is no scandal involved, and there will be no pressure on Tiffany to accept my offer of marriage."

Silly man. His mother jumped immediately. "So you've offered for her? Well, girl, why have you not accepted?"

She threw an angry gaze Wolf's way. "A lady doesn't wish to be rushed. Marriage is for the rest of my life. If I'm standing on a cliff overlooking a pond, I don't immediately jump. I take my time and work out if it's safe and right for me to jump."

Lady Wolfarth stared at her for a moment, then nodded. "Quite right. I shall say no more."

"Perhaps you could change into your gown and join me in the garden as soon as possible. I don't want the light to change."

"Am I needed?" Claire asked. "After I've helped you change, I think I'll visit with Ivy and Ashleigh." The way she said it conveyed a message that Tiffany understood. Claire would talk to them about the situation the Sisterhood found itself in because of Sprat. It might be a good idea that they talk without her. After all, this was all her fault.

∾

Wolf didn't seem able to wake up this morning. What little time he'd been able to spend in his bed trying to sleep over the past few days had instead been spent either worrying over Melville and the danger he had put them all in, or fantasizing about Tiffany. The last thing he needed was his mother interfering. Things with Tiffany were progressing nicely.

Wolf made his way outside to organize the setting up of his easel. Damn his mother. What he'd said was correct—no one would recognize Tiffany because no one saw her the way he did. A part of him hoped that when she saw herself through his eyes, she'd understand he did have a genuine desire for her. But that would not happen until the day of the auction.

He kept the painting covered on the easel until his mother was seated with her tapestry and he'd once again posed Tiffany the way he had previously.

His artist's eye immediately noticed something different about her today. Her relaxed posture and confidence. Did that indicate she was finally understanding he was serious in his pursuit of her hand?

Soon he pushed all the noise and his mother's chatter out of his mind and concentrated on revealing Tiffany on canvas.

Time flew by. He'd been concentrating for over an hour, and as his muse flowed, so did the heated blood in his veins. Posed in that invitational way, knowing what book he had put in front of her, and how he'd like to explore and introduce her to many of the positions described in its pages, his entire body heated.

Soon the sun made sweat trickle down his back and, for a moment, lightheadedness made him take a deep breath and blink hard.

"Are you all right, Slade?" His mother asked. She sat under the shade of the tree, as did Tiffany.

He straightened, and his head swam. The heat and too many late nights didn't mix, it would seem. "I might need to sit down for a few minutes." He slowly walked toward the empty chair next to his mother in the shade.

"You've overheated yourself. I'll organize for some refreshments. Tiffany, go and get changed. My son has had enough for the day. I won't be long, Slade."

Tiffany rose to her feet and came to stand beside him. "You're not sickening with something? All this stress can't be good," and she reached out and placed her palm on his forehead. "You do feel hot. And you thought it would cloud over..."

"I just need a drink and a few moments in the shade. That is all, I promise you."

He couldn't help himself. He pulled her down to sit on his knee. "You look beautiful in that gown."

"You should let me up. Your mother will be returning soon."

"She left us alone for a reason. Like me, she is certain you are the right woman to be my marchioness."

"You never did tell me why you think I'm so suited. And then there is Margo..."

Wolf's muscles tightened. He didn't want Margo's memory invading this new relationship. The past should stay there. He had come to terms with his mistakes and accepted his guilt in her death. It had taken him many years to do so and he would not open those wounds again.

Tiffany ran her hand through his hair as if she were caressing a child. "Your mother told me how Margo died, and I think I understand why you've been so reluctant to marry," she said softly. "What I cannot fathom is why she killed herself. Is there something in this story that should see me not accept your offer?"

He would have to have strong words with his mother. She could ruin everything. And he was more than certain Tiffany was the right woman to be his wife. He still refused to look too closely at why the idea of her declining his proposal hurt. It wasn't simply pride.

As he'd come to know her, he admired her. She had a quick wit. She was kind. She had a grand pedigree and he wasn't going to overlook the reason he made the impulsive offer to her in the first place—her skillful investing. However, what he'd not expected was this warm feeling she caused in the vicinity of his heart. He'd wanted to lock his heart away so he could never be hurt again. It scared him how much he was beginning to feel for her, and Sprat being on the loose only added to that fear. What if something happened to Tiffany? It would be his fault, because he refused to pay Sprat for Melville's debt.

"You've gone quiet." She looked at him with a raised eyebrow.

That's what he appreciated about Tiffany. She would never lie to him. She had no artifice. If she wanted to know something, she asked, or searched for the truth. He had no idea how to answer her, because deep down inside he did consider himself responsible for Margo's death. But he knew he'd learned a hard lesson from his reckless, stupid behavior.

"No. Nothing about her death should make you not consider my offer." Was that a lie? He tried not to let the idea that he wasn't good enough for her swamp him. Because of Melville, she was now in danger. "I would make you a good husband."

"I won't push. But one day, if I'm to stand by your side and say my vows to become your wife, I'll want to know what happened. Not because I'm nosey, but so I can understand the man I'm going to be sharing my life with. I hate secrets. If only my father had told me his doubts about Sprat, I'd not be in this position."

He tried not to let her words lead him to anger. "Are you implying that the reason you are now considering my offer is because you've lost all your money?"

She bent and kissed him on the lips. "Of course not. I can always make more money and Fane would never force me into a marriage I did not want. The reason I want to understand the man I marry is because I want to know, before I wed, if he is capable of growing to love me. Marriage is for a very long time. I can't end up being someone's polite, baby-breeding wife who lives a life separate from her husband's."

He moved restlessly on his chair, wishing his mother would return. This conversation was drifting to places he did not wish to go. It made his head pound.

She added, "And then there is the delicate question of whether we are compatible in the bedroom."

"I beg your pardon?"

"I know your reputation with the ladies, so I'm sure you are very skilled. However, will I be enough for you in that department? I'm warning you now, I won't share my husband with other women."

He'd never thought about what his daily life would become

once he married. Yes, he'd released his last mistress before courting Tiffany; he would never disrespect her that way. But no other women for the rest of his life? He looked at her. Really looked at her, and while he couldn't say he was in love with her, he liked her. He wanted her to be happy. He wanted their marriage to be happy.

His parents' marriage hadn't been a love match, but he instinctively knew they had grown to love one another. Even though his father had died when his mother was still quite young, she'd never wanted to remarry.

He slid his palm down Tiffany's bare arm and collected her tiny hand in his. He turned it over and pressed a kiss to her palm. He loved the shiver his touch provoked. "I will teach you everything you need to know about the bedchamber. It's the one place I'm confident we will be in perfect harmony."

"How can you know that? I've never—that is—your kiss is the first I've experienced."

He leaned forward and pressed a kiss to the top of one breast that was pushed up by her gown, and she shuddered. "You are full of passion—"

"Don't be ridiculous. Everyone knows I'm a bluestocking. Quiet, contained."

"And brimming with denied passion."

She looked at him as if he'd gone mad. "You shudder with just the briefest of touches," and he stroked a finger over her breasts, slipping under the edge of her gown to reach her nipple. He watched her eyes flutter closed as he ran his finger over and over the hardening bud. "So responsive. You'll come alive in my bed."

Her eyes flew open at those words. Her chest rose and fell with each fast breath and she watched his hand delve deeper inside her gown to cup her breast.

So engrossed was she in his foreplay, she didn't appear to notice the hurried footsteps of his mother returning, but Wolf did. He withdrew his fingers and placed her back on her feet. "Never fear, Tiffany. The bedroom is the one area in which we will be completely compatible. As to other women, I'm pretty sure I won't need any other but you to see to my needs."

"Slade," his mother called. "Rockwell's inside and he's been hurt. Come quick."

Wolf looked at Tiffany and then raced for the house, his mother following. Tiffany turned to look for her glasses. She was virtually blind without them. Wolf had placed them on the table next to the easel. She bit her bottom lip. She wasn't sure her legs could move. She swore she could still feel his touch. Was Wolf right? Could she throw off the mantle of conservatism that she wore like armor?

It took mere moments for her to realize this was her chance to see the painting. She pushed away the guilt, knowing full well that he had decreed no one was to see it until it was finished, and retrieved her glasses. She slid them on, then looked at the canvas in front of her. She blinked. And blinked again. This wasn't her... It couldn't possibly be her...

She moved closer, and slowly the exquisite brush strokes took shape. This woman on the canvas was—beautiful. It couldn't be her. She moved until her face was only inches away. It was her, but it wasn't. She took a step back and looked again. She covered her mouth with her hand.

It *was* her.

He was right, even she barely recognized herself. No one would think it was her...

Was this how he saw her, or was this woman his fantasy? The woman he hoped she'd be?

Affairs of the heart were very confusing. How did any woman really know how a man felt? How did any man know?

Trust. Couples had to trust in each other and share what was in their hearts. Here she was, grilling Wolf about his feelings and why he wanted to marry her, when she had not been forthcoming herself as to why she was seriously considering his offer.

Looking back, she'd been infatuated with Wolf since the age of seventeen when she'd joined the Marlowe family. The prince who'd carried her up the stairs. But infatuation had changed to something deeper as she'd come to know Wolf better. And now, after everything that had happened since their wager and the situation with Sprat, she could easily see herself falling in love with the man. Would he ever come to love her?

She wanted a chance to find out. Wolf liked her, admired her even, there was no doubting that. Now, if this painting was truly how he saw her, then his desire for her was in every brush stroke. Could desire lead to love? She had no idea and no one to ask. This was the time she missed having her mother, or even Lady Marlowe, alive. But friendship and desire were a very sound basis for starting a marriage.

Suddenly remembering Rockwell was hurt, she turned her back on the painting and moved quickly toward the house, hugging the knowledge of how Wolf saw her to her heart.

Chapter Seventeen

"I'm quite all right, Wolf. Someone jumped me from behind and hit me over the head as I was checking my horse's shoe on the way over here this morning. Luckily, Lord Shrewsbury was passing and came to my aid. He chased the attacker off."

"Did you get a look at him?" Wolf paced the floor. Rockwell shook his head.

"My attacker might not be connected to Sprat. Maybe just an opportunistic robbery attempt."

"You don't believe that any more than I do."

His mother was fussing over Rockwell, while the doctor cleaned his head wound. "You have to catch this horrible man. And soon."

"It would appear we shouldn't go riding around London on our own either. I'll organize more Bow Street Runners." Rockwell cursed as the doctor administered a couple of stitches.

"Do you feel like accompanying me to Capel Court? Or will you need to rest?" Wolf asked his brother. "I doubt we'll be in danger at Capel Court. There will be too many people around. And we'll be in the carriage there and back with four guards." At Rockwell's raised eyebrow, he admitted, "I promised Tiffany she could attend with me."

"Really, Wolf," his mother said. "Taking a young lady to the Stock Exchange...you're asking for scandal."

"That is why I think Rockwell should attend. Most will simply think I'm indulging the woman I'm courting."

Rockwell spoke before Lady Wolfarth could complain again. "Can you give me an hour to freshen up? I need to change," and he pointed to his bloodstained shirt.

"I have to change too. Blast. My painting is still on the easel." Wolf opened the door and called for one of the servants to retrieve his painting and store it safely away. "Mother, can you ensure Tiffany receives help to change? And tell her to meet us in the entrance hall in one hour for our trip to Capel Court."

~

"I saw the painting," Tiffany confessed to Claire, Ivy and Ashleigh as they sat watching Ivy's lady's maid, Mary, helping her change. She'd thought to keep her peek at the painting a secret, but she wanted the ladies to think of something other than all the money she'd lost them.

Ivy clapped her hands. "He let you look at it?"

She grimaced. "Not exactly. He and your mother rushed to see to Rockwell."

"And you snuck a peek?" Ashleigh laughed.

"I had to fetch my glasses. I can't see without them. They were by the painting."

Claire leaned forward in her chair. "And?"

Tiffany didn't know what to say. How did she describe what she'd seen? "He was right when he said most people won't recognize the woman as me. The woman in the painting is...beautiful. The colors, the setting, the dress—"

Claire giggled in glee. "He thinks you're beautiful."

Tiffany shook her head.

"He obviously does," Ivy added.

"I don't think you realize how pretty you are when your hair is less severe and you leave those old lady's glasses off." Ashleigh walked to where Mary was now redoing Tiffany's hair. "Let's soften your look. Get rid of the tight bun and let the soft waves flow down that graceful long neck of yours. It will make a man think about running his lips along that tender white skin. Mary, can you do something to enhance her look?"

Mary nodded. "You have such luscious hair. It holds most styles perfectly."

"Ashleigh, really," her sister scolded.

"I don't want any man kissing my neck." Then Tiffany smiled. "Except your brother." And she laughed.

Ivy danced round the room. "I can't believe it. We will be sisters. I really worried about who Wolf would select as his wife. I'm just so pleased it's you."

"Not so fast. I'm not saying I'll marry him, but I'm willing to consider his proposal." Tiffany could hardly believe it either. How did she end up here with one of England's most sought after bachelors courting her? "I just can't fathom what spurred his sudden interest in me. Any ideas?"

All the girls talked at once, except for Ashleigh. She stayed silent. Tiffany asked her, "Do you know something we don't?"

Before she could answer, Lady Wolfarth swept into the room. "Young ladies, you need to get some rest. It's Lady Carthor's ball tonight. Rockwell has agreed to escort us, as Wolf has some important estate work to complete. All of this fuss with my brother and Wolf's painting couldn't have come at a worse time." With that she was gone, leaving the ladies alone once more.

"Are you attending?" Ivy asked Claire and Tiffany. Claire nodded.

"I might rest tonight since Wolf is not attending," Tiffany said. "I am feeling quite drained and I still have to talk with Mr. Lane this afternoon. I can use the night to plan how to recoup our losses. Then I'll be ready to talk with the Sisterhood tomorrow."

Claire sighed and looked at Ivy and Ashleigh. "Can I go with you and Rockwell? I too don't feel like going, but I promised Farah I would. She needs help hiding from Lord Franklin. Her brother really is a bully insisting she encourage the man."

Tiffany felt guilty at leaving Claire to help Farah on her own. What she couldn't reveal was that Lady Wolfarth's disclosure that Wolf would be at home while everyone else was out had given her an idea to see just how compatible they were. It would also give her time to find the answers she needed. She would visit him tonight.

"I hope your meeting with Mr. Lane goes well," Ashleigh said. "Who knows, Wolf might even be able to get your share certificates. Surely the company you invested in has a ledger of who holds what shares. It would tell us if any were bought in your name."

"I could hug you, Ashleigh. Of course, they must do. At least I'll know where we stand. I have my list of what I ordered to be bought," and she pointed to her reticule. "Mr. Lane will be able to tell me, I'm sure."

"How are you going to speak with Mr. Lane alone?" Ivy said. "I don't think it's a good idea that my brothers hear your business dealings. They may begin to put two and two together."

Ivy had every right to worry about that. "I think I shall ask to place my orders with one of Mr. Lane's clerks. I know what shares I wish to buy and I'll suggest I do that while Rockwell and Wolf talk to Lane about Sprat."

The ladies all nodded. "Good idea. How are we going to ensure Mr. Lane doesn't inform my brother of your purchases?" Ashleigh asked.

"I'll just have to ask them to give me their word not to share my purchase requests with anyone, including Lord Wolfarth, and hope they honor their word." That made the ladies' shoulders slump. "I'm sorry, but I can't do anything else."

"Let's hope that Wolf and the other men are too busy dealing with Sprat to look too closely at what you are doing." With that Claire stood and said, "Come on. The men can drop me home on the way to Capel Court. I should rest too as I'm sure Farah and I will be escaping certain individuals in the ballroom all night."

~

The carriage ride to Capel Court was quiet. There were four Runners on the outside of the carriage. Rockwell had leaned his head back on the squab and, with his eyes closed, looked as if he was asleep. She hoped he was all right after his attack.

She could see the line of tension in Wolf's jaw and some of that transferred to her. His hand settled on her jiggling knee, stilling it.

After half an hour Tiffany couldn't stand the silence any further. She spoke quietly so as not to wake Rockwell, who was gently snoring. "Mr. Lane should be able to check the company share ledgers to see if I have any shares in my name."

"I've already asked him to do so. We will know the answer when we get there." Wolf's tone told her he doubted the news would be good.

"Have the Bow Street Runners found any signs of where Sprat is hiding?"

"No. He seems to have disappeared into the mist. Mr. Lane sent me a missive stating more and more of Sprat's clients are turning up at the Stock Exchange looking for him. I suspect Sprat has amassed quite the fortune and is leaving a trail of distraught investors but nothing leading to his whereabouts."

She didn't feel so stupid now. "But these men would have not paid in advance like I did. How have they been affected?"

"The share certificates he sent them, or held for them, were forgeries." Wolf shifted in his seat. "It's made me evaluate the whole investing process. I trust Mr. Lane, but from now on I shall check each share purchase on the company's register to see that the purchase was made in my name and I am the record of interest for those shares."

That would be a lot of work. She suddenly understood the

weight of his responsibility. Every Wolfarth in the extended family relied on his judgment and expertise. The shame of losing the Sisterhood's money would be nothing compared to losing the money to fund his estates and houses, which supported so many people.

She looked at him and the stress lines around his eyes. If she married him she could help shoulder some of that burden. She could offer him something more than being the mother of his children and another financial responsibility. She liked the idea of being able to contribute. How would she offer her skills, and would he accept them? Men were usually so full of pride.

"The one good thing about these men stepping forward is that everyone will likely believe Melville's denials now. So, really, this has turned to a matter of simply finding and prosecuting Sprat."

Tiffany's stomach clenched. "Prosecuting him for what? Swindles or murder? I want—no, need—to know if he had anything to do with my parents' deaths. Was it his men that killed them? I've never known the truth."

He squeezed her knee. "It won't bring them back."

She let the tears well. "I just need to know. The idea that I've used my parents' killer as my stockjobber... It eats me up inside."

"And if he did kill them, won't that make it worse?" As her tears fell in earnest, Wolf pulled her onto his lap and hugged her tight. "He fooled everyone. Men wiser and older than you. How were you to know that such evil exists in the world? You bear no blame for Sprat's actions. And I promise you, when I find him I will get the truth from him regarding your parents."

"Thank you. I will hold you to that promise."

The carriage turned into Bartholomew Avenue and began to slow. "We are almost at Capel Court."

Tiffany scrambled off Wolf's lap and used her handkerchief to wipe her tears. Rockwell stirred awake. "Gosh, that didn't take long."

"You've been asleep for the whole hour's drive," drawled Wolf. "But given your injury, I'll not tease."

Mr. Lane had been expecting them, and they entered his offices to find refreshments waiting. Tiffany tried not to let her hands shake as she sipped her tea. "There is not good news on your share certificates. I'm sorry, but we could find only one company holding shares in your name. They are worth only a few pounds."

It was as if the ceiling had fallen in on her, and she struggled to breathe. Her tea sloshed over the edge and dripped onto her glove. Wolf reached and took the cup out of her hands.

"I will help cover your losses, Tiffany. I won't let that man rob you."

She smiled through welling tears. "That is most kind, Wolf. Thank you. However, if Mr. Lane will help me, I fully intend to recoup all I have lost."

"It would be my honor to assist you," Mr. Lane said, looking at Wolf.

She rose to her feet. "If that is the case, may I have the services of one of your clerks? I have some shares I wish to purchase. I have the money," and she made to open her reticule.

Mr. Lane also stood. "There is no need for you to pay today. I'm happy to take your orders. If you'll come with me, I'll see if Chester is free. He can document your choices, unless you'd like me to look at your stock selections first."

"No need, thank you. I am quite sure of my picks. I'll leave you to talk with Lord Wolfarth about Mr. Sprat." With that she walked out to the reception area and was introduced to Chester, a young man who'd worked for Mr. Lane for five years. Once the introductions were done she told him what she wanted to buy and how much.

"Your choices have a bit of risk associated with them. I've tried to tell Mr. Lane to look at Armley Mill. However, your invest-ment in the Scottish railway... I'd be remiss if I didn't say it's extremely high risk."

"This is what I wish to buy. And no, I don't want this discussed with Lord Wolfarth. This is my money and my choice. Can you ensure my privacy please?"

Chester drew himself up. "My word is my bond. I don't discuss my clients' purchases with anyone unless they wish me to."

"Does that include Mr. Lane?"

"I have to show Mr. Lane what I have done and for whom. But I will ensure I stress the need for your privacy. I'm sure Mr. Lane would never speak to Lord Wolfarth unless he spoke to you first."

That would have to be enough. What more could Tiffany do? Her only other option was to use Fane's stockjobber, but she was sure the man would tell Fane everything given she was his ward, and that was too close for comfort. Wolf, on the other hand, wanted to keep in her good graces, so he would likely respect her privacy.

"Thank you, Chester. I would like monthly updates and I'd like to reinvest any dividends back into each share."

Chester raised his eyebrows. "I would advise spreading your risk by investing in something else."

"Thank you for your concern. But I have a strategy and I intend to follow it for a few months."

"As you wish. I was the one who tried to find your shares from the list you provided, and I must say I was very impressed. If the shares had been bought for you, you would have managed to build a considerable sum that most professional stockjobbers would not manage to match. I shall respect your decisions."

Tiffany blushed and would have let pride swamp her if not for the fact she'd let a man swindle her of such wealth. "It didn't do me much good, did it? But I have learned my lesson."

"I wish you had not had to learn such a lesson. I can tell you many of the men here would like to find Sprat for you."

"I think you and I are going to work very well together. I look forward to bringing you more purchase orders. I shall alert my bank to pay for the shares once I receive the purchase order note."

"Lord Wolfarth thought you might like to put your purchases on his account."

"That won't be necessary. I'd like to keep my account separate. Will that be a problem?" She wondered if they would deal with her only if her payments were through Wolf.

"As you wish. I'll open an account and we will bill you monthly."

The door opened and Wolf entered. "Is everything to your satisfaction?"

She rose and held out her hand to Chester. "Thank you. I look forward to working with you."

"And I you, Miss Deveraux," said Chester, beaming.

Rockwell and Wolf appeared subdued as they made their way back to the carriage. "I gather it wasn't good news from Mr. Lane," she said.

"Sprat is in the wind and he's taken money from many investors, some who may lose everything," Rockwell said. "It's given everyone a scare. Many lords are in their stockjobbers' offices asking for proof of purchase etcetera. It's given the Exchange a very bad reputation. The board of the Exchange is looking at introducing new processes to ensure this doesn't happen again." Rockwell entered the carriage after them and added, "I'm going to find him. I'm going to find him and wring his bloody neck. And now I have a clue to where he might have gone."

Tiffany gasped. "Really?"

"Yes," Wolf said. "From one of the clerks that used to work with Sprat. He left eighteen months back to work for another stockjobber. He heard one of Sprat's clerks mention Ireland— Cork, to be precise. Rockwell will organize sending the Bow Street Runners across."

"If they find him," Rockwell said, "I'll be on the first boat across the Irish sea."

"If he's left London, are we still in danger?"

"Good question, Tiffany. It never pays to be too careful. The ladies will have to continue to have guards for a while longer."

That meant they would have to call off the stall as the men had demanded. But Ivy needed money if she was to help her newly patronaged orphanage. "Since the risk appears to be lower, could the stall at the church not go ahead if we had enough men? Ivy really needs the money and you know she won't take charity from you. She wants to do this on her own."

"I don't see why not if they are well guarded. I'm happy to oversee it. Ivy has worked so hard to organize the day."

Wolf considered her for a moment. "As long as you follow Rockwell's instructions to the letter, and no wandering off to slip into Mrs. Buchanan's soiree."

Tiffany had forgotten all about the soiree Valora wished to attend. All she really wanted was to help Ivy raise money from the stall since Tiffany had lost everything else. "I think the ladies understand the danger both in terms of Sprat and their reputations should they go to the soiree. We really do just want to raise the money at the stall."

"If Rockwell is willing to work with Ivy then I have no objections."

"Thank you," and she pressed a kiss to his cheek. Wolf's smile was her reward, even while Rockwell chuckled.

A funny look swept Wolf's face. "Why is it so important to you that Ivy has this stall?" He knew. She could tell. Rockwell looked up too. "Have you been investing money for Ivy? Is it not only your money Sprat has absconded with?" He spoke softly, but she could see tension in his jaw. "It is, isn't it? That is why your purchase notes amounted to so much money."

"I did invest a small sum for her but that is all." That was the truth. Some of the other ladies had given her far more. Please don't ask, please don't ask... Thankfully, Rockwell interrupted by saying, "Did I mention that those Armley Mill shares are in demand? I see an order was placed today for quite a few. You don't happen to know anything about that, do you, Tiffany?"

"I may have bought some, yes. I think they are a good long-term share to hold," she uttered rather defensively.

Rockwell nodded. "I agree. I hold some. I'm wondering about buying more." He smiled at Wolf. "Lucky for you Park Mill's share price is also holding strong, but I'm not sure for how much longer." He winked at Tiffany, while Wolf growled.

Did Rockwell know about their wager? She looked at Wolf but he said nothing. She wasn't going to push in case he asked her more about her investments.

It was nearing dusk as they reached Mayfair and the men escorted Tiffany home. Wolf saw her safely in the door. "I will expect you tomorrow at ten for the final sitting. I should be able to finish the painting from memory after that. I won't be at the ball tonight. I have work to do regarding my estates. Rockwell will be there in my stead."

"I'm not going either. I...I'm a tad tired from my situation." And she wasn't only talking about the loss of her money. Her biggest fear was that Wolf was seducing her and she had no idea why. She was worried because it was working. What if she was made to look a fool? What if she lost her heart to Wolf and he kept his locked away?

Wolf took her gloved hand and pressed a swift kiss to her knuckles. "Until tomorrow then."

She stood watching him until he entered his carriage and they drove on.

"You're smitten."

She swung round, embarrassed to be caught mooning after Wolf by Claire of all people. Claire, who thought love a fantasy. She stood on the stairs, looking down in judgment upon her. "He's quite the man."

Tiffany started up the stairs. "I must admit he's impressed me over the past week of his pursuit. He's been quite the gentleman."

"You say that as if it's a bad thing."

They continued upstairs to Claire's bedchamber where she

was getting ready for the ball. "I just wish I understood why he is suddenly so keen to wed."

Tiffany flopped on the bed. "You mean keen to marry *me*."

Claire stopped Milly from pulling her gown over her head. "That is not at all what I mean. I'm more confused about the fact that there was no sign he was evaluating any of us for the role of his countess, and then suddenly he's all over one of us. Whether it was you or someone else, I'd still wonder why."

"If only I could spend more time alone with him, I'd get answers."

Claire laughed. "Isn't that what you're going to do tonight? I'm not stupid. As soon as it was known Wolf would not attend, you were not attending. We both know how to sneak into Wolfarth House to secretly visit Ivy and Ashleigh. I'm sure that is how Ashleigh escaped and fell into scandal and yet Wolf hasn't closed the secret passage up. He doesn't know about it. So don't go telling him tonight."

Tiffany sat up. "You don't think I'm silly for going to him?"

"I'd think you were rather silly if you didn't. I wouldn't marry a man filled with secrets. And I'd want to know why he picked me. I'd never let any man force me into marriage. It would be my choice alone."

Tiffany lay back down on the bed and sighed. "I feel the same. If I can't have what my parents had I don't want to wed. To be married like some of the ladies of the *ton*, no love, bored with the man you share your life with... It would be torture."

"Far better to remain a spinster."

She saw only one flaw in that plan. "I want children. Don't you?" she asked Claire.

Claire nodded. "But I wouldn't bring children into a house without love. Look at Farah's childhood. It's a wonder she's turned out so nice. But she is almost scared of her own shadow. She's letting that brother of hers dictate her life."

"I for one will help her if I can. You will keep Lord Franklin away from her tonight? I'm scared he'll propose and she'll be too scared to say no. Then she's trapped—for the rest of her life."

Claire nodded. "It looks as if we both have assignments for tonight."

"Oh, I forgot to mention. Wolf says we can go ahead with the charity stall. The men think Sprat has fled to Ireland. We still have to have men guarding us but at least Ivy will get her money."

"That's fantastic. Just don't tell Valora or she'll start on again about attending Mrs. Buchanan's soiree. This infatuation with my brother will be her undoing. The *ton* will only forgive so much because of her beauty. I thought she'd have learned that from Ashleigh's fall from grace."

Milly popped her head in the room. "Your bath is ready, Miss. Tiffany. And Lady Claire, I need to finish doing your hair."

"I'll leave you to get ready."

Claire grabbed her arm as she made to walk past her. "Be careful. If you're caught alone with Wolf you'll have no choice. Society won't be forgiving to a bluestocking orphan, even if you are under Fane's protection."

She pressed a kiss to Claire's cheek. "I love how you look after me. I'm so lucky to have you, cousin." Tiffany walked to her bathing chamber and began to plan what she would ask Wolf. Fear and excitement prickled her skin as she let the scented water cover her. If she liked what he had to say, she would agree to his proposal. However, if she thought he'd keep his heart locked away, or if he was still in love with the ghost of Margo, she would walk away, no matter that her heart would be broken.

Chapter Eighteen

Wolf had his servants bring a dinner tray to his study. The paperwork had almost taken over the room. He had a lot to get through tonight.

Since Sprat had fled and word of his swindle was out, there was no risk to the Wolfarth family of having to pay for the share transactions. His coffers remained full. But anger burned deep for Tiffany and what she had lost. He suspected she'd invested for a few of the young ladies. It was a bitter pill for them to swallow.

Earlier he'd opened an urgent missive and learned which bank Sprat had used for his swindle. It was several banks actually. What Sprat hadn't been so clever about was how he transferred the money. When Wolf had explained to the banks what had happened, they'd had no problem with divulging where Sprat's letters of funds were addressed to. Rockwell was right. It looked as if Sprat was in Ireland. He'd taken his letters of introduction and funds to the Bank of Ireland.

If he wasn't so busy he'd go with Rockwell to Ireland. But he'd ask Fane to go with Rockwell instead. After all, it was Tiffany who'd lost money. He would petition the Regent tomorrow to get a royal seal to have the Irish banks release the stolen funds. If he couldn't find Sprat, he'd at least feel better knowing he'd deprived the rogue of his ill-gotten gains. He was pretty sure Sprat would come after him for that. Then they would capture him.

He pushed the Sprat problem aside to concentrate on his estates. The latest report from his estate up north said that Melville was behaving himself as far as gambling went. He'd even taken to visiting a lady widower in the village. His uncle appeared to have a new lease on life and the shock of Sprat's allegations, the attempt on his life and Wolf's threat to send him to the Americas had been enough for him to temper his gambling. For now.

Rockwell had escorted their sisters and mother to the ball tonight, but before departing, he had left a copy of the latest share sheet on Wolf's desk. He'd circled the share price of Armley and Park Mills. He was losing his wager. Whether or not Tiffany became his countess would be entirely in her tiny hands when he lost.

It meant much more to him than he realized. For some reason he'd thought it would be easy to make a bluestocking with little chance of romance in her life fall in love with him. He smiled at his arrogance. His little bluestocking was so much more than he'd ever imagined he wanted in a wife.

He'd wanted her investing skills, but now he wanted her companionship and he... He swallowed back his fear. It would be so easy to fall in love with her. She was wonderful, delightful, kind, intelligent, challenging and so filled with yearning to experience everything in life that he wanted to give it to her.

The one drawback was she deserved love. And he didn't know if he was strong enough to give his heart again. Margo's death killed something inside him. He didn't want the responsibility of someone's heart and soul. What if he disappointed them and made their life miserable?

Deep inside he knew Tiffany was nothing like Margo. Looking back, Margo lacked strength of character. It wasn't her fault. Society had set its expectations of her. Be beautiful and charming and simply find the right husband. She'd succeed in her plan until life said otherwise. He could hardly blame Margo.

What happened to her was incomprehensible. But he thought about Tiffany and what she would have done in that position. She would have at least talked to Wolf about the situation. And he was positive she would not have killed herself. She would have fought back. But Tiffany had a weapon to do that with—her intelligence. Margo had possessed only her looks.

Tiffany could handle anything life threw at her. Anyone who underestimated her did so at their own peril. He was in peril, because he'd underestimated her too. He'd been arrogant enough to think she'd simply welcome the match.

Now Wolf couldn't fathom the idea of having anyone else as his countess. The words on the parchment in front of him blurred. What was he going to do? For the first time in his life he was unsure of himself. He pushed her out of his mind. He needed to talk to Julian. He'd gotten married last year, and to a woman he loved. How did Julian win Serena's heart?

A soft click alerted him to the fact someone had entered his study. He looked up to see Tiffany standing just inside the door. She took his breath away. Her hair was down, the soft tresses falling over her shoulders in waves. She was dressed in a deep blue velvet gown that seemed to float around her as she moved toward him. No corset!

He finally realized his mouth was hanging open. He rose to greet her. "Tiffany, is something wrong?"

"I wanted to see you."

Her eyes sparkled with wickedness. Excitement fired within him. Her lips broke into what could only be called a sensual smile, and to add oil to the flame, she ran her little pink tongue over her bottom lip. Wolf's groin instantly tightened.

As his gaze drifted down her body, his tongue almost lolled out of his mouth at the amount of pale, plump bosom on display. Her low-cut gown with its sheer silk bodice barely covered her nipples, and the tiny sleeves hung off her shoulders, leaving her décolletage bare and as inviting as newly fallen snow.

He stood there like an imbecile, drinking her in and yet

willing his body to ignore the vision of pure temptation before him.

"Come here." She crooked her finger and bade him move closer.

He didn't need further encouragement. But as he walked round his desk toward her a wave of loneliness and loss washed through him. Here was the hot-blooded woman he would marry, and yet she was not in his heart. *You don't want her in your heart. You won't let her in your heart.* The fear of letting anyone close again saw his stride falter.

"Wolf..."

Her voice took his breath away. It held such power. When she whispered his name, he stepped forward as if lured by some irresistible force. He soaked in the beauty standing within touching distance. Pure innocence wrapped in an outer coating of sin. The heat in her eyes made him feel flushed and feverish. Her intense stare set his body quivering with longing. God help him.

"What is it?" she whispered uncertainly into the stillness of the fire-heated room. The spitting flames could be heard in the silence, along with his ragged breathing.

"You are so beautiful," he choked out.

"No, I'm not," she whispered with a sensual smile, her uncertainty vanishing in an instant. "But you make me feel beautiful." Slipping her arms around his neck, she hugged him close.

He was in heaven, wrapped in her heat. Slowly he let his hands slide down her back, his palms molding to her curves, her softness beckoning him.

Through his jacket, he could feel her ripe, firm breasts pressed into his chest, and he had to touch them. One hand slid up her side, and with a shudder that rocked him to his core he cupped her breast and gently squeezed.

"I wanted to talk with you. In private. About—us." Her voice was scarcely a whisper.

"We don't need words. You feel this pull of attraction too.

How can you deny we'd make an excellent couple?" He'd never felt this driving need for any other woman.

Then his mouth covered hers. He kissed her with a fever, hard and demanding, and desperate at the same time. He let his dark need for her overwhelm him as his tongue slid urgently into her mouth, stealing any chance she had to catch her breath. He'd never experienced anything as molten as the fire in her lips.

Long, passion-filled moments later, he broke off, and she groaned. Shutting his eyes, he rested his forehead against hers and struggled for control.

She pulled him closer. "I don't want you to stop," she said shakily. "I wanted to talk to you, but your kiss stole my words."

He couldn't respond. For several pounding heartbeats he stared into her eyes. "You coming to me dressed like this...with no corset... Does this mean you agree to become my countess?" he said.

"I need answers. What happens when this desire burns out? What will be left between us?"

"Desire and passion are excellent building blocks for a happy marriage. Can that not be enough?"

He saw her hesitation and ruthlessly took advantage. His hands slipped under the neckline of her gown, his palms pressing against her nipples, which were pebbled into tight, hard peaks.

She let out a whimper, and her head dropped back.

Striving for sanity, he closed his eyes. He didn't want to move too fast and scare her, yet he wanted her to feel what could be between them. He tugged on the neckline of her gown, dipped his head, and took her nipple into his mouth.

She whispered his name, kissed his bent head, and caressed his arms as they held her.

He should stop this now. He'd pledged to do nothing that would force her to wed. He was a man of his word, even though she tempted him more than wine tempts a thirsty man.

He went very still, her nipple resting between his lips. Then she shuddered and begged, "More, please, Wolf..."

He moved across to her other breast and she groaned, digging her fingers into his arms as she arched her back to push her breasts up to meet his mouth. For long minutes his lips and tongue set about arousing her. It was tantalizing and intoxicating, and his body thrilled as he felt the shivers of response he drew from her body.

~

When Wolf's mouth covered hers, it was as if lightning struck— heat and sizzling desire. Tiffany could barely breathe. Then he made her lips open for him.

The scent of him filled her senses, and his taste stole her reason. It was exactly like the last time, and she loved it. She should stop him and get the answers she needed before she gave herself to this man. She needed to protect her heart before he stole it completely.

It was hard to think while wicked and wonderful sensations bombarded her, leaving her giddy and wanting more. Her head swam with erotic images from her dreams. Images of his hands on her belly, his lips on her breasts, skin to skin as he sought to ease the ache inside of her.

She clung tightly to his massive shoulders as he thrust his tongue deeper, inciting delicious, melting weakness in her limbs.

Suddenly Wolf drew her hard against his body, and the kiss changed. Became hot. Possessive. Glorious.

The sinful thrill of being captured against this warm wall of muscle and bone should have unnerved her. But it didn't. Instead, need, impossible to resist, surged through her.

When he suddenly broke off the kiss she cried out in protest. Then she saw the desire shimmering in his hooded eyes. She trusted in that desire. Wolf would never be false. She could hardly believe it, but then she remembered the painting and how he saw her, and her body came alive under his gaze.

She saw the exact moment he surrendered to his need to taste her again. His eyes darkened and his mouth claimed hers once more.

This kiss was not one a man gave a woman he intended to let remain a virgin—and that thought alone should have scared her because it would mean...

She snuggled into him and was rewarded when he swept her into his arms and carried her across to the chaise longue, his lips never leaving hers.

He lay her gently down before following, his heavy body pressing her deep into the cushions. She loved the feel of his weight on her. Loved the marvelous mouth that continued to drive her desire higher.

Wrapping both arms round his neck, she returned his feverish kisses in kind. She strained against him, delighting in his body's hardness, as his hands began to roam her person.

She forced the guilt away. She'd come dressed to call to the man in him. It had worked. But when his fingers found she'd left off her stockings, his intake of breath was worth the risk. The feel of his fingers on the bare skin of her leg was exciting, scandalous, stimulating.

His other hand undid the hook on the front of her gown, and he rose up enough to pull the material apart.

Only then did he break the kiss.

He was breathing heavily and as aroused as she. His eyes never left hers as he peeled the material back and kissed the top of her exposed breasts. Then his fingers went to the second hook, and the third, and the fourth, until her breasts were fully exposed to his gaze—and his mouth.

Eyes gleaming with satisfaction, he drank in her disheveled state. She should have been embarrassed at his study, but she wasn't. In fact, it made her hot and bothered. She arched her back, almost demanding his attention.

When he lowered his head, took one peaked nipple tenderly into his mouth and suckled, she thought she'd reached heaven. She cupped his head and held him there, pressed against her as she panted and writhed. Who knew she would become such a wanton for this man?

His hand continued molding the contours of her breasts while his mouth tortured her. She barely noticed that his other hand was pushing her legs wider to allow him to settle between her thighs.

Her body couldn't help but move beneath him, seeking some form of relief. She almost cried out when she felt a finger slide through her wet folds.

"So responsive. So beautiful," he assured her, drawing back to look down her body to where his hand stroked her intimately. "I knew you would be. I can see the passion trapped inside."

His gaze flicked to her and she locked onto his hypnotic stare. "I want…"

He pressed a kiss to her bared stomach. "You have no idea what you want, my darling, but I'll show you."

With that promise ringing in her ears he moved lower, pushing her gown out of the way, baring her body completely to his heated gaze.

She was not a coward. She wanted him in every way a woman could want a man. Had she even lived before he touched her? She longed for him, and a shudder of excitement rippled through her. But when his hot breath blew on the most intimate part of her, she froze.

This was too decadent—*he* was too decadent. What was she doing?

With his dark and stormy eyes fixed on her face, as if daring her to stop him, he lowered his mouth. The kiss between her thighs was beyond intimate.

She could not believe that he was kissing her there. She could not believe she was *letting* him. It was mortifying, yet at the same time she knew she'd beg him to continue if he stopped.

Tiffany's fingers threaded through his thick curls, tangling in their silky softness as she clutched his head, urging him closer.

Anticipation sent a series of tremors ricocheting through her, but it did not prepare her for what he did next. Gently he parted her folds, and his heated lips tasted the very heart of her womanhood. When his tongue slid through her curls and licked the most intimate part of her, she moaned, and her hips lifted in desperate need.

When he draped one of her legs over his shoulder, opening her wider to his ministrations, her body exploded with want and desire.

And still his talented tongue licked at her with exquisite expertise, sucking and teasing and nibbling until she lost any sense of time or place and let her dark, dangerous lover take her where he willed.

She hovered on an airy precipice, her soul teetering on the edge of nothingness. Sensations overwhelmed her. Her limbs went taut, her body shook, and she felt as if she were losing her mind to the pleasure. Then his wicked tongue entered her, and she came apart, plunging over the edge into an abyss of bliss. Writhing against his mouth, her fingers clutched in his hair in the sweet, amazing tide of her release. She cried out his name. "Oh, Slade. Oh, God."

At this moment she would let this sensual man do anything to her. She tried not to listen, but her heart begged her to let it love this man.

She was still humming with the joy of it when he began to move up her body.

"Beautiful. You are so beautiful," he whispered.

She reached for him, and slid her palms slowly up muscled biceps to his shoulders. She wished he were naked; she wanted to feel his skin. Then she wrapped her arms around his neck and held him close. "That was incredible."

He smiled and brushed her lips with a kiss so tender she wanted to weep. "There is more, so much more, but not tonight. I promised you I'd never put you in a situation where you had to marry me. If I go further, that promise will be broken. I want you too much."

"I really only came to talk." How could there be more than this perfection? No wonder women flocked to him.

"With your legs bare and no corset?" He nuzzled her nose with his own. "You only have to say 'I'll marry you' and I can show you how good lovemaking can be."

She sighed in resignation and disappointment. "I can say those words, if you can tell me what is in your heart."

"I do care for you. I can give you the most wonderful life. Friendship. Children. A home. Investing to your heart's content. But I don't know if I'll ever be able to give you my heart. If not for the fact blood still pumps in my veins, I'd swear my heart had been stripped and torn apart. I'm not sure it will ever mend."

She knew this had to do with Margo's death. Did he feel responsible? What happened to her? "If you want me to marry you and trust you enough to be part of your life, can you tell me about Margo?"

He sat back and ran a hand through his hair, looking as if he wanted to flee. She sat up and began to hook her dress back together while he talked.

"Margo was a typical well-bred young lady. Beautiful beyond words, and I fell in love with one look." He laughed. "Not love. I don't think I really loved her. I was simply young and infatuated. I asked her to marry me the first night I met her, so how could I have loved her? I didn't even know her."

He stood and began to pace the room. The pain bottled up in him was evident from the tension in his shoulders. "I was young and arrogant and had no idea of the real evil in the world. I thought my position in society, my title, my money protected me. I was very wrong and Margo paid the price."

A coldness washed over her at his bleak words.

"On an outing in Richmond Park, I left the servants to follow us home and, with just Margo, set off in the phaeton."

What happened hit her before he said another word. "You were attacked?" He flopped into the chair by the fire, his head in his hands. "What happened?" But she knew.

"They raped her and I could do nothing to stop them. The sounds. Her cries. They haunt my dreams." A lone tear fell down his cheek. "She could not live with the consequences."

Consequences...

"When she learned she was with child—no, not mine, I'd not touched her in that way, happy to wait, and then after the attack... she wouldn't let me touch her and I understood why. I thought with time she would heal. I would never have abandoned her. This was my fault."

"No. It wasn't your fault. It was the men who attacked you."

"I should never have gone so far from London without an escort. Margo paid the price."

"And if her child was a boy, he would have become your heir." Tiffany understood the dilemma Margo had faced, but to kill herself... "She could have had the child in secret and then married you."

He looked up at her, anguish on his face. "Yes. That is what I thought, but maybe she didn't believe in me. She didn't believe I'd stand by her."

Tiffany went and sat at his feet. She placed her hands on his thighs and rubbed. "You were right. You didn't know each other. For if she really knew you, she'd have known you would never have abandoned her."

He placed his large hand over hers. "I tried to get her to postpone the wedding until she was ready. Maybe she thought I was trying to back out of the engagement. The day our wedding was supposed to have taken place, she killed herself. She slashed her wrists in her bedchamber." He squeezed her hand. "When I got the news, my heart literally shriveled in my chest, and I can't seem to bring it back to life."

Tiffany understood guilt, but she'd never faced something like this. She rather thought if he could just forgive himself, his heart would heal and he could learn to let love back in. But she also wondered if he was scared. Scared to be responsible for another person's wellbeing ever again. No wonder he was so worried about what Sprat might do. He would feel responsible for any action Sprat took in retaliation for Wolf not paying Melville's debt and bringing Sprat's actions to everyone's attention.

At least she now understood what she faced where Wolf was concerned. She was not prepared to give up on the idea that he could come to love her. He just had to heal from his past. *Just!* Was she a woman that could help him heal? He was older and wiser now, and she was perhaps stronger in spirit than Margo. She knew one thing. She would not have killed herself if she'd been in Margo's place. That was letting evil win. And she'd never allow that.

"I have always known that in life good things take time. Investing is not an overnight win. You need patience and skill and perseverance. Trust is the same. You don't trust overnight either. Trust develops and grows. Relationships appear to be the same. Love, real love, takes time to grow."

He tweaked her nose. "Is this your way of telling me that my heart will heal?"

"With the right person, I know it will. What I have to consider, as do you, is whether I'm the right woman to help you mend your broken heart."

He stared at her for a long time. "Do you want to be that woman?" he asked in a whisper, as if her answer might shatter the silence.

Was he ready? With everything going on around them, it would be risky. "Why don't we deal with Sprat and then see what develops between us? So far I'm liking the idea of becoming your marchioness more and more. Especially after tonight's stolen delights."

Finally, a smile broke over his lips. "Speaking of which, if you don't sneak home soon there may be no choice but to wed. If Mother catches you here, that's all she'll need. You know how keen she is for the match."

He was right, of course. Tiffany rose and stood looking down at him. "We can tick trust off our list. I've known you for years and I trust you. I know the man you are. Thank you for trusting me with your story." She bent and kissed his forehead. "I will see you mid-morning for my final sitting."

~

He needed a drink. He poured himself a brandy and sat back down at his desk, but all thought of work vanished. He hadn't expected to go so far with her tonight. But the feel of her, the scent of her, the sight of her in that enticing gown had loosened his control. She'd come to test him. And he hoped he'd passed the test.

The warmth in the area of his cold dead heart told him she could be right. Could he come to love again? Would he risk it? He thought she just might be worth the risk. What kind of marriage did he want? He wanted what his parents had shared. He wanted that intimacy. The feeling that you had a friend walking beside you, supporting you.

He was still as hard as rock. He wanted to race to his bedchamber while her taste was still on his lips and pleasure himself. He'd been doing that a lot lately. In his dreams, Tiffany was always lying naked before him, like he saw her in his painting. He kept the painting in his room where he could see it.

From now on he wouldn't have to imagine. He would remember. And memory was worse than imagination, because imagination had not gifted him with the innocence of her response. His armor was punctured, and now his fractured heart wanted to break free.

What he needed to decide, and soon, was if he could let his heart mend, and love again.

Chapter Nineteen

shleigh, Ivy and Claire joined Tiffany for the final painting session. They wanted to go over the last-minute arrangements for the stall the day after tomorrow. Tiffany missed most of the conversation, distracted because she would be facing the Sisterhood directly after the sitting, and she didn't know what she would say to them. They were meeting at the Marlowe townhouse under the guise of the stall.

"I think Valora should be on the stall for the men's clothing. Husbands will gravitate toward her table. You know how men are around her. She could sell a man poison with a smile and he'd drink it."

Tiffany heard Wolf chuckle at Ashleigh's words.

"I think Farah should join her. She will ensure Valora doesn't get carried away with flirting. I don't want men dropping down on bended knee and declaring their heart to her." Claire's words were said in jest—sort of. Valora tended to have that effect on men, except for the one man she wanted—Fane.

"I'm happy to be on any of the stalls," Tiffany offered.

Ivy said, "You'll be handling all the money. We need someone who can add quickly in her head. I've never seen anyone add up numbers faster. No one will be able to slip anything by us."

Tiffany would like that job. She did love numbers, and raising money for such a good cause would help alleviate her guilt just a tad.

Suddenly Wolf stood back from the painting and looked up at the sky. "Just in time. Here come the clouds. I thought we'd been lucky to get a full week with no rain. If I were you, ladies, I'd help Tiffany change and get home before the heavens open up."

Tiffany stood and stretched. "Wise words, my lord. Come, ladies."

"No demand to see the painting?" Wolf teased. Tiffany could not look at him. She felt her face heat. "You've seen it," he said, correctly interpreting her blush. "But how..." He paused, eyes narrowed, then answered his own question.. "Yesterday, when Rockwell was hurt." He sounded...disappointed.

"I had to collect my glasses... It helped me understand a few things, and it's why I came to..." She almost let it slip that she'd gone to him last night. She looked at her three friends. Ivy's mouth formed an O while Ashleigh simply shook her head.

Wolf coughed to cover her slip. "Then you are forgiven."

"So we can see it?" Ivy asked.

"No. Not until I'm ready. It's not finished."

"Why are older brothers no fun?" Ashleigh said. She linked arms with Tiffany and the ladies made their way inside. "I'm not going to ask what that private conversation was about, but it would seem you are warming to my brother."

"You sound as if that's a bad thing."

Ashleigh hugged her tight. "I'd love to have you as my sister-in-law. I just hope my brother deserves you."

"I'm not sure any of the men we are related to deserve any of us." Claire laughed as she and Ivy ran up the stairs toward the bedchamber.

Tiffany hung back, wanting to defend Wolf to Ashleigh, but the look in Ashleigh's eyes made her hesitate. Was Ashleigh bitter about the fact Tiffany's relationship with Wolf was going well, when Ashleigh and her brother's relationship appeared strained? Was she scared Wolf would reveal the details of her scandal?

"I would never ask him to reveal your confidences."

Ashleigh looked at her. "One day, when it doesn't hurt so much, I'll tell you."

"I'm always here for you. And I never judge. Gosh, I have been funding a criminal when I thought I was being so clever. I'm in no position to judge anyone."

"What does God say? He who throws the first stone..."

"Then why are you so worried for me? Is there something I should know about Wolf and his offer?" Tiffany pressed her friend.

Before she could reply, Claire leaned over the banister. "Hurry up, you two. I don't want to get my slippers wet walking home and the clouds are looking blacker."

The moment was lost, but Tiffany would have another conversation with Ashleigh. Something about her and Wolf was troubling Ashleigh. Tiffany didn't want to gain a husband and lose a friend.

~

Soon the ladies were back at Marlowe's and organizing afternoon tea in the drawing room.

As each of the ladies arrived she didn't sense any anger or blame, but it was hard to face her friends knowing what had happened.

Tiffany sat in a chair by the fire, ignoring the happy chatter around her. Her stomach was clenched so tight she couldn't eat a thing. Once all the talk died down, Lauren, who had lost the most, spoke. "Before we begin, all of us have talked and we want to make it very clear that we do not blame you for the situation we are each in. As I'm the one most affected, I can't stress your innocence enough. Sprat took in men much older and wiser than you.

Each of us knew the risks involved in investing and we will not have you bear the burden of this situation alone."

Tiffany let tears flow.

"Please don't cry," Farah urged. "We have every faith in you to win the wager with the men and earn back our losses. Gaining access to Wolf's stockjobber is a blessing. I bet you wanted to marry Wolf the minute he offered Mr. Lane's services. A husband who would allow you to invest. That's a man to admire. My brother barely lets me breathe without his permission."

Claire handed Tiffany a handkerchief. "Tears won't help us beat the men. Please tell us you have a plan to do that at least."

She dried her eyes and tucked the handkerchief in her sleeve. "I do wish to apologize for being such a fool as to trust Sprat, but I thought my father valued the man. I just wish Father had told me of his doubts before that fateful trip to London. The trip from which he never returned. Sprat is smart. He told me he'd lent Father some money to help him, and my mother's lady's maid said she'd seen him do that, but then the highwaymen stole it. So I assumed he was an honorable man. It was all a trick. I think he set the highwaymen on my parents. I suspect my father, like Wolf, refused to play his game, and Sprat killed him and my mother."

"Oh, goodness," Valora said. "No wonder Wolf is being cautious. We should all be on our guard." She added, "I'm more than happy to provide funds to help us win the wager if others are a bit short."

"Me too," Farah chimed. "I really want you to beat my brother."

"Thank you, but I have already invested the one thousand pounds. I had some savings and extra pin money. It's the least I can do for creating this mess."

"There was no need to do that," Courtney said. "We stick together when any of us are in trouble. This is not your fault. I wish you would stop implying that it is."

"I'm happy to invest on your behalf at any time, but the one-thousand-pound challenge has begun, and I'm funding it and will share the winnings—if we win. I have taken a risky strategy, but I am monitoring it daily, and should anything change I'm ready to move the investments around."

"Are we still to listen in on those around us for tips on their strategies?" Ivy asked.

"Yes. I'll adjust our risk profile depending on what we hear and learn." Tiffany was not about to tell them of her concerns that Wolf might learn what she was investing in. Would Chester tell Mr. Lane, and would Lane tell Wolf? If Lane did, and Wolf chose to follow what she purchased, he would be their biggest competitor.

"We trust you. And if for some reason we don't win, at least we will have given the men a good fight. That in itself will make them notice us as more than simply women to marry off."

"Hear, hear, Claire," said Ashleigh. "Well said. Tiffany, you are not to take this too seriously and feel pressure to win. If at any time we feel you're getting upset or stressed, we will call the whole thing off. We help each other, and God knows the few dividends Sprat did pay out saved some of us. We are thankful for that at least. This is supposed to be fun and quite frankly, right now it doesn't feel like fun at all."

The girls all nodded in agreement.

Claire said, "Moving on then. If you have any information to share, let's hear it. Tiffany is ready to write it down."

The ladies had managed to collect a fair amount of information. Tiffany learned that no one had mentioned the two shares she'd invested in: Armley Mill and Kilmarnock and Troon Railway. The railroad was a risk, but if the Marquess's plan came to fruition, she'd earn a fortune.

An hour later the talk ran out.

Claire moved to pull the bell. "More tea, I think. Now that is over, who would like some of Cook's fabulous strawberry sponge with cream? The charity stalls are all organized, but I think we should go over the plans for the day."

Tiffany approached Lauren and pulled her aside. She pushed

some money into her hand. "The shares I purchased for you would have earned this sum this quarter. Wolf made good on one of my investments. The money hadn't been paid into Sprat's bank. They found it at his office, so I'd like you to take it."

She could tell Lauren wanted the money. The way she was eyeing the food on the table made Tiffany wonder how much she'd had to eat of late. "Thank you. I'm not really in a position to say no."

"I'll ensure you soon will be. I have a sound share plan for you. Some that produce good dividends and others that may see some price growth."

"Thank you. I don't know what I'd do without this group. My brother only joined the army to earn some money. He just couldn't get through to Father. I think Lucien dying in the Irish Rebellion only made my father's fall into despair worse. He gambles and drinks even more to forget. He blames himself for Lucien's death."

So he should. The thought was unkind, but really, who would let their only heir join the army because pride would not let them divulge their need for money? The army had sent Lucien to Ireland never expecting the uprising to occur, and suddenly Lauren had lost her brother and the only person in the family earning any money.

She squeezed Lauren's hand. "You and Madeline will always have a home with me if ever you're in need. Please let me know if I can do anything. Anything at all. When my parents died, if I'd not had Lord Marlowe, I don't know what would have happened to me. Sometimes we need to let others help us."

Lauren hugged her. "I promise. Now, if you'll excuse me, I'd like some cake. And I may take some home for Maddy."

It was early dusk as the ladies took their leave. "I shall see you tonight at Lady Stonewest's ball," Valora said. "Are we all attending?"

Only Lauren shook her head. "Stay for a moment, Lauren," Claire whispered in her ear. Lauren hesitated but agreed.

Once everyone had left, Claire said to Lauren. "Come to the ball with us tonight. You can stay the night here and have Dayton's room since my brother refuses to come home from India. Rest and then we will get dressed and have a quiet supper before heading out. I have a dress which would look gorgeous on you."

"Oh, please do, Lauren. You deserve to have some fun. It would be nice to have the Sisterhood all in attendance for once," Tiffany added.

Lauren nodded. "If I go home, Father may well find this money you've given me and tomorrow I need to pay what little staff I have left or they will leave. I'll pen a note to Maddy and let her know."

Tiffany flicked a concerned look at Claire. They should do more for Lauren, but they weren't sure what. Money was what they needed, and that could have been achieved if not for Sprat. Perhaps she could swallow her pride and accept Wolf's offer to make good some of the money Sprat had stolen from her. She'd give the money to Lauren. She prayed they would find some of her absconded funds so she could help her friend, but she wasn't so stupid as to believe the money would solve all of Lauren's problems. As fast as she earned it, her father found and spent it. Lauren had one goal—to see Madeline married so she was financially secure.

The Sisterhood needed to come up with a long-term plan to help Lauren. As Tiffany followed Claire and Lauren up the stairs, her mind worked. For once, the usual option available to a woman in dire financial straits—marriage—appeared to be a viable one. Lauren had no dowry but she was very pretty, and perhaps Wolf would have an idea of how to help her or, at the very least, Madeline.

It struck her like a cold blast of hail. She was turning to Wolf more and more, as if she was already his wife. And yet she could not bring herself to mind. Wolf didn't force his opinions on her.

He listened. Offered advice. He really would make a wonderful husband.

She hugged that thought to herself and, as she lay in her shift on the bed trying to get some rest before the ball, dreamed of their kiss from last night.

~

As usual, Fane escorted the ladies into the ballroom and then made a hurried escape to the card room. Claire led them toward Lady Vale and Valora, who stood with Courtney and her brother Lord Julian Montague and his wife, Serena. They had taken up position near the open doors to the terrace. Even though it was raining, the night was warm and the ballroom was stifling.

Serena fanned herself. She was with child and probably had only another month before she would have to cry off such engagements. If any couple was a walking recommendation for a love-match marriage, it was Julian and Serena. He was even keeping their investment challenge secret. He thought it a hoot.

"I see your brother has deserted you again. He's such a coward. Scared of the mothers," Julian teased Claire. "And it's lovely to see you tonight, Lady Lauren. We should see more of you."

"You are most kind, my lord. I am hoping to dance if not my troubles away, then at least the evening."

Scarcely had she finished that statement when a few young men encircled the ladies to fill their dance cards. Tiffany had never known the men to have so much interest in her. Wolf had raised her popularity. Or was it that they wanted to learn what Wolf saw in her? She did keep the two waltzes free for him just in case. Speaking of, where were Wolf and his sisters?

For the first hour Tiffany danced with a few young men, but for the most part she kept her attention trained on the top of the stairs, waiting for Wolf to arrive.

"Do stop staring. Many are noticing. You know what Ivy's

like, she's always late," Claire whispered in her ear. "I'm happy for you. Happy that you seem to like Wolf's attentions. From the way he's behaving, he's obviously enamored of you—"

"Enamored? I hardly think so. He likes me, that's true. Desires me? I think he does. But you and I said we'd not marry unless for love."

Lauren came to stand next to her. "Well, judging by the look on his face, I'd say he's more than 'in like' with you. He's searching the ballroom for you, look."

She looked up and there he was at the top of the stairs. He looked so handsome she almost forgot to breathe. His hair shone blue-black in the candlelight. His jacket hugged his broad shoulders. And his eyes... They found her in the crowd and burned for her. The look he sent her had Claire and Lauren sucking in a breath.

"Oh, I agree, Lauren. That's the look of a man completely smitten," Valora said.

Tiffany stood as if turned to stone as Wolf made his way through the crowd until he stood before her. She couldn't tear her gaze from his handsome face, not even to greet Ivy and Ashleigh.

The music played for a waltz. "My dance, I believe," and he held out his hand. The path to the floor seemed to clear before them, as if all present were aware of the significance of this dance.

She placed her hand in his and he enclosed it possessively, pulling her closer than was truly respectable. Then he preceded to twirl her around the floor. It wasn't the dance that made her dizzy. It was the look in his eyes. *You belong to me,* they screamed. And for the first time in her life she wanted to belong to a man. This man.

"You look delectable," he whispered in her ear. "I see I'm going to have to stake my claim before other men turn your head."

She laughed. What other man could ever turn her head? "Perhaps. I suspect you'll head to the card room with the other men. Cowards, all of you. Hiding from mere women."

"I shall be by your side all night, sweeting. I want to spend more time with you, even if it is under prying eyes."

"I won't complain about that. I like being in your company. Preferably in private," she added wickedly, knowing she was safe in the crowded ballroom.

This time he laughed. "You think you're safe to tease me here at the ball? I'm sure I can find any number of private spaces to grant you your wish."

Her pulse skipped in her veins as she considered the idea. She could not deny it was tempting. Very tempting. She thought it best not to poke the wolf when he was in this hunting mood, however. She didn't wish to find herself compromised. Even if she was beginning to see him as husband material, the choice would be hers and hers alone.

The dance was coming to an end and she wished it could go on all night. "There is one thing you could do for me tonight. Could you dance with Lady Lauren this evening? It will do her social standing a world of good."

Wolf looked over his shoulder as the final strains of music played. "Her brother, Lord Lucien, was very close to Rockwell. My brother took Lucien's death hard. I think he has been keeping an eye on her father, Lord Danvers, but I agree, we should do more for Lady Lauren."

"This is why I like you so much. You are kind to others without judgment."

"I'm hardly in a position to judge anyone." He escorted her back to her friends and Lady Vale, and true to his word he asked Lady Lauren to dance.

Valora took her aside. "I still want to sneak into Mrs. Buchanan's. Will you come with me? I can't ask anyone else. With Lord Wolfarth courting you, you're likely to be forgiven if we are caught."

"If we are caught, both of us could be ruined." She gentled her words. "Can you not see that this is not the way to gain Fane's attention. Besides, if you have to work so hard, is he worth it?"

Valora chewed her bottom lip. "I don't know of any other way to gain his attention. Like tonight, he comes to the balls but never dances. I never have a chance to be in his presence."

"I hardly think that attending an entirely unsuitable soiree will increase your chances of him looking on you favorably as wife material. You know he's not thinking of marrying soon. The *ton* would be a hive of twittering mothers if anyone thought he was wife hunting."

"I just...I just look at you and Wolf. Wolf never looked at you until that carriage ride. You were able to spend time alone with him and you piqued his interest. I want that chance with Lord Marlowe. Tell me how I can find time with him alone."

"You won't find him alone at Mrs. Buchanan's soiree. There will be women there looking for protectors. Do you really want to see Fane scouting for a new mistress?"

Valora's bottom lip trembled and Tiffany could tell tears were about to fall. She took her friend's arm and led her away from prying eyes toward the retiring room.

They weren't in there for long. She hoped she'd made Valora see sense, though she wished she could help her friend find the happiness she craved. But, like Claire, she wondered if Fane was the right man for Valora. She loved her cousin, he'd been very good to her, but he was quite selfish.

As they strolled back through the crowded ballroom and drew nearer to their friends, Tiffany heard Ashleigh say, "Oh, for goodness' sake. I'm sick of all this talk of romance and love. My brother has offered for Tiffany so that Fane will offer for me and take Wolf's scandal-ridden sister off his hands."

"That's not true," Ivy cried.

Claire shrugged. "Sounds like Fane."

Tiffany stood rooted to the spot, and it took the other ladies a few seconds to realize she'd overheard Ashleigh.

"I'm sure that's not true," Valora whispered in her ear.

Ashleigh turned and saw Tiffany, and her face went deathly white. She stepped toward Tiffany, her hand outstretched. "I'm sorry you had to hear it this way. I've been trying to find a time to talk to you. I hate what my brother is doing."

Tiffany's mind raced, her thoughts all jumbled. Ashleigh's words made sense. Wolf had yet to tell her why he decided to pursue her. But the way he treated her, the way he looked at her... It couldn't only be about protecting Ashleigh—could it? Her heart started to put up its fortress. The one thing she'd learned about Wolf was the lengths to which he'd go to protect those he loved. If he thought Ashleigh would be left on the shelf...

There was only one way to find out. She needed to talk with Wolf. Where was he? She searched the room and, as if he knew she was looking for him, his eyes locked with hers. He smiled, but she didn't smile back. Instead, she turned and moved toward the rear of the room. She couldn't go outside, it was still raining, but she knew a corridor ran along the back of the ballroom and led to a small orangery. Would he follow?

She'd barely made the corridor when strong arms drew her back against a solid chest. She held herself stiff. "What's happened?" he asked.

"Not here. I'm not having this conversation in a corridor."

He took her hand in his and strode toward the orangery, but then turned left and entered a small study. He closed and locked the door behind him.

"You locked the door?"

He turned her to face him. "If you are caught here with me, you will have no choice but to become my countess. Is that what you want?"

"At this moment it definitely is not." She folded her arms across her chest.

"I repeat. What has happened?"

"Ashleigh had an interesting theory as to why you have suggested I become your countess. I'd like you to tell me why you decided on me for that role."

He groaned and ran a hand through his hair. "I didn't think anyone had overheard Marlowe's stupid conversation."

"Apparently your sister did and she's very angry."

"Well, she can't have heard the whole conversation, because if she had, she would have heard me saying no."

"So you did discuss this idea with Fane?"

"It was well before I really knew you. Dayton jokingly suggested it and Marlowe grabbed hold of the idea, saying he'd marry Ashleigh regardless of the scandal surrounding her."

"Why did you say no?"

He groaned. "Bloody hell. Because if you must know I don't think Marlowe would make Ashleigh happy."

She let out a breath. So it wasn't because he didn't want her. "Then why suddenly decide I would make you a good countess?"

"I didn't suddenly decide you were the woman for me." He drew up to his full height. "You really want to know what made me offer the stupid wager to marry me?"

She nodded, her lip sucked between her teeth. Did she want to know? Would it shatter the bond forming between them?

"It was a spur of the moment offer because I'd had bad news from Mr. Lane about some investments, and I suddenly felt out of my depth. Everyone assumes I have the ability to make money as if it falls from the trees, but I struggle with the decisions every day."

"Oh, dear God. You offered because you thought I could help you with investments." And she burst out laughing. "I never knew my talent would land me a husband. I invested so I wouldn't need one."

"It's not funny. Besides, it may have started out that way, but as I got to know you, I grew to like you. Admire you. Hell, I think I love you," and he was almost yelling.

She stopped laughing and looked into his handsome face and saw the truth. He wasn't lying. "You love me?"

"I'm just as surprised as you. I thought my heart was so broken it would never spring free and love again. But then I got to know you." He cupped her cheek. "How could I not fall in love?"

She turned her face and pressed a kiss into his palm. "I think I love you too."

"Think?"

"I've never been in love before, so I'm not sure what I'm feeling. But I like it. I like how you make me feel when you look at me. When you pull me into your arms and when you kiss me," she added breathlessly.

His smile saw her knees go weak. He gathered her close and slowly lowered his head until his lips took hers in a soft, tender kiss. Her arms slipped to his shoulders and she ran her hands down his back, feeling the strength coiled there. The kiss soon swept them both away. Her hands wound into his hair while his roamed her body as if he had every right to it.

The kiss grew in passion and soon all she could hear, and feel, was the man who was making her wild with uncontrollable desire. A man she was pretty sure would become her husband—and that didn't frighten her. It thrilled her. She clung to his broad shoulders, swept along by the sensations his tongue created as it conquered the inside of her mouth.

Tiffany got lost in the kiss, bombarded by his fresh sandalwood fragrance and his ruthless lips, which demanded her submission. A groan rumbled deep within his throat, echoing the cry she held back; she badly wanted to let the sounds escape.

He drew back. "You know you're mine. Since I caught you at Capel Court you've belonged to me."

Her gaze focused on his lips. She watched, mesmerized, as he drew in another breath. He opened his mouth to speak again but she silenced him.

She stretched up, drew his head down, brought her lips close to his and murmured, "I've always been yours. Since the day I came to live with the Marlowes and you carried me up the stairs. You were my prince keeping me safe in my new home."

"I barely remember that night. I wish I did."

"I remember it plenty for both of us. I wanted you to kiss me, but it was the longing of an infatuated and scared young girl."

"You're not a young girl now. And I hope you're not scared."

"I'm never scared when I'm with you."

With that he covered her lips with his, kissing her voraciously, all consumingly. Hands splaying, sliding over her person like a whispered caress. Reverent. Worshipping. Claiming...

He closed his arms about her, pulling her close, molding her to him. Any thought that he might stop died the instant she set eyes upon his face, on all he said with just one hot, burning gaze.

Soon she found herself scooped up and carried to the small chaise longue near the fire at the other end of the room. He gently laid her on it, following her down. She loved the weight of him atop her as she clung to his shoulders. She couldn't wait for him to pleasure her, but instead he stopped kissing her and simply cuddled her into his side.

"Not here. Not like this. The first time I make love to you, I want it to be in my bed, as my wife."

"I don't want a big wedding."

He ran a finger down her cheek and lifted her chin. "I'm the Marquess of Wolfarth. Society will expect a big wedding. If we don't have a big wedding it may look as if we have something to hide."

"They'll think that anyway. Why else would you marry a woman like me?"

"Don't keep saying that. You're beautiful. Besides, all will be perfectly clear when they see my wedding gift. The painting I created of you. Every man will envy me."

"I thought that was for the Royal Academy auction to raise money for the society. You said no one would recognize me."

"It is, and how else could I get you to see how beautiful you really are? But who do you think is going to buy it? I'd not let anyone else hang that on their wall. It shall hang in my—our—bedchamber." He pressed a kiss to her lips. "When can I announce our betrothal?"

She pushed out of his hold and sat up, her head spinning.

"Gosh, this is moving very quickly. You know I'll help you with your investments without becoming your wife."

"When I'm with you my investments are the last thing on my mind. Right now my driving need is to get you naked and make you mine. I don't care about your financial skills. I'm not marrying you for those. I'm marrying you because I think you and I will make a perfect love match."

"Thank you. What about Sprat? Can we marry with him still out there? Or should we wait until he's caught?"

Wolf lay back upon the chaise longue, a delicious feast for her eyes. At the mention of Sprat he suddenly looked tired. "You're right. I would prefer to have Sprat dealt with. Rockwell's off to Ireland in a few days. I think the key to finding Sprat is to follow the money. If the money is in Ireland, so is Sprat. He has too many people hunting for him here." He stood up and held out his hand to help her rise. "We should return to the ballroom before there is too much talk. We can still announce our betrothal. May I call on Marlowe tomorrow to organize the marriage contracts? And I'd like to host a ball at my home to make the announcement."

"Can you wait until after the charity stall tomorrow before speaking with Marlowe? I'd like to be present for the conversation."

He tapped the end of her nose. "Don't you trust me?"

"It's not that, it's just... This is my life. I think I should have the right to be part of the process." She held her breath. If Wolf was who she believed him to be, he'd—

"If you want to be there I have no objections."

She hugged him tightly and let love flood her heart. "I feel like the luckiest girl in the world."

Wolf beamed. "As my wife, I'll make it my goal to ensure you feel like that every day."

They rejoined the ball and Wolf didn't leave her side all evening. If society was in any doubt of his intentions toward her, those questions had been answered.

Ashleigh tried to talk with her, but Tiffany merely hugged her friend and said it didn't matter. Tonight she basked in the glow of being wanted and finally feeling as if she belonged in the world she inhabited.

Wolf walked her to the Marlowe carriage. As he helped her ascend, he kissed her hand and said, "You'll never be invisible again. You will be forever in my heart." He turned to Marlowe. "If it's convenient, I'll call on you tomorrow evening after the ladies are back from the charity stall."

"You are not attending Mrs. Buchanan's soiree?"

"No. Rockwell and I plan to help the ladies at their stall. I shall escort them home."

"Then I shall see you for a light supper." Marlowe looked at Tiffany and smiled. "Are you happy for me to have this conversation with Lord Wolfarth?"

She leaned over and pressed a kiss to Fane's cheek. "Thank you for asking." She smiled over her shoulder at Wolf. "Yes. I'm happy."

"Then tomorrow it is."

Wolf stood watching them until the carriage left the drive, and then Tiffany finally sat back and turned her attention to her cousins and Lauren, who were all smiling at her.

"Congratulations," Lauren said. "He's a wonderful choice for a husband."

"If I have to lose you to anyone, I suppose Wolf is better than many."

"You're not losing me, Claire. I'll only be living a few doors away."

Claire shook her head. "Not all the time. Our estates are miles apart. Cornwall to Yorkshire takes days to travel. And how will we run..." Claire looked at Fane, who appeared to be asleep.

"I'm too happy to think about all of that right now. Can't you let me bask in this glow for a few hours?" She reached and squeezed Claire's hand. "We knew this couldn't last forever. We are grown woman who have to live the lives we want. I want to become his marchioness. I will be happy with Wolf."

She sat back and tried to relive how she'd felt in Wolf's arms, but the sadness on Claire's face ruined it. They had talked about being spinsters together in a little cottage in Cornwall.

She wished Claire could find a man to love. Try as she might, Tiffany couldn't think of a single man of their acquaintance that Claire favored. Fane's behavior made Claire view marriage with distaste. Maybe Tiffany's marriage to Wolf and Serena's marriage to Julian could change those views. She hoped so. She didn't want her friend to end up alone and miss out on the joys of motherhood and family.

Chapter Twenty

The church square hummed with adults and children. Tiffany had to concentrate every time she had a bill of sale to organize. She was tired from little sleep last night and the early start to set up the stall. In her dreams she'd danced with Wolf all night, instead of only two waltzes. She'd woken tangled in her bedsheets.

Today she was going to become betrothed to the man of her dreams. And her body hummed with joy. She couldn't wait for the stall to be over.

The churchyard was still full of people two hours later. The stall was a huge success. They had been busy the whole time, and soon all the clothes and other items they had available would be gone. They had raised so much money for Ivy's orphanage.

"Do you need a break?" Wolf asked. He'd stayed by her side the entire time. "I'm sure I could manage your duties for a few minutes."

"I could use a cup of tea and a chance to stretch my legs." She looked over to the busiest table, Valora's. The crowd had dispersed, as most of the gentlemen's clothes and items had sold first. The ladies would remember this idea for next time. Then it struck her. Valora was not at the table. Tiffany glanced around. She couldn't see Valora anywhere. *Please don't let her have gone alone to Mrs. Buchanan's.* "Thank you, Wolf."

She leaped to her feet and almost ran to Claire's side. "Where's Valora?"

"She went to the retiring room." Claire straightened from rummaging through the last pieces in one of the boxes. "But that was a while ago." Claire looked at her. "Oh, no. She wouldn't."

"Who wouldn't what?" Farah asked.

"Valora is missing," Tiffany said quietly.

Farah began looking around. "Oh! We have to stop her. Have we got time? When did she leave?"

"I don't know."

Farah peered over her shoulder. "There's Rockwell. Let's ask him to go after her." Before they could stop her, Farah was off.

"If Rockwell tells Vale, Valora will be married off immediately." Claire sounded close to tears. "I could strangle that girl. Why didn't she tell one of us?"

"She told me at the ball last night that she still wanted to go, but I thought I'd convinced her not to."

"You should have told us and we would have kept a closer eye on her."

Tiffany didn't want this day to be spoiled. It was supposed to be her day. She was getting engaged. "This is not my fault. You know that no one would have been able to stop her."

Farah arrived with Rockwell. "I'll find her," he said. "I just hope no one sees us or I could end up married to her." Farah's face turned pale.

"Perhaps you could take Lord Axton Fancot with you, Valora's other brother," Claire suggested. "He's here with Lord Julian, who is helping in place of Serena."

Farah's eyes opened wide. "What if Axton tells his brother, Vale? Valora will be in so much trouble."

The girls stood there arguing, and it took them a moment to

notice Rockwell had left and collected Wolf. They walked back to the ladies. Wolf stopped in front of Tiffany. "I'll make sure we stop Miss Valora from doing anything foolish. Stay with Axton and Julian. We'll be back soon. We have a meeting to attend."

Farah said what they were all thinking. "I hope they get to her before she is ruined. My brother will not let me visit at the Wolfarth's. I don't want to add the Vale residence to the list."

"I'm just going to slip to the retiring room before rescuing Julian," Tiffany said. "I think the ladies buying goods are flirting with him and he's too shy to stop them."

They looked across to where a very red-faced Julian sat taking orders, and they all giggled. "I can't wait to tell Serena. He looks adorable," Claire said.

Tiffany slipped into the tiny room set aside in the church hall for the ladies. The young maid overseeing the room smiled at her. She was holding a pair of gloves that Tiffany thought were an old pair of Ivy's. "Those are beautiful," Tiffany said.

"My beau bought them for me. I haven't even been stepping out with him for very long and look what he gives me. They are the softest leather I've ever felt," and she ran the leather over her cheek.

Tiffany inwardly smiled at the young maid's dreamy-eyed look. Tiffany knew exactly how she felt. She couldn't wait to announce to the world that a man like Wolf loved her. Actually, she didn't care what others thought. Just knowing he loved her was enough.

She slipped behind the screen and took care of the necessary. On her way out, she dug into her reticule to find a tip for the maid. She had just reached the entrance when a hand covered her mouth and she was lifted off her feet. For a moment, shock and confusion rendered her immobile, and then instinct kicked in and she started to struggle. But her captor was too strong. Another man appeared in front of her and shoved a rag into her mouth, silencing any attempt to scream. As the two men carried her out, she saw the young maid prone on the floor, the gloves her beau had bought her lying by her feet.

~

Wolf and Rockwell found Valora pacing on the corner of Mrs. Buchanan's street. She looked relieved when she saw them.

"I couldn't go in. I am such a fool." Rockwell placed her hand on his arm and turned her back toward the churchyard. "Please don't tell my brother. And oh, dear lord, don't tell Lord Marlowe."

Rockwell smiled. "Tell them what? That you needed some fresh air after working so hard at the stall?"

Wolf accompanied them on her other side. "Any man would be honored to have you bestow a smile on him. A man who doesn't notice you is a man too tied up in himself, and is probably not worth your devotion."

Valora laughed. "Marlowe is your friend."

"I know. But that doesn't mean I'm blind to his faults. Just that I accept them. No one is perfect." Wolf thought back to Margo's death and how Marlowe had been there for him every day during that bleak time. And he'd helped rescue Ashleigh. And had kept the family's deep, dark secrets of that day.

"I'm certainly not perfect. I've risked my reputation, friendships and the orphanage by using the stall as a means to be foolish beyond measure. Why can't I fall in love with a man who wants me?"

"They say men always want what they can't have. Would it be any different for a woman?" Rockwell said.

"Interesting. You are implying that I want Marlowe because he's never been one of my many admirers." She walked along in silence for a moment. "You could be right. I can't say I know him particularly well." She smiled up at the two men. "And there are plenty of handsome gentlemen for me to flirt with." And she batted her eyelashes at Rockwell.

"See, brother. No beautiful woman is going to flirt with you now you're practically married."

"And I do not care." And Wolf didn't. He'd never felt this content with his life. Tiffany's love filled the deep scar in his heart.

"I hope I find what you've found with Tiffany," Valora said as they neared the church. "And you'd better treat her like a princess or you'll have all of the ladies to deal with."

"I'm sure you'll find your prince. From my experience it happens when you least expect it," Wolf replied.

They entered the church courtyard to find it in an uproar. People were being asked to leave, and Claire and the other young ladies were sobbing in the corner. Julian came racing over. "Tiffany is missing. We found a young maid in the retiring room. She was knocked out. That's the last place Tiffany was seen entering."

The world swam, and he thought he would be sick. "Sprat. It has to be Sprat. He's taken Tiffany."

"You don't know that," Rockwell said, "but it's likely. He won't harm her, she's too valuable."

"How do you know that? He might simply kill her for revenge. I've destroyed his swindle and he's a wanted man."

"I've got the men checking the whole area. A young lad saw a carriage racing away up the mall. Axton took some men and have followed on horseback. They shouldn't get too far." Julian looked as if he'd aged ten years. "I'm sorry, I should have kept a better eye out."

"It's not your fault. We all thought Sprat had fled to Ireland." Once again Sprat had bettered him. A black haze clouded Wolf's vision. "Which direction did they go?" He had to get to Tiffany. He could not bear it if anything happened to her. It would be his fault. He'd tried to take on Sprat and failed. He'd failed, once again, to protect the woman he loved.

If he lost her... He wanted to hit something—no, someone. Sprat. He'd kill him if he touched even a hair on her head. He blocked out the memory of what had happened to Margo. It couldn't happen twice. Could it?

Rockwell read his mind. "He won't hurt her. He won't have time. We'll get him. Come on, Julian has organized horses for us." If Rockwell was trying to hide his fear, he was failing. Wolf could read his brother better than a book written in English.

Chapter Twenty-One

Tiffany didn't need her eyes uncovered to know who sat on the seat opposite her. Her captors had blindfolded her before shoving her roughly into the carriage. Her knees had hit the floor, but her cry of pain was muffled by the rag in her mouth.

She tried not to panic as she fought for breath through her nose.

"I underestimated Lord Wolfarth. I was sure he'd pay Melville's purchase orders. He's never struck me as a man who likes scandal."

Shows how little you know him. If she could just get her hands free of her bindings. They'd stupidly left her feet unbound. They had also not removed her gloves, which gave her the ability to work her wrists without the rope cutting into them. If she could just slip even one hand free.

Luckily the carriage was clattering along at a good pace, rocking and bouncing over the jagged cobblestone streets, hiding her movements. The rope seemed to slide over the fine leather gloves, and with building elation Tiffany realized she could slip her right hand free.

Suddenly the rag was tugged out of her mouth. She didn't

scream; her cries would not be heard over the pounding carriage ride, and he'd simply shove the rag back in. Would he remove the blindfold? She hoped so. It would be so much harder to escape without her sight.

"Unlike me, Lord Wolfarth wasn't so gullible."

He laughed in her face. "Who would have thought a lady of some social standing was one of my most successful investors. I got very wealthy from following your advice. A pity it's going to have to end."

Her limbs went rigid. That didn't sound good.

A hand landed on her thigh and she could smell Sprat's breath near her face. "Then again, I could keep you alive for a while and use that mind of yours. The risk of Wolfarth finding me would almost be worth it."

It took all her self-control not to whip her freed hand round to slap his face. "So you'll kill me, like you killed my father and mother."

He tore the blindfold off and she was staring into the eyes of evil. "My, my, that mind of yours is too sharp. I have plans for you —while you're useful you'll live. Who else knows about your parents?"

"Everyone."

He sat back then, chewing his bottom lip. "That changes things. Does Wolfarth know about..." He eyed her warily. "No. He couldn't know. He'd have searched harder."

"Know what?" she asked, not expecting him to answer.

But Sprat surprised her. "It was Wolfarth who made my career change into stockjobbing possible. My previous career was a tad more unsavory and risky to my personal health. I was part of a gang that used to rob naïve pansy gentlemen."

Wolfarth had never been a pansy. "It was you in Richmond Park. Your gang attacked and raped Lady Margo and stole from Wolfarth."

"Yes, the rape was unfortunate, and one of the reasons I left the gang. Not my cup of tea. The man who raped the young lady was dealt with. I didn't want to kill your parents either, but your father didn't care about the scandal and he called my bluff. I couldn't have that. All the other men I was blackmailing would band together and my income would fall away or worse I'd be run out of London."

"Like you are now?"

"Yes. I thought it clever to send the money to Ireland. Did they really think I would have only one bank account, at one bank? I chose the account with the least funds and transferred it to Ireland, knowing Wolfarth would believe I'd fled there."

Tiffany fought back nausea. Sprat would never let her escape now. She knew too much—enough to hang him. If she didn't rescue herself, she would not live long enough for Wolf to find her. "So where are you fleeing to?"

"The Americas, of course. The land of opportunity for a man with money."

"My money," she ground out.

"I must admit I did feel a bit guilty. Your plan of financial security so you didn't have to marry... But now it appears you are quite keen to marry. Wolfarth is a wealthy man, and with your skills his fortune can only grow. I can't have that."

She looked at him blankly.

"Wolfarth has taken money from me, so I'll ensure he doesn't make any extra from his marriage to you. You'll come with me and while you keep making sound investments, you'll live. And Wolfarth will suffer knowing I've bested him and have what he wants—you."

She wanted to tell him to go to hell, that she'd never give him advice again. But she would do whatever she must to stay alive until she could escape—however long that took.

∾

Wolf pulled on his horse's reins; they needed to pace the animals. At least they could travel faster than a carriage, but were they even going in the right direction?

"I bet he's heading to the docks. He must have a ship standing by," Rockwell yelled at him.

Wolf had never prayed so hard. The thought of what the man could do to her had his heart retreating behind its fortress. He couldn't go through this again. Couldn't fail. He had to rescue her.

"What if he's not?"

"Julian and the rest of the men have each taken a different road out of London. However, Sprat knows a carriage cannot outrun men on horses. Fleeing by carriage is too dangerous. He'll need to flee London faster. A ship would do that."

"What if he's not fleeing, merely hiding?"

Rockwell's jaw grew taut. "Then we check escape routes at the docks first and then if we need to, we regroup. Tiffany is strong and smart. We will find her."

She's not Margo! The more he kept telling himself that, the more he feared it would make no difference. She was strong and smart, but so was Sprat.

Why had Sprat taken Tiffany? To punish him for exposing his swindle? Once again, he'd put a woman in danger, and he'd not been robust enough in his protection.

"If he's hurt her?"

Rockwell grimaced. "I doubt that. She's too valuable. I have a feeling Sprat needs her for her skill set. I'm sure he's made plenty of money off her investment skills."

Rockwell was right. She was too valuable for Sprat to kill. An even worse thought hit him. Sprat was taking her with him. Wherever he was fleeing to, Tiffany would go. If Sprat set sail, Wolf might never see her again.

Wolf wanted to howl. The pain racing through him almost saw him come off his steed. He loved her, and no matter what Sprat did to her, he would shower her with his love and help her heal. He would not let others keep him from her side, like they had with Margo.

~

Tiffany had no idea in what direction they were traveling. He'd removed her blindfold but not the coverings on the windows. She'd have only one chance to escape. Jumping from a fast-moving carriage onto hard cobblestones was risky. If she hit her head, or broke a leg...they would capture her again, but at least there'd be witnesses who could tell Wolf they'd seen her if he came looking.

Soon the rocking lessened. The carriage was definitely slowing down. To her joy, Sprat pushed the window covering aside, and she could see they were in a high traffic area, carriages and wagons everywhere. She could hear gulls. They were near the docks. If she didn't go soon it would be too late. She couldn't let him reach the dock where she assumed he had more men waiting. If he got her on a ship, she'd never escape.

Both hands were now free of her bindings. All she had to do was reach into her pocket where she'd hidden a small Queen Anne pistol. It might not be powerful enough to kill Sprat instantly, but it could do some damage. Especially where she would point it.

Her moment came when Sprat pulled down the window to talk to his man. She slowly reached one hand toward the door. With his attention diverted, she made an instant decision to run. She flung the door open and jumped. Thankfully the carriage had to stop to let a wide wagon pass, and she landed and rolled. She didn't even have time to catch the breath that was knocked out of her, because Sprat was already scrambling from the carriage, yelling at his men.

One of them jumped from the back of the carriage and came after her. She ducked behind the lumbering wagon and into the crowd, running as fast as her skirts would allow, back the way the carriage had come.

Unfortunately, she stood out in the crowd. Her clothes, hair, and the fact she was clean made blending in difficult. She wasn't about to dive into an alley though; she had to stay in the open and hope someone came to her aid.

She glanced over her shoulder. The man was gaining on her. Another carriage was moving swiftly toward her and, timing it perfectly, she nipped across the road, right in front of the wheels, and made it to the other side. The driver yelled at her, but the maneuver had bought her some time as her pursuer had to wait to go around the carriage.

Her lungs burned with each deep breath. She'd never outrun him. Her legs couldn't go any faster. She glanced behind. He was almost within arm's reach. She saw another large wagon, coming fast up the other side of the road, and decided to dash back across. If she timed it perfectly, he'd never make it.

To her horror he tried, and the noise as the horses hit him and he fell under their hooves would live with her always. She didn't stop. Didn't look back. She kept running up the street, and only when she was sure no one still followed did she slow to a walk, chest heaving and her trusty pistol still in her pocket unused.

Looking around, she didn't have any idea of her location. She needed someone to help her. A quick glance at those around her, however, and she decided that trusting anyone here wasn't a good idea. Even now, walking at a regular pace, she was drawing significant interest.

She kept her hand in her pocket, on the handle of her pistol, and kept walking the way the carriage had come. Anyone trying to rescue her would likely come down this road. Her slippers were in tatters and she felt every sharp stone through their soles. Her feet were wet, too, but she refused to notice what she was treading in. She forced herself to keep moving, and prayed that Wolf and the others knew she'd been taken.

～

Wolf's stomach tightened the closer they got to the docks. Would they get to Tiffany in time? So lost was he in his misery, he almost missed the fact Rockwell was slowing his horse and pointing down the street.

He pulled on the reins so hard his horse reared. He shook his head and looked again. Tiffany was walking, head down, slowly up the street. She was limping.

He leaped from his horse and raced across the road, dodging wagons and carriages. "Tiffany."

Her head snapped up, and as soon as she saw him she came running. He scooped her into his arms and held her tight. "I knew you'd come for me."

They stood hugging at the edge of the road, and he couldn't care about anything except the fact she was safe in his arms.

Rockwell arrived with both horses behind him. "Let's get her home."

Wolf pulled back. "Where's Sprat?"

She pointed down the street. "His carriage is way back down the road. I assume he's reached his ship by now because he only sent one man after me and…the man was hit by a wagon. I don't know if he's dead, but if not, he'll be badly hurt. No one else came after me."

"He can't have set sail yet. The tides are not in his favor until this evening." Wolf looked at Rockwell. "Do we have time to take her home before going after Sprat?"

Tiffany placed her hand on Wolf's arm. "I don't want you going after him. He's not worth it. He told me he's sailing to the Americas, and I believe him. Too many people here are after him. Powerful people. He knows it's too risky to stay. Especially after kidnapping me."

Wolf was torn. "What if he comes after you again? I need to know he's either dead or sailed on that ship."

"Take your betrothed home, brother. Send more men to the

docks and I'll go and find which ship Sprat is on. I won't do anything until the men arrive, but at least we will have an eye on his movements."

Wolf hesitated. He didn't want Rockwell to have to clean up his mess, but he also couldn't bear to let Tiffany out of his sight. "I'll see Tiffany home, but I'll come back with the men. Don't approach the ship until I return. Safety first."

Rockwell nodded his agreement. Wolf swung into his saddle and Rockwell helped Tiffany onto the horse. Wolf made her sit side saddle in front of him. He didn't want to let her out of his sight.

As they set off for home, he said, "I can see your feet have taken a battering. Are you hurt anywhere else?"

"I suspect I'll have a few bruises from jumping out of the carriage and hitting the ground. And my palms are scraped from breaking my fall. But other than that, I've escaped with relatively few injuries."

"How did you manage to escape?"

"They stupidly bound my hands behind my back without taking my leather gloves off. The gloves were always loose on me, and I simply worked the bindings until I could slip my hands out of my gloves. Then I sat and waited for the carriage to slow a bit and Sprat's attention to be diverted. I was thinking of using the pistol in my pocket but I didn't need to. Sprat didn't expect me to get free."

She really was quite the woman. A pistol in her pocket. "Was he going to take you to the Americas too?" A shudder ran through him at the idea.

"Yes. He said you had cost him money and he didn't want me marrying you and helping you accumulate more wealth. He wanted me to be his investment adviser once we reached the Americas. I certainly would have helped him lose money. But I would have done anything to stay alive until you found me, or I could make my own way back to you." She cupped his cheek. "I would never have given up, no matter what Sprat did to me."

She bit her lip. "I learned something I think you should know. It was Sprat and some other men who robbed you and Margo all those years ago. The money and jewels he stole helped him set up as a stockjobber. It was your robbery that gave him the idea to stop Father. However, he played no part in Margo's rape and in fact made a point of telling me the man who raped her had been dealt with. What happened to Margo was one of the reasons Sprat decided to abandon thieving—only he didn't leave thieving behind, he just stole in a different way."

"He can steal all my money as long as I have you. If I'd lost you..."

"But you didn't. I just want to go home and have a long hot bath and soak these aches away. I wish you'd reconsider going after him. If I lost you over a man like Sprat, then I'd be—well, I'd be very angry. He's already cost me my parents."

"I was reconsidering until you mentioned Margo. He deserves to be punished. He might not have raped her, but he didn't stop the man who did. I owe it to Margo. And your parents."

Would Tiffany, could Tiffany, understand the guilt that he'd lived with? Dealing with Sprat would go a long way to putting his past to rest, and let him move on with her.

"I want to avenge my parents too. But not at the expense of your or Rockwell's or anyone's life. I've learned there is something far more valuable than money or revenge—love. The people you love and who love you. A family."

Wolf said nothing more. A part of him wanted to see Sprat in the flesh to either kill him or arrest him. Only then could he be sure Tiffany would be safe.

She fell asleep just as they neared home.

His heart still pounded in his chest even though he held her safe. This was what love did. It made you fear. He didn't know if he could live his life afraid. Afraid to love and face the loss.

Chapter Twenty-Two

Tiffany awoke to find Claire leaning over her bed, shaking her. "Wolf is downstairs with Fane. I think he's here to arrange the marriage contract. Didn't you want to be at that meeting?"

She tried to sit up and her body protested. "How long have I slept? What happened to Sprat?"

"You fell asleep in the bath after Wolf brought you home. I helped you to bed and you've slept for over twelve hours. They captured Sprat. He'll stand trial and likely hang for his crimes." Claire pulled the sheet back and exclaimed at the bruises and cuts on her knees. "Perhaps I should ask the men to hold the meeting in here. I don't think you're in any condition to move too far today. Those scabs on your knees need to heal."

She did feel as if a bull had trampled her.

"I'll call for Milly and she can help make you presentable. I'll order some food and suggest the men visit you in your bedchamber. Scandalous, I know, but you are marrying him. I'll also send your apologies to Lady Hawthorn. All of society has heard of your adventure and the ladies found it very romantic. Wolf to the rescue. They will be sorry that you have to miss the ball tonight, but I'll explain about your injuries." As she turned to leave, Claire added, "Wolf also made an announcement of your betrothal in The Times today. I suspect he is protecting your reputation given the abduction is the talk of London."

And he wouldn't want a repeat of the Margo situation. He'd want Tiffany to understand he would marry her regardless. Silly man. She already knew that and she was fine—apart from a few bruises and scrapes.

Milly arrived to help with her ablutions and make her presentable, and soon after a servant brought her a pot of tea and a plate of eggs and bacon. She ate every last bite, not only because she'd missed dinner and was hungry, but because she was happy— her ordeal with Sprat was over, she was safe and she was going to marry the man she loved.

Tiffany sent Milly to advise the men she was ready to receive them. She organized two chairs to be set beside her bed.

She didn't have to wait long before a knock came at the door and Fane and Wolf entered. She smiled at Wolf and immediately recognized something was wrong. He did smile back, but it didn't reach his eyes, and there was no warmth in his gaze.

She sat up straighter and looked at Fane. Her cousin didn't seem to notice anything was amiss. "I hear you managed to capture Sprat. I hope no one was hurt?"

Wolf laughed. "Sprat's tightness with money was his downfall. He didn't buy his own ship, merely passage on one, and as soon as the captain saw us arrive with constables and night watchmen, he turned Sprat over without a fight."

Marlowe added, "He'll go before the magistrate later this week. I expect he'll hang for his crimes against the peers."

She looked at Fane. "But not for my parents' murders?"

"I don't think it wise for you to testify. He'll hang either way." She knew Wolf was merely thinking of her sensibilities and reputation. Besides, he was right. You couldn't hang a man twice.

"So it's really over."

Wolf leaned in and took her hand. "You're safe now. I swear

I'll do everything I can to ensure nothing bad happens to you ever again."

That's when it hit her. The look in Wolf's eyes was guilt. He blamed himself for her kidnapping. Was he thinking of Margo? God, what must he have gone through upon hearing she'd been abducted? This wouldn't help. Was that fortress around his heart building again? She needed to talk with Wolf alone.

Fane's words interrupted her thoughts. "All seems to be in order, Tiffany. Wolfarth has been extremely generous. He's agreed to keep the small dowry your father set aside in trust for any daughters you may have. Any possessions you bring to his house will remain yours, as will any income you earn from the shares you invest in. Your pin money is a substantial amount and so is your clothing allowance to spend however you see fit."

She looked at Wolf. "That *is* very generous, Wolf. Thank you."

"I want you to be happy and well looked after."

She wanted to say his love was all she wanted and needed to make her happy, but she needed to convince him that while life held no certainties, love made the journey bearable, enjoyable and wonderful.

"Fane, would you allow me a private word with Wolf?"

Wolf opened his mouth, no doubt to protest, but Fane stood and said, "I'll be just outside the door."

As soon as Fane stepped out, Tiffany threw back the covers and tried to stand. Her legs didn't wish to co-operate and Wolf caught her as she was about to fall. They stood looking at each other. "Don't do this to us," she whispered.

He didn't even try to deny it. "You could have died or been taken away from me—or worse," he choked out.

"But I wasn't. I'm here standing in front of the man I love, wanting him to have the strength to love me back."

"I—I can't. You don't know the pain..."

"I know the pain of loving someone who doesn't have the courage to love me back. I can't marry you knowing you'll always keep a part of yourself locked away from me. What if we have children? Will you keep them at arm's length too? I couldn't bear to see that."

She cupped his cheek. "I know you carry the guilt of what happened with Margo, but it wasn't your fault. It was a tragedy of circumstances and you have to let it go."

"It's my fault you were taken by Sprat. If I'd just paid Melville..."

She clung to his arms as they supported her. "Is that what you think? I was in trouble the minute I gave money to Sprat. Even if he never approached you about Melville, at some stage he was going to have to deal with me as I began to notice things. I ended up at Capel Court because he didn't send my statements." She pressed a kiss to his lips. "If he hadn't used Lord Melville I'd have been totally in the dark as to Sprat's character and the threat he posed. He could have killed me before anyone knew. So, in a way, your intervention saved me."

"I hadn't thought of it like that."

"You are not God. You are not there to know everything and to protect everyone." She sat on the bed and pulled him down next to her.

"I just want to keep you safe. If something happened to you... But you're right, I'm not God. I wouldn't want to be."

They stretched out and lay cuddled together on her bed.

"All I want to do is love you," she whispered in his ear.

"I fought against loving you," he murmured. "My heart held so much fear, but your strength made me see that perhaps loving you would not be a mistake. Then Sprat took you. And I panicked."

"Love should never be feared. I can't marry you if you fear it. I couldn't live with that guilt. To make someone afraid to love would be a terrible punishment."

Wolf drew back, gazed down at her, seeing her lashes glitter with tears. Gently he touched her face. "I want to love you so much. I want to give you my heart, my soul—everything I am."

"Oh, Wolf. I'm here waiting for you. All you have to do is believe in the power of my love. Love is supposed to conquer all. Can you be the man who banishes his dark shadows and moves into the light so he can love me?"

He took a deep breath, seeking courage. "I have wealth, titles, all the privileges money and rank can buy, but they are all worthless if I lose the one thing that matters most. You."

"Then don't push me away."

His brows drew together. "I might as well cut out my heart if you leave me."

She sighed. "That sounds a tad dramatic. It also sounds like a man who is in love but won't admit it."

He drew her into his arms, pressing his lips to hers, relief coursing through him. "I'm an idiot, aren't I? A coward. I feel stronger just having you in my arms."

The soft light in her eyes reflected her quiet smile, catching his heart and sending it thudding in his chest. "Fear doesn't make us cowards. Not facing your fear is cowardly. And you faced your fear. You love me despite your fear. All you've had is a little setback. But I can feel it in your touch. You love me." Her words were spoken true and clear.

"I love you more than life itself." Only now was he realizing how desperately he needed her love, how rare and precious that love was. "I'll never forsake you. I'll never deny my love again."

Tiffany lay in the warmth of his embrace, cherishing the feel of his hard body against hers. She could sense his fear easing. She'd ensure he never feared again.

"I love you so much," she murmured. "No more living in the past. We have only the future ahead of us."

For a long moment they simply held each other, until Wolf broke the silence with a quiet question. "Will you marry me? I think I should ask again given how badly I mucked this up."

"Yes. Yes, I will marry you. I can't wait."

He bent his head to kiss her, to seal their pledge. Fire flowed between them as their lips met, fire and want and need. Fierce desire burned through him for the woman he loved.

They would make a new beginning, Wolf vowed solemnly. He'd let nothing ever make him fear her love or his love for her. He would prove himself worthy of a woman as strong and kind as Tiffany. And he'd spend the rest of his life making up this lapse in judgment to her. He'd never let her doubt she owned his heart.

"Because Marlowe is standing outside the door, I cannot show you how much I love you. So put me out of my misery and agree to a short engagement."

Her laughter filled his soul, and the fortress deep in his chest crumbled to dust, never to rise again.

Chapter Twenty-Three

Two months on, Tiffany stood in her bedchamber while the dressmaker put the finishing touches to her wedding gown. All the girls fussed around her and she took a sip of brandy to calm her nerves. Soon she'd be walking down the aisle of Saint Paul's Cathedral in front of hundreds of people, including Prinny. She still couldn't get used to having the eyes of the *ton* upon her.

She was marrying the man of her dreams, her prince from that night long ago, even though she'd won their wager. Armley Mill's share price had increased the most. She teased Wolf about her win constantly and Wolf didn't mind. That's why she loved him.

Milly had done her hair and layered in so many jewels she felt like a walking jewelry box. She looked the best she'd ever looked. For once she didn't feel as if she would let Wolf down. Wolf! She could never have dreamed of a better lover, friend and husband-to-be. They had waited two months to wed, until her cousin Dayton could return from India. She was surprised but pleased he'd agreed to come home for her wedding.

All these months Wolf had doted on her. He'd spend most of his day with her and then she'd sneak into his house, or he into hers, and spend the night making wondrous love. They read the scandalous book *Memoirs of a Woman of Pleasure* from cover to cover and, just as he'd promised, he demonstrated the learnings, much to Tiffany's pleasure.

He had kept his word and let her invest with Mr. Lane. And she'd already helped him increase his share portfolio with excellent results.

The Sisterhood's challenge against the men was going well. She was pleased with her investments. If Mr. Lane had told Wolf about the shares she'd purchased, he didn't let on. Nor, as far as she knew, had the men discovered the Sisterhood's secret—that they were the challengers.

Now she had another secret.

She pressed a hand gently to her belly. Thank goodness they were marrying, as she was sure she was with child. She'd missed her monthly courses last week. And she was never late. She hadn't told Wolf yet. She would tell him when they reached Cornwall. It would be her wedding present to him.

She hoped it was a boy, and that he would look just like his father: thick black curls, mesmerizing blue eyes, and a smile that could soften the hardest heart. A wave of sadness filtered through her joy. She wished her mother and father could be here with her. Perhaps they were watching from heaven.

Tiffany's veil was in place and her nerves calmed with another sip of brandy. Finally, the dressmaker declared she was ready and left the room to give her a moment with her friends.

"You are absolutely glowing," Valora declared.

"It's the brandy," Tiffany replied with a wink.

Farah and Lauren looked at her and sighed. Courtney teased her. "I bet you can't wait for the wedding night."

"I can vouch for how wonderful it will be," Serena added.

Tiffany's face heated.

Ashleigh choked back a snort, and Ivy dug her in the side. The two had caught Tiffany slipping from Wolf's bedchamber numerous times.

Claire stood quietly looking at her. Claire, her cousin, who she loved so much. Claire, the sister she'd never had. A small tear escaped Claire's eye. Tiffany moved to embrace her. "Please don't cry or I will too, and I don't want to walk down that long aisle in front of everyone with red eyes."

"For many years I've never woken up and not had you sleeping in the bedchamber next door. You're the first person I speak to every morning and the last I say good night to. You're my rock, my friend and my... I don't know what I'll do without you. I shall miss you."

"I'm only going two doors up the road. When I go to York-shire you'll probably be pleased to see the back of me." Tiffany wished Claire could find someone as wonderful as Wolf. Then she wouldn't be lonely. But with Fane as an example of how men behaved, Claire had lost faith in marriage. Maybe Dayton was returning at exactly the right time. Claire needed her other brother, since Fane paid her little attention.

"Just promise me you'll be happy," Tiffany said. "One day this will be you." She turned to all of them. "One day each of you will marry the man of your dreams. I know it."

"If I found a good man, an honest man who made me as happy as you look, I'd grab him. Not everyone is so lucky. And not every man is good," Ashleigh said.

"I had the best man ever, but I lost him. If men birthed a child, they'd never let them go to war." Courtney still mourned her fiancée, Lucien—Lauren's brother—who had died in the Irish Rebellion.

"I believe your heart is big enough to love more than one person. You'll see."

Courtney smiled at Tiffany. "I hope so."

Tiffany turned away from her friends and walked toward the mirror glass. She looked at herself in her wedding dress, not quite believing this day was here. "He does make me very happy."

Valora stepped forward. "Then let's not keep him waiting. He might be getting nervous and think you've changed your mind."

~

The cathedral was filled to overflowing. All of society was here to see Lord Wolfarth marry his best friend's ward.

As she entered on Fane's arm, Tiffany's nerves vanished. She'd never felt surer of the step she was taking. She loved Wolf so much, and when she saw him gazing at her with such pride and love shining from his eyes, she knew he loved her.

Fane handed her into Wolf's keeping, and her almost-husband smiled and said, "You look beautiful beyond words, my love," and her heart went soft at the warm endearment.

She smiled, and replied with perfect truth, "So do you."

The service flew by. Once they'd exchanged vows and the Bishop pronounced them man and wife, Wolf took her arm and she let him guide her down the aisle toward her new life. There would be a small breakfast at the Wolfarth's for a select few, and then in one month they would hold a ball. She'd host her first ball as Marchioness Wolfarth. But they had a trip to make before that.

Wolf beamed with pride. He had the woman of his dreams by his side to share his life with and to love, whatever the world threw at them. Tiffany was beautiful. In fact, he could hardly wait to take her home, strip her of her gown, and make love to her until she fell into an exhausted sleep.

Ignoring the now cheering crowd around them, he pulled her into his arms and hugged her fiercely. "I'm the luckiest man in the world."

He led her to the carriage and helped her climb in. The cheers were deafening as they moved off toward Wolfarth House.

~

The wedding breakfast was noisy and fun, and like a dream. She'd formally met all the staff on her arrival, although she'd known most of them for years. It was clear they thought Wolf had made a good choice in his wife. She had a new lady's maid, Anna, since she'd left Milly with Claire.

The party didn't look as if it was ever going to end. She felt the brush of Wolf's lips at her temple and her breath faltered.

"It will soon be time to leave, sweeting. You need to change and gather your things?"

Fane had given them the cottage on the beach at St. Ives in Cornwall for a week of privacy, away from the intrusive and gossiping *ton*. It had been Claire's suggestion. It was somewhere familiar for Tiffany, but also a place where she and Wolf could move into this new relationship with no interruptions. They could swim in the sea in private and pretend they were the only two people in the world.

He spoke softly but with a hint of impatience. "I think it will be easier on Fane if we slip away quietly. He's struggling with the fact that you are now in my care." He pulled her into an embrace. "*My* responsibility."

Her stomach fluttered wildly.

She couldn't form a coherent word. She simply nodded and slipped out of his arms and through the door. With her mind racing about what was to come—revealing her secret on her wedding night—she made her way quietly to her room. The countess's apartments. She didn't know how often she'd sleep in her own bed. Wolf had made it perfectly clear she would sleep with him every night.

As she entered the bedchamber she saw Wolf's wedding present on the wall above her bed. The portrait of her in the garden below. He'd said he wanted her to see it every day so she would always remember how beautiful she looked to him.

He'd spent a fortune buying it at the Royal Academy of Art auction. The picture had created quite the stir as people quickly understood the woman in the painting was her. Society now looked at her in a different light.

She loved her husband so much.

She would miss the Sisterhood over the next few weeks.

However, they had their instructions and they would write. The ladies knew all her secrets, but she had a husband to share her secrets with now. That might be difficult given most of her secrets revolved around him and the challenge.

The door opened and Ashleigh, her new sister-in-law, slipped into the room. "How are you holding up?"

"On the outside, perfectly well. On the inside, I'm terrified. I hope I don't let Wolf down. Everyone will be expecting much from me, and I've never enjoyed being the center of attention. I'm not very good marchioness material. I never paid much attention to the ins and outs of running a house this size. I never expected to marry, or ever marry a man of such social standing. I'm hoping you and Ivy will help me."

"You are the perfect woman for my brother, and that is what counts. He loves you. As do Ivy and I. I'm so happy you are part of our family. And I wanted to thank you."

"Thank me?"

"Thank you for helping my brother open his heart and love again. Margo's death saw him living in the shadows. Too scared to risk his heart again. Then he met you. And even after your capture by Sprat, you made Wolf overcome his fear and let you into his heart."

"And you? Seeing Wolf and I find love, has it made you unlock your heart a little bit, perhaps enough to let someone worthy of you come near?"

Ashleigh smiled sadly. "Perhaps. I'm not sure my reputation encourages any man who is worthy. But I will try."

She squeezed Ashleigh's hand. "Look after Claire for me over the coming weeks. She will be lost for a while. Thank goodness Dayton is home. I think he understands Claire's loneliness. She has no other female in the house now."

"Ivy and I will keep her busy until your return. Valora is up to her usual tricks. She seems to think Vale and Claire would make the perfect couple. Can you see those two together?"

Tiffany shook her head. "Who am I to give an opinion? I

would never in a million years have thought Wolf and I were suited. Perhaps Valora is right. I hope so. Vale is a nice man."

A knock sounded and Wolf poked his head around the door. "Ready to leave. We should make it half way to Devon by nightfall but we need to leave now.

Tiffany linked arms with her sister-in-law, and they walked down the stairs. She waved to all her friends as she held her husband's hand, and together they set off on their honeymoon.

He pulled her onto his lap. "Happy?"

"Immensely. I love you."

He kissed her, and soon she barely noticed the miles flying by.

~

Three days later they reached the cottage on the beach and Tiffany knew tonight was the night she'd reveal her wedding gift.

While Wolf sorted out the staff and their trunks, Tiffany stripped off her stockings and slippers and paddled her feet in the cool water.

She decided to lie in the shade and wait for Wolf, but soon her eyelids grew heavy and she succumbed to sleep, tired from three days of travel over bumpy ground and sleeping in strange beds— when they'd slept at all. They couldn't get enough of each other.

Wolf had taken longer than he'd anticipated, as he'd organized a light supper and given the staff the night off. He wanted his bride all to himself for what would likely be their only spell of privacy for a good while.

He strolled down to the beach in pants and shirt only, and found Tiffany fast asleep under the tree. He stood watching her sleep and his heart swelled with love. She'd made him see that love was worth any risk. Love fed your soul and made life worth living rather than merely existing.

He lay down beside her and pulled her back against his chest. He pressed little kisses down her cheek and neck. Slowly she woke and turned into his embrace.

"Hello, husband."

"Hello, wife."

Then he kissed her. He deepened the kiss and his desire ignited as it always did when he held Tiffany in his arms.

She broke the kiss. "The staff will be scandalized on the very first day."

"I've given them the rest of the day and night off. They won't be back until early tomorrow morning."

"Such a clever husband."

He rolled her over until he rose above her. He unhooked her gown and undressed her. Then he shed his pants and shirt. "Time for a dip in the sea." He scooped her up and carried her into the waves, kissing her as they went.

She clung to him as he walked into deeper water. Soon they were swimming and romping in the sea and enjoying the freedom of their private space.

Finally she swam back to him and hooked her legs around his waist, lying back in the water, her hair floating around them.

"I have a secret."

Wolf looked at her grinning face. "If your secret is that the Sisterhood is the anonymous investment challenger, I've already guessed. Mr. Lane thought I should know what my wife was up to in the investing arena. But don't worry, your secret is safe with me. I'm quite looking forward to Blackstone's horror when he learns he's been beaten by a woman."

"That's not my only secret."

He frowned as he pulled her up so her arms wrapped around his neck. "I think we should make a pact that we have no secrets."

"That's only because you want to know what my secret is."

"Are you going to tell me, or will I have to tickle it out of you?" With that he began to tickle her sides, and she fell back in the water and quickly swam away.

"That's not fair. If you promise to take me to bed and make love to me, I'll share my secret with you."

He threw back his head and laughed. "That's the easiest promise to make."

She swam back to him. "My courses are late. And I'm never late."

It took Wolf mere moments to understand. "You're with child."

"Most likely. We'll know for sure in another month."

He pulled her to him and carried her out of the water, past their clothes, into the cottage and up the stairs to their bedchamber.

"Don't put me on the bed, I'm all wet."

He set her on her feet and found some towels and dried her off, gently running the towel over her stomach. "I'm going to be a father. What could be more perfect than that?" And he pressed a kiss to her belly.

She wrapped her arms around his neck and kissed him, leading him to the bed, and proceeded to show him what else was perfect—their love for each other.

Epilogue

Rockwell hadn't seen his brother look so happy for a long, long time. Wolf and Tiffany had returned from their honeymoon in Cornwall last week. Married life obviously agreed with the happy couple. In fact, Tiffany was glowing tonight, even though he understood how nervous she was about hosting her first ball as the Marchioness of Wolfarth.

The night was going well, with most of the *ton* present, many no doubt wanting to evaluate Tiffany. How had she captured the attention of the Marquess of Wolfarth? That was the question top of their minds. The answer was easy—with love.

That's why he hid in the shadows. He was now the only eligible Wolfarth left. Most knew he'd accumulated his own fortune from his travels and investing. He was now sought after by mothers of young debutantes. While Rockwell held no fear of love—in fact, he loved a lot of women—he wasn't ready to find "the one".

He'd taken immense satisfaction in cleaning up Sprat's crimes instead. While the newly married couple were in Cornwall, Sprat had been tried and hanged. The saga was over, and he hoped Wolf could get on with his life and put the terrible past behind him. If his contented, smug smile was anything to go by, he had.

The heat of the ballroom hit, and just as he was thinking of taking a stroll on the terrace, a feminine laugh caught his ear and he knew whom it belonged to—Lady Farah, the younger sister of the Duke of Blackstone, his best friend. "Stone" to everyone who knew him, because he had about as much emotion in him as a stone did. But Rockwell knew that underneath Stone's ducal persona there lay a man who was all heart. Or he hoped so.

He searched the crowd and found her with the other ladies who surrounded Tiffany. But his eyes saw only Lady Farah.

He loved the sound of her laugh. It was warm-hearted and filled with joy. He shook his head to clear the image of Farah standing in his bedchamber with his Hessian boot on her long slender leg, her skirts hiked up to her waist. He'd never seen anything so erotic. Was that why he couldn't get her out of his head?

Rumor was, Stone was marrying her off to Lord Franklin. That wouldn't be a happy match. Perhaps he should talk to Stone. But there had been no announcement yet. Franklin was as dreary as a cold winter's day, and quiet, shy Farah needed a man who could draw out the real woman inside. The woman who wasn't scared to assert her own wishes and desires. He felt sorry for Farah. If Stone pushed ahead with this match, she would marry a man who didn't know how to spell "fun", let alone enjoy life.

As if Lady Farah had sensed him watching her, she turned and glided across the floor toward where he hid from the crowd. He couldn't help the seductive smile that broke over his lips. She was very beautiful in a pixie-ghost sort of way.

"Good evening, my lord. I hear you're traveling to Ireland tomorrow to retrieve the money Sprat stole from Lady Wolfarth."

"That's correct. I need to sign some papers at the bank to have the funds transferred back to Wolf."

Farah nodded thoughtfully. "Do you think it will take long for the funds to be returned?"

This made Rockwell curious. Why was Lady Farah so interested in funds? "It should not take more than a few weeks."

She bit her lip. "That long?" She rubbed her hands together.

"Is there a reason Tiffany may need the funds sooner?"

She shook her head. "No. Not Tiffany," and before he could ask more, she brushed past him and out into the corridor.

How strange. Had Tiffany invested funds for Farah? Why would Farah, of any of the ladies, need funds? Her brother was very wealthy and she was soon to be married to a wealthy lord.

Before he could give the strange conversation any further thought, Tiffany arrived at his side. "I think it's time to dance with your sister-in-law instead of hiding from all the ladies in the corner of the room. Why are men so afraid of marriage?"

"Wolf has shown me there is no need to be afraid of marriage, only of choosing the wrong woman."

"Well answered, Rockwell. Is there a right woman for you, do you think?"

An image of Farah in his Hessian flashed through his head.

She chuckled. "Oh, I think there might be." And as they danced, Tiffany ran her eye over the ladies present, only Farah had not returned to the ballroom yet. Tiffany turned her attention back to Rockwell. "I will work out who it is. I'm so happy. I want everyone to find what I have found with Wolf."

※

Nearing dawn, Rockwell entered the bedchamber he kept at Wolfarth House. He was too tired to return to his bachelor quarters after Tiffany's successful ball. He'd told Wolf's valet, Simpson, not to wait up for him. He was perfectly capable of undressing himself.

He pictured Farah helping him undress. He'd love to undress her and leave her standing naked except for his Hessians. For God's sake, he had to pull himself together. He wasn't ready to marry. He had his big safari through Africa to do next year. He wouldn't marry and go off on a dangerous twelve-month trip. It wouldn't be fair to his wife. A pity really, as he suspected Blackstone would have Farah married off by the time he returned, if not before.

Rockwell slid naked between the sheets. He was already hardening, thinking of a naked Farah in his arms, when his head hit the pillow and...something else. He sat up and turned to look. It was a roll of parchment tied with a pink ribbon. As he picked it up he could smell a fine scent of roses. Slowly he undid the ribbon and rolled out the sheet.

Safe travels to Ireland. I shall miss you while you are away.
But my dreams are free and I shall dream of you...
Yours F.

He put the parchment to his nose, closed his eyes and sniffed. It smelled of the fragrance Farah had worn tonight.

Fancy little mousy Farah sneaking into his room to leave this saucy note on his pillow. What the hell did it mean? He didn't want to examine too closely why he was so pleased.

It made him not want to leave for Ireland tomorrow. As he began to stroke his cock, picturing Farah in his room, naked, in his bed, he thought it would be the quickest trip to Ireland and back he'd ever made.

The End.

The Adventure Doesn't End Here...

Dive into the SISTERHOOD OF SCANDAL series set in the Regency World.

**A Lady Never Presumes
Book #2**

How do you create a scandal?
Lady Farah Perrin, younger sister of the Duke of Blackstone has earned the nickname 'timid mouse' because being the only daughter, she's been brought up to be the demure, perfect *ton* diamond. But when her overbearing, stuffy brother announces she is to marry the odious Lord Franklin, the timid mouse is replaced by the sly fox. Publicly challenging the duke won't work. However, creating a scandal that cannot be ignored is very achievable. Now all she has to do is ascertain which of the current London rakes will unwittingly aid in her plan.

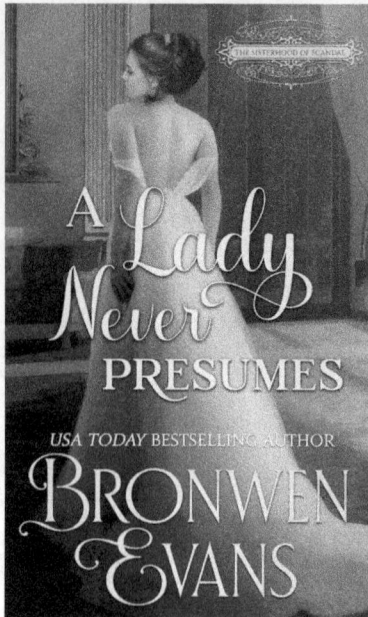

How do you avoid temptation?

Lord Rockwell Ware, the younger brother of the Marquess of Wolfarth, loathes being known as 'the spare'. If that's how he's viewed he'll enjoy living his life on his own terms, amassing a fortune, taking on many wagers or dares, and doing whatever he bloody well pleases. It appears someone else lives life on her own terms—Farah. His best friend's recently betrothed little sister begins sending him private missives of the most intimate nature. He should hand them to Blackstone to deal with, but as each note arrives he finds himself falling further into temptation. Yet, Rockwell soon learns, every wicked game has its price.

BUY NOW

HAVE YOU READ THE FREE PREQUEL - A LADY NEVER CONCEDES

A **FREE Regency Short Story** to launch the Sisterhood Of Scandal Series.

Lord Julian Montague, the second son of the Marquess of Lorne has been Miss Serena Fancot's best friend since childhood. When Julian starts talking about taking a wife, Serena is very aware they are no longer children.

Why does she suddenly notice just how lovely his dimples are and how tall and handsome he is? His clothes fit him like a tight glove and he has a body to rival Apollo. Suddenly, she can't help but notice how the women in society's ballrooms drool over him.

Worse still, he's not once tried to kiss her, or hold her hand, or whispered words of love in her ear. Does he not see her as the love of his life? Has she left it too late to make Julian realize he is the only man she'd ever wish to marry? Has she left it too late to show him he's the love of her life? That won't do. But how do you make your best friend fall in love with you?

GRAB A FREE COPY HERE

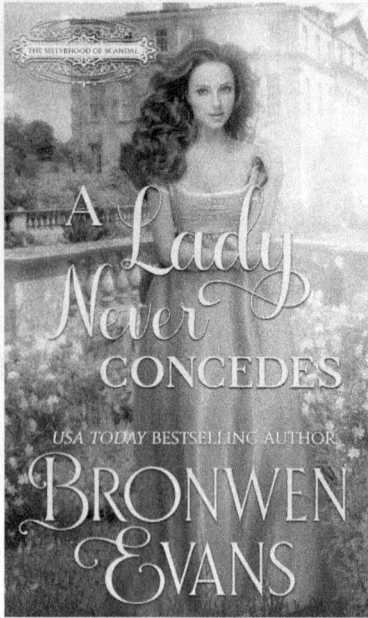

About Bron

USA Today bestselling author, Bronwen Evans grew up loving books. She writes both historical and contemporary sexy romances for the modern woman who likes intelligent, spirited heroines, and compassionate alpha heroes. Evans is a three-time winner of the RomCon Readers' Crown and has been nominated for an *RT* Reviewers' Choice Award. She lives in Hawkes Bay, New Zealand with her dogs Brandy and Duke.

Thank you so much for coming along on this journey. **Reviews are always welcome** and help authors immensely. So does talking with your friends about what you enjoyed in the book.

If you'd like to keep up with my other releases, my newsletter coupon codes for specials, or other news, feel free to **join my newsletter** and receive a **FREE** book too. You can also join the newsletter on my website.

www.bronwenevans.com

Also by Bronwen Evans

A Love To Remember – August 2017

A Dream Of Redemption – February 2018

Imperfect Lords Series

Addicted to the Duke – March 2018

Drawn To the Marquess – September 2018

Attracted To The Earl – February 2019

Taming A Rogue Series (Was the Invitation To Series)

Contemporaries

Lord of Wicked

Lord of Danger

Lord of Passion

Lord of Pleasure

The Reluctant Wife

(Winner of RomCon Best Short Contemporary 2014)

Coopers Creek

Love Me – book #1

Heal Me – Book #2

Want Me – book #3

Need Me – book #4

Drive Me Wild

Reckless Curves

Purr For Me

Slow Ride

Fast Track To Love At Christmas - novella

Other Books

Baby It's Hot Outside: A Christmas Down Under Box Set

The Duke's Christmas List - novella

A Scot For Christmas - novella

To Tempt A Highland Duke - novella

Highland Wishes And Dream - novella

Regency Delights Boxed Set

Join Bron's Bold Belles

GET UPDATES DIRECT TO YOUR INBOX

Subscribe to my newsletter for updates about new releases, sales, freebies, giveaways and Buy From Bron discount coupon codes. Plus each release month I draw an active subscriber and gift you a $10 Amazon.com Gift Card.

CPSIA information can be obtained
at www.ICGtesting.com
Printed in the USA
LVHW100435240123
737768LV00004B/242